ALSO BY HENIA KARMEL-WOLFE

The Baders of Jacob Street

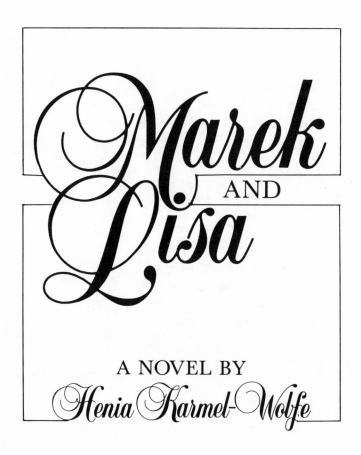

Marek AND Lisa

A NOVEL BY
Henia Karmel-Wolfe

DODD, MEAD & COMPANY

NEW YORK

Copyright © 1984 by Henia Karmel-Wolfe
All rights reserved
No part of this book may be reproduced in any form
without permission in writing from the publisher
Published by Dodd, Mead & Company, Inc.
79 Madison Avenue, New York, N.Y. 10016
Distributed in Canada by
McClelland and Stewart Limited, Toronto
Manufactured in the United States of America
First Edition

Library of Congress Cataloging in Publication Data

Karmel-Wolfe, Henia.
Marek and Lisa.

1. World War, 1939-1945—Fiction. 2. Holocaust,
Jewish (1939-1945)—Fiction. I. Title.
PS3561.A675M3   1984   813'.54   83-25322
ISBN 0-396-08287-4

To Leszek,
and for Aaron and Sarah

Part One

*I*t was the pain that told her she hadn't died, signaling the message from her legs to her brain.

"Pain," she cried out in recognition. "Pain."

Out of a milky mist, slowly a shape emerged, then eyes, a nose, lips. "*Schmerz*," the lips said.

Now that her pain had been translated and pronounced in two languages, it seemed to double.

Pain, pain, pain, *schmerz, schmerz.*

Her hand reached out, trying to grasp the vanishing shadow. Then warmth flowed through her body, and in the warmth the pain dissolved. The shape reappeared, the face, the lips.

"What is your name?" the lips said.

Her name . . . Lisa Unger, Elisa Wysocki, Lisa Rodwan, Elisa Rodwanski . . .

Like dresses hanging in a closet, each one for a different occasion, her names were stored away, waiting for her to choose the proper one. But how could she if she didn't even know what the occasion was?

"Tomorrow," she said. "I'll tell you tomorrow. . . ."

Tomorrow there was a white flatness over her head with shadows, now stretching, now shrinking, like images in a funny mirror. Then the pain came back, like a persistent, yelping puppy at first, then like an old, nagging shrew.

"Down," she said to the puppy. Then to the shrew, "Enough, you told me already, I know . . ."

Pain, *schmerz* . . .

A sound of bells came from afar, then the warmth carried the pain away.

Like a conditioned animal, she learned to associate the shadows with the pain, the bells with the warmth, the warmth with oblivion.

"Hurts?" another voice asked. The voice came from a dark ball of fleece that rested on a white rectangle. The ball rolled over. The ball had a face. The face had round, black eyes, like the shiny buttons of Maxie the bear. . . . Lisa had pulled one button out. It had left a hole big enough for the tip of her finger. . . . Bad girl, Lisa, look what you did to Maxie . . . Sawdust, sawdust . . .

"Who are you?" she said to the face.

"Natalia. They call me Natka."

Lisa wanted to say she preferred Natalia, for it sounded like a flower, but it was too long and too hard to say.

Natalia–Maxie, pain, pain, *schmerz*! . . .

"Don't," Natalia said. "You were out for so long, don't . . ."

"I have to," Lisa said firmly, as if it was an appointment she had to keep, and sank in again.

Then came other faces, other shapes and voices, and hands. The hands were important. There were gentle hands, and rough hands, careful hands and the uncaring ones.

Then some of the awareness came back. The flat surface over her head she recognized as a ceiling, the white rectangle as a pillow, the head resting on it as belonging to . . . the name escaped her, then came back, welcomed like a loss recovered.

"Natalia," she cried. "Natalia."

4

Her tongue felt swollen, stiff, heavy.

"Drink," she said. "Water."

From far away the ringing came, upsetting the sequence of shadows, bells, and pain. For the shadows hadn't crept out yet, and the pain was still slumbering.

"Bells," she said, "bells . . ."

Natalia, arm propped, head on the upturned hand, eyes shining and black, said, "The Russians marched in. The war is over."

"I'm thirsty," Lisa said, her voice that of a petulant child.

"Wait," Natalia said. Then, "*Schwester*," she called. *Schwester* . . . sister. Whose sister? *Schwester* . . . sister of mercy . . . a nurse? a hospital?

"Drink, mercy, drink!"

Light and tiptoeing, white and rustling, the nurse seemed to float in through the open door. She brought mercy up to Lisa's lips. "Suck," she said.

It wasn't enough. "More," she begged. "More."

Natalia asked something in German.

"*Nein*," the nurse said.

"More, drink, more . . ."

The scent was what hit her first, of vodka, sweat, and new leather. Her eyes caught a glimpse of rawhide boots, then moved up the khaki breeches to the brass buttons on the jacket, the red star on the collar, all the way to the pock-marked face with a smile that glittered, to the hair like a porcupine's quills.

The voice was guttural and melodious at the same time.

"I'm Sasha," the voice said. "The war is over, everybody is free."

"Sasha," Natalia cooed. "Sashenka."

Free . . . freedom . . .

Sasha, the freedom man. . . . He handed out freedom the way an ice-cream man hands out an ice-cream cone. If she

5

had an ice-cream cone, her tongue would become a serpent that would coil around it, twirl around it, lapping it, cool and smooth and wet. She would know what to do with an ice-cream cone. She did not know what to do with freedom.

"Thirsty," she moaned. "Water . . . "

"Don't," Natalia's warning voice said. "She will get sick."

What did she mean, " 'She will get sick' "? . . . She *was* sick. That's why she was in a hospital.

"Thirsty, water, drink . . . "

Now Natalia, the fleecyhead, Natalia, the linguist, was telling Sasha, the freedom man, in his own tongue, that Lisa had been shot when she broke out of the line to pick up a potato.

"A beet," Lisa corrected her angrily.

But Natalia, now busy presenting Sasha with a leg, gift-wrapped in bandages, didn't seem to hear her. "They shot me too because I couldn't march anymore." What the connection was between the march, the beet, between Natalia's bandaged leg and her being refused water, Lisa couldn't see.

"Drink," she whimpered. "Drink . . . "

When she had been granted water in careful sips, the room slowly came into focus.

In the narrow passage between her bed and Natalia's was a table. On the opposite wall a window, through which tree branches could be seen. Farther down, another bed, around which white figures flocked like big, fluttering birds, repeating in frightened chirps. "*von Dresden*," "from Dresden," which to Lisa sounded like a proper name with an aristocratic prefix. They flapped toward her, and when they came closer they did not look like birds anymore. The one with the white mustache seemed rather like a benevolent big cat, and the other, like a long-snouted hound. At a respectful distance, the nurses waited.

"The chart," the fat one commanded in a booming voice.

6

A nurse handed him a framed rectangle.

He looked at it and passed it to the other. "What do you think, Dr. Luther?"

"Hmm," Dr. Luther said. "The fever is still jumping." Then turning to the nurse, he asked, "Is she conscious?"

"Off and on," the blond nurse replied.

Dr. Luther pushed the cover away. They were all bending over her now.

"What is *your* opinion, Dr. Boesel?"

The big one said something in Latin.

Careful now, she wanted to say. She had studied Latin.... Why do doctors talk Latin? So that the patient should get used to a dead language ... A joke ... Ha, ha ...

They put the cover back; they were already moving away.

They forgot something. Her throat. They forgot to look at her throat. Her throat was hurting her. It was dry.... Now open your mouth, Lisa, wider, say aaaah.... The tonsils have to come out, Mrs. Unger. You see how lucky you are, Lisa? You will be eating nothing but ice cream. What's your favorite flavor? ...

"I want ice cream," Lisa said in a loud, distinct voice.

"What did she say?"

"*Sie will Eis*," Natalia, the linguist, translated.

They were at Natalia's bed now, hovering over her. They moved away. The nurse began rolling off the bandage, stepping backward as she did. The gauze was hanging between her hand and Natalia's leg like a ribbon on a new bridge. The other nurse stood there, waiting, scissors in hand.

Ladies and gentlemen, we are assembled here for the solemn dedication of Natalia's leg....

The roll in the nurse's hand grew thicker, the layer of bandage on Natalia's leg thinner. Then it came off, showing the naked, reddish-blue skin.

"*Schön*," the big one said.

7

"*Schön*," the thin one repeated.

"*Schön*," the nurses chimed in.

And Natalia lay there smiling modestly, accepting the praise gratefully but humbly.

Now Natalia was sitting up, her bony back turned to Dr. Boesel, who listened to it, then stepped aside and with an inviting gesture offered it to Dr. Luther.

"*Die Lungen*," she said.

Lungen? Lungs?

"The postmaster was asking questions. He wanted to know why you never went out. I had to say something. I told him you had bad lungs."

"What are you trying to do, ruin my reputation? Mother wouldn't hear of sending me to school in Switzerland, any place but Switzerland. She was afraid someone might start a rumor that I went there because of 'bad lungs,' and I might have trouble finding a husband."

"Aren't you lucky I married you?"

Married you ... married you ...

"Marek," Lisa cried out. "Marek."

"Who is Marek?" Natalia asked.

But that was later. That was when the thirst had been quenched, when the pain had been quieted, when she realized she had remained flat on her back because her right leg was elevated under the white sheet with something heavy weighing it down. It came when Natalia's hair had grown long enough to be combed.

She was combing it with short, impatient jerks, sitting propped up on two pillows in a half-reclining position, when she posed the question.

Lisa didn't answer. She didn't feel she had to. She hardly knew Natalia, and although she understood that she must have been in the same camp, it was in this room that she had seen her first.

"Were we in the camp together?" she asked to make sure. And after getting an affirmative answer, she said, "Why don't I remember you?"

"I was one of many," Natalia said. "I remember you, though. You were the one who sang."

Sitting on her bunk, legs pulled under, eyes closed, she would hum softly to herself, each melody a picket in a fence that separated her from the stench of the barracks, from the dirt, from the noise. Encouraged, she would sing louder, her voice gradually drowning the sounds of the shrill bickering. There would be silence except for her singing and the occasional raging of the half-demented woman with wiry, disheveled hair, whose name has been forgotten ever since she has been dubbed Cassandra, and who, pointing a bony, accusing finger at her, would rave, "She sings, damn her, in hell she sings, on our graves she will be singing." Once she came closer and spat.

She sang over the sound of warfare, so close the earth seemed to tremble, until the news came that the guards had just climbed the trucks and fled. As if in suspended motion, they waited. Then stillness came and with it the anticipation that turned to excitement and, when they saw the German lorries return, panic. Then, under the cover of darkness, they were marched out of the camp.

Days later, when the need for sleep became so strong that she couldn't fight it anymore, and only moved forward pushed by those walking behind her, her eyes closed like those of a somnambulist, Lisa began to sing just to keep awake. This time it wasn't only Cassandra who cursed her. The angry, hostile voices seemed to be coming at her from every direction. "People are dying all around and she sings. People are dying and she sings. Damn her." Angry, hostile voices ... "Whore!" A stone hurled ... "Whore!"

9

Why did they call her that? It wasn't fair. . . . She had never . . . It just wasn't fair. . . .

She remembered passing through a village that seemed to be untouched by the war. Behind picket fences the houses, white but for the colorful shutters, stood in a neat row. The trees were covered with moist new leaves, and in the flower beds daffodils began to bloom.

The warm April day brought the people outside, and they stood in front of their houses—women, children, and old men—staring at them, with a mixture of curiosity and fear.

A child hid his face in the folds of his mother's long skirt.

"Don't cry, love," the woman said, patting his head. "These are just criminals."

Some handed them water from tin pails when the guards were not looking. A woman stepped out into the road carrying a round loaf of bread. A forest of arms stretched out, clawlike fingers fluttered.

Bread, bread . . .

Lisa's stomach had been reduced to a painful pit, her legs refused to carry her.

Like a wanderer in a desert, she would see mirages: a barn would loom on the horizon in which she hoped to rest, a huge kettle would steam over a fire—both dissolving as she got closer.

But the sugar beet she suddenly noticed between the furrows of the freshly plowed field was real. Covered with mud, it was lying only a few feet away. No one else seemed to notice it. It was hers. She broke out of the line in a leap.

A bullet cut the air with a swish, then another. She fell, her body twitched, and she passed out.

When she came to, she was lying in a pool of blood. Disconnected, as if outside of herself, a thought formed: she was dying. It came without regret, accompanied by a feeling of relief. At least she wouldn't have to march anymore.

*   *   *

10

"There was one song I really liked," Natalia said. She hummed a few notes trying to recall the melody, then sang a bit off key:

> Everything passes,
> And all goes away,
> After each December
> There will be a May.

"Anyway," she said, "May is over now."

Lisa looked at the window. The tree that she remembered budding was now densely covered with moist, green leaves. Without realizing it, she had turned twenty. On May 15 she became twenty years old. She remembered the fuss her parents would make on her birthday—the secret preparations, the whispers, the extravagant presents, the cakes and ice creams, the candles and balloons, the first cherries and bunches of lilies of the valley in all the vases. Twenty years old ... What a party that would have called for. If she was twenty, Marek is going to be twenty-four; in October he is going to be twenty-four years old if ... she stopped, not allowing the end of the thought to form.

"How long have we been here?" Lisa asked, turning to Natalia.

"A little over a month." Natalia said.

"How did we get here?"

"A farmer brought us over on a hay wagon."

"I don't remember a thing."

"You were unconscious most of the time. You were so feverish that you were delirious. And the things you said!"

"What things?"

"First you insisted you were Queen Sabbath. 'I am Queen Sabbath' you kept saying over and over again. And that was when the war was still going on. Luckily you said it in Polish and no one could understand you. But another

11

time you were saying to Boesel, in purest German. 'You were not a Nazi, Doctor.' Of course he was, the old baboon. They all were. And then that name, over and over—Marek. Who is he?"

"We got married."

"You are married? When did you get married?"

"After the winter," Lisa said and closed her eyes.

$\mathcal{I}$t was winter when they first met during a registration, its purpose according to most—to determine the number of Jews now living in Krakow; to others—to decrease that number by granting permits of residence to some, forcing the rest to settle elsewhere. As he walked into the dimly lit hall and took his place at the end of the line to her right, the snow was still on his jacket. She looked at him curiously. Blond and blue-eyed, he could be easily taken for a Pole, even a *Volksdeutscher*, an ethnic German, the way he was dressed in high boots and breeches and a green loden jacket. But it was more than just his looks, or the smug outfit that seemed to set him apart. It was the way he carried himself, a poise, aloofness almost, as if he did not belong there and merely graced the frightened, hunched crowd with his presence. The pursed lips gave his face an angry, stubborn look, unredeemed by his eyes, which rested on her in a fleeting, indifferent glance. He brushed the snow off his jacket with the back of his hand; it fell on the dirty floor and glittered before melting.

"Is it snowing?" she asked.

"No," he said without looking at her. "That's manna from heaven."

Not sure whether to laugh or to take offense, she turned

away, but still could not help stealing glances at him, and when their eyes met, she felt herself blush. Embarrassed, she blurted, "Why don't you go and yodel or something," referring to the way he was dressed, and waited for a reaction. To her surprise, he just looked at her and smiled. The smile transformed his face, now gentle, almost vulnerable, and Lisa, in spite of herself, smiled back.

Her line moved faster, and she had already registered and turned to leave while he was still awaiting his turn. As she passed him, he stretched out his arm, stopped her, and said, "Wait for me."

She walked out through the hallway into the street. The snow was falling thickly and calmly.

He came out after a while, looked around, and smiled when he saw her.

"You waited," he said.

"I wasn't waiting."

"Just standing here, turning into a snowman?"

"I happen to like snow."

"In that case, let's go to the park," he said, taking her by the elbow. "There is plenty there."

The trees stood tall and white, the park benches were covered with a fluffy layer, and the poet's bust in the middle of a fenced-in area looked like something children might make out of snow. A black bird flew in, sat on the top, then took off.

"An hour ago it didn't even look like snow," she said.

He agreed politely. "Now that we have covered the subject of weather," he said, "what would you like to talk about?"

Suspecting he was trying to snub her again, she looked at him only to discover that he was smiling.

"People are worried. No one seems to know what this registration is all about. There are all kinds of rumors going around," she said, thinking that snow and registration were

14

all they had in common so far.

"There are always rumors," he said.

"They say it might be a trap."

"It probably is."

She felt her irritation return. "Why then did you bother to register?"

"I am guided by the law of averages."

"How is that?"

"The first time I registered was about a year ago. It turned out to be the wrong thing to do. Then, back in October, I didn't, and it wasn't right either. I figured that according to the law of averages—"

She interrupted him. "There was no registration in October."

"There was where I came from."

"Where was that?"

"Lodz."

"There is a ghetto in Lodz," she said.

"In which I couldn't stay because I didn't register."

"It's different here," Lisa said vehemently. "There will never be a ghetto here. . . . Krakow is the capital now where foreign dignitaries visit, the International Red Cross . . ."

He was about to argue the point, then caught the look in her eyes and said nothing.

"When did you come here?"

"Not long ago."

"Where have you been until then?"

"All over."

They walked on. "Where do you live?" she asked after a while.

He told her.

"Alone?" she asked.

"With a family."

"Your family?"

"My family is in the ghetto: my mother, my uncle, his

15

wife, and their little girl."

"Are you here with your father?"

"My father died in April, a normal death."

She noticed he said "normal," not "natural." Here they called it "one's own death." "He must have been a righteous man," they would say, or "She was a woman of valor," to earn the privilege to die one's own death. She had heard it so often that she almost said it now, but afraid he might mock her again, she said nothing, only touched his arm lightly with the tips of her fingers.

He reached over, covered her hand for a moment before taking it into his. She left it there, warmly nestled. After a while she asked him what his name was. "Marek Rodwan," he answered.

"I am Lisa," she said, "Lisa Unger."

The snow gleamed in the bright sunshine as they walked through the park the next day. It was soft and powdery, except for the narrow path in the middle. Between the snow-covered bench and the poet's bust the question she didn't ask the day before seemed to be waiting.

"What did your father die of?"

He contemplated the question as if there was more than one answer and he was trying to choose the right one.

"If you asked my mother," he said, "she would probably tell you that he died of the war, and she would make it sound like a disease. My father fell ill shortly after he was denied access to his factory. He owned a textile mill before the war. It was put under Aryan management. He worked there in the beginning, then they didn't need him anymore. Shortly after, he began to feel sick. Somehow my mother tied the two together. 'A man should have something to do,' she would say, 'or he withers away.' That's what was happening. My father began to wither away. Only not because of idleness but because of melanoma."

16

"What kind of disease is that?"

"A form of cancer. It would have destroyed him, war or no war, but my mother never accepted it. 'I have to build him up,' she would say. 'What he needs is protein,' and she would buy meat and milk at black-market prices, even though my father could not so much as look at food. After a while he didn't look like himself anymore, and when he finally did die, all I could feel was relief."

"Because he didn't have to suffer anymore?"

"Because I did not have to watch him suffer," Marek corrected her. "I've never talked about this before," he added, making her feel as though she had just been given a gift.

They were approaching the bench. He stopped, swept the snow off, and sat down, pulling her next to him. He took a photograph out of a brown wallet. "That's him," he said, handing it over to her. "My father."

She looked at the man of medium height, in pinstripes, hand resting on the ornate handle of a walking cane, at the woman in a polka-dot summer dress, her face partly covered by a wide-brimmed hat, and in between, towering over both of them, Marek, his student cap askew. It was like one of those pictures that would appear in a newspaper under the caption, ". . . And in happier time," next to another depicting a disaster.

"You look like him," she said, returning the picture. "Your mother is darker."

He nodded.

"Were you a student at the university?"

"At the polytechnic."

"Engineering?"

"Architecture."

"After the war you will build me a house."

"Strange you should say that; those were exactly my mother's words just before I left."

She looked at him puzzled.

"It was decided, that is, my mother and the rest of the family decided, that I was the one to stay 'on the outside.' They bribed a clerk in the municipal office to provide me with Aryan papers. My mother sold everything she had to pay for them. I couldn't bring myself to leave, but she insisted, saying that I owed it to myself, then that I owed it to my father. As it turned out, there was no reason to argue, for I couldn't stay anyway.

"I helped them move, the five of them. It was one tiny room, and the window faced a dirty brick wall. My mother must have known exactly what I was thinking because she said, 'After the war you will build me a house.' "

From the time she learned Marek had Aryan papers stashed away someplace, Lisa lived in constant fear that he might suddenly leave. She kept reassuring herself he would do so only if faced with immediate danger—why else would he have bothered to register?—and repeatedly went over his description of what living "on the outside" was like.

"You have to adopt a whole new personality," he had told her. "You put distance between yourself and others, you learn to be silent. The less you say, the better off you are. Just 'yes' and 'no,' and if you have to say more, you crack a joke. That catches the other fellow by surprise and gives you a few moments to size him up. After a while you are afraid you might have forgotten how to talk. It drives you crazy. I mean literally crazy. It came to a point that I once locked myself in a lavatory just to talk and hear my own voice. When I realized what I was doing, I decided it was time for a break and I came here."

Remembering all that, Lisa managed to convince herself that he was not going to leave, not for a while in spite of the persistent frightening rumors, that he would rather take his chances than resume what he had referred to as a "schizophrenic existence."

18

But her fear returned with increased force as they walked their usual path, a foreboding silence between them. The snow was coming down heavily, a fact she found ominous, thinking that on a snowy day they had met and on a snowy day they were going to part, for there was little doubt in her mind that that was what was going to happen. Dusk began to fall. The snow gleamed in the light of the streetlamps. He slowed down and stopped next to one. He reached into his pocket, took out something, and handed it over to her. It was a postcard. She held it up to the bluish, quivering light of the gas lantern and read, "Dear Mama."

Uncertain whether to go on, she skipped over the lines and looked for a signature. "Marek," it said on the bottom. She turned the card over. It was addressed to Mrs. Eugenia Rodwan. To the left of it, a red stamp across read, "Addressee unknown," and underneath someone added in bold block letters, "Deported."

She held the postcard in her hand thinking nothing, except that the snow was falling on it, making it wet.

He took it from her and folded it before putting it back in his pocket.

"It will smudge," she said. "The ink will smudge." Then, fear getting the better of her, "What are you going to do now? Are you going to leave?"

He placed his hands on her shoulders, turned her around, and holding her at arm's length, he looked at her and shook his head.

Later—it must have been much later, for the snow had melted, and in the park, stalks of new grass began to sprout—when they stood on a bridge arched over a lily pond, he told her he had been refused a permit to stay in the city.

She looked at him without understanding. "But you registered," she said.

19

"So much for the law of averages." He managed a faint smile. "Besides, as a newcomer, I had little chance."

"You can't," she said and wanted to say more, but her head was empty of every word she had ever known. She leaned against the railing and closed her eyes. The spring breeze made her shiver. He gathered her in the folds of his open coat and held her close. "Come with me," he said. "Let's get married."

She freed herself to look at him. "You are not joking. You do mean it."

He nodded.

Feeling her fear and the dark portent dissolve in the warmth of unexpected joy, she threw her arms around his neck and clung to him for dear life.

Her mother's face resembled a tragic mask, the corners of her mouth drooping, when Lisa broke the news to her.

"Married, in times like these? When God only knows what tomorrow will bring? And what kind of wedding is this going to be?"

Her mother had it all planned for her. Lisa was to attend a university, preferably in the West—the West was where culture dwelled—where she would meet a young man who would fall in love with her. (Who would resist Lisa, beautiful as she was, her hair wavy and dark, her face delicate and pale, her eyes the color of amber, her daughter whom she had named after a famous authoress rather than any of the deceased grandmothers, the source of her pride, the perfected continuation of her own self?) The wedding would be lavish and huge, with many guests arriving from abroad, Lisa in a long white dress, carrying a bouquet of roses and baby's breath, the ceremony performed by a rabbi from an old dynasty.

The rabbi who married them had no fame and no following. There were no guests, for they were strangers in the small town Marek had moved to, followed by Lisa, soon joined by her parents who had refused to stay behind, still believing their love would guard and protect her. Her mother cried all through the ceremony, but not her father. He welcomed Marek as the son he had always wanted and never had, and stood there erect, a happy smile in his eyes.

It did not last long, her father's happiness or her mother's discontent.

The news of the roundup reached Lisa on the nearby farm where she was working, picking apples in the orchard. A barefoot, flaxen-haired peasant girl brought it. "Something is going on in the Jew Street," she had said and added something else, something that Lisa didn't hear, for she was already running across the road to where Marek worked. She found him next to the wheat-thrashing machine and pulled him away. They crossed the field, stopping between the tall, swaying stalks so as not to be spotted.

The street they lived on was deserted. They entered the rickety, wooden house without seeing a soul. The apartment they had shared with her parents was empty. On the kitchen table two bowls were half-filled with soup, a slice of bread with teeth marks next to one. Near an overturned chair, a spoon, caked with dried food, was lying on the floor. Lisa picked it up and put it on the table. She straightened the chair and sat down, her arms limp. "They should have never left. They should have stayed where they belonged."

Marek touched her shoulder. "Don't," he said. Then, "We cannot stay here."

She said she knew.

In the evening, when it got dark, they left. Marek's good, safe identification papers were in his pocket. Lisa's recently purchased documents, issued in the name of Elisa Rodwanski, née Wysocki, had been hurriedly manufactured and were so amateurish that they could hope only that no one would ever check.

21

he next day it was Lisa who asked the first question. "How is she?" she asked, pointing at the bed down the room.

"The same," Natalia said. "Nothing changes with her."

"What is she like?"

"Don't you know?"

All that Lisa could see from where she lay was the white frame of the bed. "I can't see from here," she said.

"She looks like a mummy—nothing but bandages. Just an opening for the mouth, for the nostrils, and for the eyes. They shoot her full of drugs and feed her liquids through a straw, and from time to time they wheel her down to embalm her again. They shake their heads and talk about her and sigh. Sometimes I think they keep her alive so they can talk about her, shake their heads, and sigh. She comes from Dresden, you know."

"I know," Lisa said. "I heard them."

"They" were Dr. Boesel; Dr. Luther; Marianne, the head nurse, with a smile plastered on her face as though she were posing for a photograph; Suzanne, the one with gentle hands; Irmgard, with a face like a red polished apple; and Dorothea, the Valkyrie, Germanic and strong.

After the floor was mopped, looking shiny and new as

long as it was wet, then cracked and dull again, they would march in. Boesel and Luther, Marianne and Suzanne, Irmgard and Dorothea, standing like soldiers according to rank. One day someone else joined them, standing between the doctors and the nurses, wearing a white coat, her head uncovered, the gray hair contrasting with a very young face, with a slightly upturned nose and a full mouth.

"This is Dr. Kamin," Dr. Boesel introduced her to Lisa, then took the X ray from an envelope and handed it over to her. As she held the slick, shiny negative against the light, Lisa caught a glimpse of the white shadows that were her bones, looking like fossils excavated from a cave.

Dr. Kamin said something technical, and then they talked in hushed whispers that Lisa did not try to follow. Then they left.

Later Dr. Kamin came back alone and sat down on the chair between Lisa's and Natalia's beds.

"How did it happen?" she asked.

"I was shot," Lisa said.

"Me too," Natalia said quickly, as though afraid to be left out.

"Why?"

Natalia shifted uneasily.

"I wanted to pick up a beet," Lisa said. "I was hungry. You see, we were in a camp."

"For smuggling," Natalia interrupted.

"Not for smuggling," Lisa said, "but because we were Jews."

She knew why she had said it. It was pity she wanted from Dr. Kamin, and more than that, she wanted the woman's guilt and her shame. She watched her face. A quick shadow passed over it, then disappeared. *Now*, Lisa thought, *she will suddenly remember something she has to do, and she will leave . . . or she will say something about "the Dresden" . . . or, like photographs out of a wallet, she will bring out her personal losses.*

23

But Dr. Kamin said nothing.

"What is wrong with me?" Lisa asked.

Dr. Kamin didn't answer right away. "To start with, you were undernourished."

"Oh, really," Lisa said.

"Then you lost an enormous amount of blood," Dr. Kamin went on, ignoring the interjection. "There was a bullet in your abdomen. It was removed. There was no damage, and the wound healed nicely. But the leg doesn't seem to be mending. There is an infection that is not going away."

"Why?" Lisa asked.

"We don't know."

"Oh," Lisa said.

"I myself think that the tibia—the shin bone—is splintered. And it's the splinters that are causing the infection. Keeping it in traction, in my opinion, doesn't do any good. It is not the position of the bone that causes the trouble."

"I see," Lisa said. Then, pointing to Natalia, "And she?"

"Her wound was only superficial. But she has lungs like someone who has worked in a coal mine."

"I was breathing poison for two years," Natalia said. "I worked filling grenades."

From the corridor came the clatter of dishes and the voices of nurses going off duty, bidding good-bye to one another loudly, as if together with their uniforms they shed their whispers. Supper was brought in. Dr. Kamin rose, ready to leave.

"Goody," Natalia said, grimacing as she sniffed the sour-smelling food. "Dishwater soup for a change. Why," she called accusingly after the doctor, "are we still on a camp diet?"

Dr. Kamin, already at the door, turned around. "Because," she said, "there is famine in the country."

*　　*　　*

24

Lisa woke up in the middle of the night. Over her head the ceiling hung like a black shroud. Somewhere at the edge of her consciousness images gathered, like an angry crowd against a bolted gate. Out of the shadows crept the primeval fear of darkness and night.

"Natalia," she called. "Natalia."

But Natalia, submerged in the depths of drug-induced sleep, did not hear her.

From her silence, loneliness came, and joined the fear. Lisa felt abandoned and cold, like a shipwrecked survivor on an iceberg floating on dark waters.

Behind her, she knew, hung a cord, which, if tugged, would mobilize a nurse, just as a string pulled by a puppeteer would put a marionette in motion.

She stretched her arm over her head, her hand tapping in the dark. Her fingertips touched the end of the cord, but it slipped away before she could grasp it. The cord seemed to be playing evasive games with her, teasing her, now coming closer, now escaping her again. Her breath came rasping and short. Her face was covered with sweat. There . . . Her fingers closed tightly over the cord. She tugged at it again and again, involving every muscle in her body, as if she were pulling at a heavy rope in a belfry. The door creaked. Following the yellow, widening beam of a flashlight, the nurse tiptoed in. The light traveled searchingly along the wall.

"Here," Lisa called softly. Her hand let go of the cord, and her arm covered her eyes in a reflex, protecting them from the sudden glare.

"What's the matter?" the nurse whispered, coming closer. It was Suzanne, the one with the gentle hands.

"I can't sleep," Lisa whispered back.

"Anything hurt?"

"I just can't sleep. Give me something to make me sleep."

The light shifted, illuminating the chart at the foot of the bed.

"You got a shot at eight. I can't give you anything else without the doctor."

"Then ask the doctor."

"The doctor wouldn't give you anything either. Besides, there is no one here." Her hand touched Lisa's forehead. "You are perspiring. Your pillow is wet." She lifted Lisa's head with one hand, the other turning the pillow. She placed Lisa's head down carefully, like a fragile object.

"What's going on?" Natalia mumbled, waking up.

"Nothing," Suzanne said. "She just can't sleep."

"Do what I do," Natalia said drowsily. "Recite verses. It works for me."

"Better now?" Suzanne asked Lisa.

Lisa nodded. The fear was gone, and the loneliness was carried away. "Could you turn on the little light and leave it on?" she asked.

"I'm not supposed to. It would disturb the others."

"Then at least don't close the door all the way."

"That I will do. Go to sleep now. Good night."

"Good night," Lisa said, and following Natalia's advice, she whispered softly:

> For many reasons
> And for sorrows many,
> Give me a pillow,
> Stuffed with hops.

Beer was made out of hops. Stored in huge burlap sacks, they filled the place with a strong, sweet aroma. The place was the brewery where Marek was working.

FOUR

*T*hey got off the train; everyone did. It was the last stop. They waited, letting the others go first, the men sweating in their sheepskins, the peasant women, kerchiefs tied under the chin, pushing their way through with wicker baskets. After everyone had left, the station empty but for an attendant, they too got off.

The attendant, in a faded uniform and a visor cap, swinging a lantern to and fro, was walking up and down. Marek approached him.

"Excuse me," he said. "Is there a place around here where we could get something to eat?"

The man pointed at a house across the road. They thanked him and started toward it.

A sign in a window of the roadside inn advertised, "Home Cooking." The heavy door squeaked when pushed open. The large room was darkened, the tables, covered with cracked oilcloth, empty. They sat down.

"Anyone here?" Marek called. A short, balding man wearing a huge apron came in.

"Good day," Marek said. "Could we get a bite to eat here?"

"A bite it will be," the man said. "We don't serve until five." He disappeared into the kitchen.

27

Marek reached across the table and removed a wisp of straw from Lisa's hair. They had spent the previous night in a barn, hiding from a patrol.

The innkeeper returned, carrying a plate with thick slices of buttered dark bread and a generous portion of farmer cheese, wiped the table with a corner of his apron, and put the food down.

Marek rubbed his hands. "That looks good," he said. "Now, if we could only have some coffee."

"Only ersatz," the innkeeper said.

"That would be fine."

"Nothing like the smell of real coffee," the innkeeper said. "But what can you do. . . . You here to work?"

Marek hesitated but for a moment. "I sure hope so," he said.

"There is plenty of work in the brewery here. The crop was good. They need people, they bring them from all over. Good for business too."

Marek followed his eyes, which seemed to be looking under the table. "Oh, the luggage," he said. "You're not going to believe it. My wife here—did I introduce myself? My name is Rodwanski, Marek Rodwanski, and this is my wife, Elisa—Lisa for short. Anyway, she went to the washroom on the train. It took a long time, and I went to look for her. I asked a nice young man to keep an eye on our suitcase and when we came back . . ."

"No man and no suitcase?"

"You guessed it."

"Yah," the innkeeper said, shaking his head. "These are crazy times we live in."

"We will have to write home for some things," Marek said.

"Where is your home?" the innkeeper wanted to know.

"Warsaw."

"The Germans barbecued the Jews in the ghetto there,"

28

the innkeeper said.

Lisa, her head bent, was busy following the cracks on the tablecloth with her forefinger.

"So I heard," Marek said. "We were not coming from Warsaw; we were coming from Lodz—that's where we got married." Then to change the subject, "You wouldn't know of a place we could rent?"

"I just meant to suggest one. Nothing fancy, mind you. An artist's studio. My niece, a bit crazy I must say, used to paint there. She went to England just before the war. Never made it back. I happen to have the keys. As I said, the place is not much, isolated. You'll be needing a bike."

"I suppose one cannot be too choosy."

"Not with all the people coming here. I'll take you there after you finish eating, if you want me to."

"Sure."

"I hope the pictures won't offend you," the innkeeper said and chuckled.

FIVE

*W*hen she opened her eyes, it was morning, and Dr. Kamin was sitting next to her bed. She must have come in right away, before even putting the white coat on. The dress she wore was a faded blue and too heavy for this time of year.

"What happened last night?" the doctor asked.

"I woke up. I couldn't go back to sleep."

"Was that all?"

"All?" Lisa said. "It was enough. I don't like lying awake." Then, "And I know the reason," she added, for suddenly it became clear to her. "You changed the medication."

"I took you off morphine."

"What did I get then?"

"Something we call a placebo."

"I don't need a pacifier, I need the real thing."

"No, you don't," Dr. Kamin said firmly. "You are not in pain anymore."

The door opened and the nurse peered in. "Here you are, Doctor," she said. "I've been looking for you all over. The Krantz woman is vomiting blood."

"I'll be back," the doctor said, and hurried out.

"You talk to her," Lisa said to Natalia. "Tell her how I

30

kept you awake."

But when Dr. Kamin came back, Natalia wasn't in the room, having been taken down to have her dressing changed, and Lisa was dozing.

"No wonder you stay awake at night," the doctor said. "You nap too much during the day."

"You have it all wrong," Lisa said, opening her eyes. "I nap during the day because I can't sleep at night."

"It would be good if you did something during the day to make the time go faster."

"Like weaving baskets, for instance?"

"How about reading?" Dr. Kamin said. "You do read German, don't you?" She handed her a book.

Lisa turned to the title page, looked at the stilettos of the Gothic lettering and then at the doctor. "Thomas Mann?" she said.

"I guess I couldn't resist the temptation of letting you know that I had a book by a banned author on my shelf—a credit I don't really deserve. It belonged to my husband."

Lisa smiled. "Just as I couldn't resist throwing my personal plight at you the first chance I got."

Dr. Kamin laughed nervously. "Now," she said, "that we've exchanged calling cards, perhaps we can talk."

But they knew it was hard, if not impossible, to do so without falling back into the same pattern—one making accusations, the other presenting an alibi.

"Is your husband a medical doctor too?" Lisa asked after a while.

"He was killed on the Eastern Front, and he was an artist, a painter. Abstract."

"Oh," Lisa said, then paused, not knowing what else to say. "Abstract? The 'decadent art'? Wasn't he persecuted for it?"

"Not really. He wasn't well enough known. He was not a great artist, I'm afraid."

31

"After I got married we lived in what used to be an artist's studio," Lisa said. "There were canvases all over the wall. I think you would call it cubism. I couldn't tell. I don't know much about art."

The unframed canvases depicting male and female nudes covered every inch of the wall. The elongated and one-dimensional figures looked unreal, except for the eyes, which seemed to follow Lisa around the room. The room was flooded with light but was drafty, the wind blowing through the large, unprotected window. Outside there were marshes and a muddy pond, full of frogs, whose loud, monotonous croaking lulled them to sleep.

The room was sparsely furnished—a bed with a straw mattress, a pillow, and two army blankets, some shelves, a stand with a basin, a pail, a double-burner cooking plate, and a wood-burning stove.

The stairs led to a basement (the strange structure, squatting in the middle of nowhere, seemed to consist of an attic and a basement, with nothing in between), the assorted junk covered with dust and cobwebs, which Lisa promised to clean up "one day."

"When was that?"

"In 1943."

"Don't you know what happened to him?" Dr. Kamin asked.

"It isn't hard to guess. The same happened to him as happened to the others. Except for Natalia and myself, perhaps. Two of the species, like after the flood."

"If I remember my Bible correctly," Dr. Kamin said with an attempt at a smile, "it was a male and a female."

"Just another blunder."

"You said 'guess.' That means you don't really know."

"What's the difference?"

"Hope."
"Hope is for fools."

Lisa had hoped at first. She would write letters, paying the "contact" with her bread, hoping that if she sent ten, one might reach him. She would hope for an answer, and when the first transports of men began to arrive, she would search for him, looking at the sunken faces, hoping to find his. "Excuse me," she would say. "Please," she would say, the polite niceties from another life sounding almost offensive in the stench of the barracks. "Do you know . . ." "Yes, tall . . . yes, dark blond . . . do you?" She would hold her breath waiting for an answer, for a moment feeling alive again. A head shake. "No, but the other men might. . . ." Another man, another barracks. She would walk through the mud, through the slush . . . "Do you know what happened to . . .? I was told that you might . . ." A head shake again. . . . Once she was sure she spotted him in the crowd. He was standing with his back to her. She ran toward him, holding a piece of bread out. When she reached him, he turned around. The eyes of a stranger looked at the bread. She gave it to him, then ran back.

Hope reborn, hope dying again. And each time it died, Lisa died.

Talking became futile, and it was with relief that they noticed Natalia, who, standing in the open door, leaning against the frame, waved at them as if she were returning from a long trip.

"Tomorrow you will take a little ride," Dr. Kamin said in a tone of voice reserved for children and the infirm. "We'll be taking new X rays."

When she was refused breakfast the next morning, Lisa knew it would be more than X rays.

33

"What are they going to do to me?" she asked Marianne.

Marianne's perpetual smile acquired an air of mystery. She stood next to the bed, saturated cotton in one hand, syringe in the other. She rubbed Lisa's arm vigorously, then slid the needle into it easily, as if it were a block of butter.

"Here," she said, withdrawing the needle with equal skill, "relax now."

Every thought drained out. Lisa's head felt empty and light. But her tongue grew stiff and heavy in her mouth.

Two orderlies lifted her onto a stretcher and started toward the door. As they passed by von Dresden's bed, Lisa saw her for the first time. The white of the bandages blended with the white of the pillow, and it was hard to tell where von Dresden ended and the pillow began. In the round openings, eyes shone, immobile, unknowing, the eyes of an animal on a taxidermist's shelf. It was one thing to be told about her and another to see for herself, and the orderlies seemed to slow down to make sure that she saw.

"How are you today?" The voice was that of Dr. Kamin, but the face leaning over didn't seem to belong to her, so changed was it, the hair covered by a surgical cap.

Lisa moved her lips.

Dr. Kamin touched them with a wet sponge. Lisa sucked greedily.

"It's horrible," she managed to say. "I saw her, von Dresden. It's horrible."

Dr. Kamin put something over her face. "Count," she said.

Lisa counted to twenty, then became confused and began to lose consciousness.

When she came to, she was back in the room. Natalia, lying in bed, was watching her.

"What did they do to me?" Lisa asked.

"They put your leg in a cast," Natalia said.

Her leg was not elevated anymore, and out of the thick,

white layers, her toes peered, blue and stiff. She wiggled them to make sure she could.

"What did you do to me?" she repeated later to Dr. Kamin, who had come to see her.

"We reset the bone and put it in a cast. We are going to keep it there for a while. Then we shall see."

Lisa asked no more questions. She did not mind, nor did she care, all she knew was that she was very tired. She closed her eyes and went back to sleep.

When Lisa opened her eyes, she saw Natalia sitting up, looking at her.

"Welcome back to the land of the living," Natalia said.

Lisa said nothing. She closed her eyes again.

"I couldn't help overhearing what you said to Kamin yesterday, about Marek, I mean. You said he was dead, then you said you didn't know. I have been thinking about it. Which is it?"

"I don't know," Lisa said, her voice still heavy with sleep. What did she want of her? Why didn't she let her sleep?

"It makes no sense. When did you see him last?"

"I'm tired. I can't think. . . . Even when I am not tired, I can't think about it. Only in dreams . . . I am having those dreams."

"Maybe if you talked about it you wouldn't have those dreams."

"Maybe," Lisa said and went back to sleep.

*T*hen the dream came. It was not the way dreams usually are, when on some level of consciousness one knows one would wake up. It was more like watching a movie seen many times before, every scene anticipated, knowing exactly how it was going to end, but still unable to walk out. It was a vivid dream, each detail sharp and precise, from the sound of the voices to the foreboding that had been with her ever since Marek had been promoted from the stockroom to the office.

"I don't like it," she had said then. "I don't like it at all."

It was as if her mother was talking through her. "Jews should stay in the background, they shouldn't be seen," her mother would say each time a Jew had arrived at a position of prominence.

"I don't like it," Lisa repeated in her mother's voice. She didn't trust the Poles Marek had been working with. She had heard about them enough—Mikulski, the foreman; the redhead Smolka; and the rest of them.

"You wouldn't believe the things they say," Marek had told her. "The other day, Smolka bemoaned the loss of his Jewish neighbor. Want to know why? You'd never guess. He and his neighbor had shared an outhouse and, 'Jewish shit is a good fertilizer,' he had said."

"How did they react to your promotion? What did they say?" Lisa wanted to know.

"Oh, they patted me on the shoulder, called me a big shot, said it would be below my dignity to associate with them. The usual."

"And the redhead, Smolka, did he make any remarks? Has he looked funny at you?"

"Stop worrying," Marek had said. "None of them had any ambition to work in the office. Besides, there is nothing I can do."

"Perhaps there is."

"Turn down the promotion and the extra food rations—it would look suspicious."

"We could run."

"In the middle of the winter? Where to? The worst thing we could do is panic."

But worry she did, sharing her fears with Marek at first, then bearing them alone.

That day Marek was late. It's probably nothing, she told herself. He had to stay longer. After all, he had a more responsible position now. She would start supper, she thought, and by the time she finished peeling the potatoes, he would come.

The potatoes were already boiling and soon were soft enough to eat, and Marek still hadn't come back. She was overcome by the same feeling of abandonment she had experienced as a child when she would wake up in the middle of the night, walk into her parents' room, and find it empty. She remembered the bargains she would make with God. "Good Lord," she would say, "if you make them come back, I promise, I will never tell a lie, I will never say a bad word, I will give all my pennies to the blind beggar. . . ."

Now she had nothing to offer in return, and so "Good Lord," she said in her mind, "if you make him come back, I promise, I will never ask you for anything again."

As if in answer to her prayer, she heard the sound of footsteps. The steps sounded heavy. He must be tired, she thought.

"Marek?" she called down.

And when there was no answer, she knew. She had imagined it often enough. The sound of footsteps, then the stranger.

The stranger wore the blue uniform of a Polish policeman.

"Elisa Rodwanski?" he said, breathing heavily from the climb. And when she nodded, he said, "You will have to come with me."

"Where is my husband?"

"At the commissariat. I am taking you there."

Lisa reached for her coat.

The policeman pointed at the boots near the door. "Wear these," he said. "It's slushy outside."

Lisa put them on.

They walked down the stairs. On the street he turned to her. "I'm really sorry, miss," he said. "I hate to do it. I wish I could let you go, but if I did . . . It's either you or me. You understand . . ."

Lisa said she did.

At the corner, sitting in a horse-drawn cab, a civilian was waiting for them. They got in.

At the police station, in a big bare room, next to the dust-covered table, Marek sat, his face ashen.

Across the table, in a brown uniform, wearing a swastika on his left arm and with the bored expression of one forced to watch the same performance too many times, sat the investigator. Two policemen, one German, one Polish, stood at the door.

The civilian looked around. "Where is the interpreter?" he asked in German.

38

The policeman said there was no need for one. The investigator had lived in Danzig and was fluent in Polish.

The investigator nodded affirmatively.

"What are we waiting for then?"

"The informer," the policeman said.

When she saw the freckled face, the head of red hair, Lisa was not surprised. She expected him, Wacek Smolka, looking just the way she had pictured him.

He walked in with a solemn awareness of his importance.

"Mr. Smolka . . ." the investigator started, but he didn't have to finish the sentence, for Wacek Smolka, waiting and ready, had the answer prepared.

"Well," he began, "I was suspicious of him." He pointed at Marek. "Since the first time I saw him. I have a good nose; I can smell a Jew. Even if this one didn't look like one, he was still different, not like the rest of us, if you know what I mean. I was so suspicious, I would even follow him to the men's room, thought I might get a peek at his . . . you know what, but he was careful. Then before Christmas we rented the bathhouse. Everybody got excited. It was a big deal, you know. *Now I've got him,* I thought. But he didn't show up. He had a cold, he said. 'What's the matter,' I said to him the next day. 'Are you afraid to show off your birdie?' I have this sense of humor, you know. He gave me that high and mighty look of his, but I could tell that he was scared. And when he pushed himself up to the top, I said to myself, *You and I are going to have our day in court yet.* I am coming to the point," he said quickly, seeing the investigator wince impatiently.

"I went to Lodz to visit my godfather. I waited for the streetcar in front of the photographer's. The tram didn't come right away, so I looked at the pictures in the window. And suddenly, who do you think grinned at me from the golden frame? Him," he said triumphantly, pointing at Marek.

39

"He looked younger in the picture, the hair wet-combed, elegantly, with a part. A tie, a jacket, a real dandy . . . I forgot the tram and walked in to talk to the photographer.

" 'I want the picture,' I said, 'and the name too.' You see, I read these detective stories, so I know how it's done.

"The photographer wouldn't hear of it at first. The picture was taken in 1939 and he wasn't going to bother, he said. Then I told him I had to have it. He wanted to know why, and I said the reason was patriotic." He paused, waiting for approval. Then he reached into his pocket, took out a photograph, and placed it on the table.

"His first name is Marek, all right. But not Rodwanski." He turned the photograph around. "Here it is, in the photographer's own handwriting—Rodwan."

He finished. He breathed in deeply and let the air out, puffing up the freckled cheeks.

The investigator, who until then had busied himself by rolling narrow strips of paper, looked at Marek.

"It's true," Marek said. His voice was low, not even quivering, just extremely tired.

"My name is Marek Rodwan and I am a Jew. But my wife is not."

The interrogator rose.

"Nice try," he said.

The German policeman walked Marek out of the room. The other led Lisa into a cell that made her think of a chicken coop. It was about that size, and there was straw in the corner.

When the door closed behind her, a thought flashed into her mind that she should pray. She didn't. In her head there was a mixture of voices, faces, pictures.

She sat down on the straw. She sat there through the night awake.

When dawn broke, the door opened again. There was the policeman who had picked her up.

40

They walked down the corridor. *The friendly policeman,* she thought.

Suddenly a picture popped into her mind, the one from her primer, of a smiling policeman helping a little girl across the street. And underneath in calligraphic script, "A policeman is your friend."

"Where are you taking me?" she asked.

"To the truck. You are going to a camp, a work camp."

"And my husband?"

"He too, to a different one, a men's camp. It could be worse, you know," he said. "You are both young. You might survive."

There were two trucks standing in the prison yard. One was already filled with women. The men were lined up next to the other.

She climbed the step. She didn't look back. It seemed as though she was already dead. She felt nothing.

Lisa woke up, covered with cold sweat, her heart pounding. She closed her eyes waiting for it to calm down, then opened them, afraid she might fall alseep and dream again.

Natalia was sitting on the edge of the bed, her legs dangling.

"Thought you'd never wake up," Natalia said. "You slept forever."

The room was filled with twilight.

"What time is it?" Lisa asked.

"Suppertime," Natalia said. Then with a note of mystery in her voice, "What would you say to a piece of crisp chicken, a slice of white bread, and chocolate cake for dessert?" Making up imaginary menus was Natalia's favorite game.

"Fine," Lisa said, playing along.

Natalia hopped over and put the food down next to Lisa, using a flattened brown paper bag as a plate.

41

Lisa gasped. "Where did this come from?"

"Sasha brought it."

"The freedom man?" Lisa asked. She tore off a piece of chicken and put it in her mouth. She crumbled the cake between her fingers. She found it profoundly symbolic that after years of dreaming about food, now that it was in front of her, she had no taste for it. "I will eat later," she said, putting it away.

"We got something else," Natalia said. "Look at the night table."

Lisa turned her head and saw the side of a brown wooden box.

"A radio," Natalia said. "I haven't had a chance to play it yet. You were asleep; I didn't want to wake you up." She turned the knob. First came a static sound, then a man's voice recited in a monotone a list of names; another turn, and the room was filled with music.

"Isn't it beautiful?" Natalia said, closing her eyes. " 'Für Elise' . . . Listen how beautiful."

Lisa listened. And a room came back to her, and the big piano in the corner, and herself so small her feet could hardly reach the pedals, playing the very same tune. Next to the piano, leaning against it, they stood, her parents, nodding in rhythm, exchanging smiles and misty looks, and it was for those smiles and for those looks that she had tried so hard, stretching her fingers to reach an octave.

"Turn it off," she said hoarsely.

"Don't you like it?" Natalia said in an offended tone of voice.

"Turn it off."

Natalia obeyed.

Was there a connection, Lisa thought, between herself now and that little girl, between herself and the thin adolescent, herself and the young woman who was Marek's wife? It seemed as though she had died many times, to be repeat-

42

edly reincarnated.

She could ask Natalia to turn off the radio, but she could not turn off the images. They were still there, faceless, blurred, nodding shadows. Two lives, she thought, and nothing left, not a trace, not a proof that they ever were, not even a photograph or a scrap of paper with handwriting. Nothing. Only she. Suddenly she felt it as a burden that they had imposed upon her out of their nonexistence, to bear witness that they had been.

From the radio came lively accordion music. "How is that?" Natalia asked.

"Better," Lisa said.

"For someone with a voice like yours, you sure have peculiar taste in music."

he next morning Lisa saw von Dresden's body being carried out. Two men—one tall, the other short—rolled it off the bed onto a canvas stretcher. It fell and bounced up, as if on a trampoline. The short one said something, the tall one laughed. "One, two, three, go," the tall one said. They lifted the stretcher off the floor and started toward the door, the body sliding down because of their uneven heights; they were still talking, still laughing.

Von Dresden is dead, Lisa thought. She remembered a time when death was regarded with reverence, accompanied by tears and despair, followed by a long period of mourning. Then it had become a guest frequent enough to forego formalities.

Von Dresden is dead, Lisa thought once again. She looked at Natalia, still asleep. "Natalia," she called. "Natalia."

Natalia stirred. "What is it?" she asked sleepily.

"Von Dresden is dead," Lisa said.

"What?" Natalia exclaimed and sat up, suddenly awake. She stared at the empty bed. "Is that why you woke me up?" she said after a while. "What's the matter, nobody ever died on you before?" Then she lay back and turned to face the wall.

Von Dresden's bed had been stripped. After that the routine went on unchanged. The doctors came in for a short round. Nobody mentioned Von Dresden. Later, Nurse Irmgard, with the help of an aide, wheeled the bed out of the room.

"Dr. Kamin wants you to have more air and privacy," she said by way of explanation. The floor was mopped, and where von Dresden's bed used to be, the linoleum was unscuffed and lighter in shade.

Natalia kept looking in that direction, and Lisa followed her glance. The room was strangely quiet.

"She didn't really die today," Natalia said finally. "She was dead a long time ago. Say something. I don't like it when it's so quiet." And when Lisa remained silent, she slid down the bed, reached out, and switched the radio on. "Let's have some music at least."

A woman soprano cut the air with a shrill sound. Natalia turned the knob and stopped at a newscast. "The British Parliament opened its session today. Now for the other headlines. A synagogue was dedicated in Leipzig, and in Berlin, Marshal Zhukov—"

Natalia switched the radio off abruptly and looked at Lisa.

"What did he just say? Just before Berlin and Zhukov?"

Lisa swallowed, for her voice seemed to be stuck in her throat.

"They dedicated a synagogue in Leipzig."

Natalia was sitting on the side of the bed, both feet touching the floor, the left leg limp and thinner than the other. "My God," she said, leaning forward.

Lisa lay quietly, her eyes fixed on the ceiling, thinking how strange it was that on the same day that von Dresden died this news should reach them, and how the two would stay with her, inseparably linked together.

A dedication of a synagogue, she thought. But the words failed to evoke a mental image; they remained words, wavering in her mind like skywriting in the wind.

Only after a while did they dare to talk about it, in short, breathless questions that bounced between them like a rubber ball. "What do you think it was like?" "Where did the people come from?" "Who were they?" "Where do they live?" "How?" And again, "What was it like?"

With no recollection to fall back on, not even secondhand knowledge, for it was without precedent that the remnants of a destroyed people should be coming together to worship, Lisa came up with a haphazard composite of a holiday service she remembered and an armistice-day celebration borrowed from a movie she once saw.

Later, that vision came back in her sleep. She saw a dark, dense crowd, waving and swaying, separated from her by a wall of haze. She tried to walk through it in order to join it, but couldn't, for the haze was thick and sticky, like molasses. And then she began to fall, just like von Dresden, only in slow motion, knowing all the while she would wake up once she hit the stretcher.

"Wake up, wake up." Natalia was sitting on the edge of her bed, shaking her. "You're having a nightmare."

Lisa opened her eyes and looked at her.

"You called for Marek."

"I did?"

It seemed strange. He wasn't even in the dream.

Like color postcards found in a mailbox, words, snatches of conversation, and phrases caught in passing brought Lisa greetings from the outside world.

Natalia soon became another liaison. Clad in a hospital gown so wide it could be wrapped twice around her small waist, the sleeves rolled up at the wrist, she would set forth, shuffling her feet in the oversized felt slippers, and would slide uncertainly like a beginning skater into the expanded world that now included the corridor. She would set out with the excitement of a traveler and come back carrying reports

46

and gossip like souvenirs from a journey.

The girl in the next room had had pieces of shrapnel removed from her thigh; another one with third-degree burns on her arms, who had been rescued from a bombed-out house, would be released shortly; two women in the room down the corridor had been raped by Russians; and the elderly patient with gallstones was mentioned so casually that it was obvious Natalia regarded her as a parvenu.

Another link between Lisa and the world was the tree outside her window, which served as both a weather vane and a calendar. The branches calm or swaying in the wind, the leaves dusty or slick with rain, indicated the weather; the buds that flowered, the flowers that withered, told of seasons passing. And now, the first golden leaves heralded the summer's end.

The shrunken days passed faster now, and the time grew shorter between Natalia's reports, and between Dr. Kamin's visits and the books she brought Lisa to read.

But the nights stretched, long and heavy, crowded with dreams. In them she would have to flee and couldn't move, or she would be walking an endless road to a shelter that would disappear the moment she got close. There were dreams of death. There was one in which she was forced to swallow sawdust, which filled out her legs, her torso, and her arms until she was like Maxie, the toy bear she had once had. And when it reached her neck, she began to choke. She was awakened by her own scream.

One night in her sleep, she could feel worms crawling down her body. She knew that she was dreaming, for if she were dead, she wouldn't feel it. She opened her eyes. It was already daylight. She was awake now, and the crawling feeling persisted, now concentrated under her cast.

"Something is crawling on my leg," Lisa said to Nurse Irmgard, who had just walked in with the basin.

"I'll look at it in a minute," she said. She put the basin

down, pushed the cover away, and gasped, "My God." She touched the cast with the tip of her finger, replaced the cover, rushed out, and came back with Dr. Kamin.

Nurse Irmgard threw the cover off with a sweeping gesture, as if unveiling a work of art.

Dr. Kamin leaned over. Her gasp was the same, only she did not invoke God. She cursed.

She called the nurse aside, who then went out and soon returned with a male attendant who carried a pair of scissors in his hand.

The leg must have gotten thinner, for there was enough room between it and the cast for the blade to fit comfortably. There was a sound like a cracked nutshell, and the cast fell open, exposing the leg resting there, a wrinkled, livid kernel. Lisa looked at it with detached curiosity. Somewhere on the calf, between the knee and the ankle, from an opening no bigger than a small coin, transparent liquid oozed in a thin stream.

Dr. Kamin looked at it with an exasperated sigh.

"It didn't work out the way you hoped, the cast, I mean," Lisa said, the sympathy in her voice directed at Dr. Kamin's frustration rather than at herself.

"How do you manage to stay so indifferent?" Dr. Kamin asked incredulously.

Lisa shrugged.

"Don't you mind lying here? Don't you want to get better?"

"What kind of stupid question is that?"

Dr. Kamin said, pointing to Natalia, who was sitting there without saying a word. "You've been up and around for a while now, and I've been waiting for the obvious question, for you to ask when you will be allowed to go home."

Natalia's brows rose in mock surprise. "Home?" she said. "Home?"

If Dr. Kamin was disconcerted, it was only for a moment.

"You know very well what I mean. Have you made an effort? Have you tried to think beyond one day?"

"Your people," Natalia interrupted, "took care of me for over four years. They made all the arrangements for me, so naturally I assumed—"

"Oh, what's the use." Dr. Kamin rose abruptly. "Don't move the leg," she said to Lisa. "The nurse will clean it and put a dressing on." She walked out the door and closed it behind her less carefully than usual.

For a while they were both quiet. Then Lisa said, "She's right. She has something there."

"About what?"

"About us not doing anything."

"What could we do from here?" Natalia said.

"Not much, I suppose. But the point is, we haven't even tried."

"Try what, for heaven's sake?" Natalia said.

"Getting in touch with the Jewish community, for instance. Ever since we've heard about the synagogue being dedicated, we've known that there were Jews there. And we haven't done anything about it."

"It hasn't really occured to us."

"I remember a woman who slept next to me in the camp," Lisa said. "Not young anymore, a nice woman. I always admired how she took everything in stride. Then, the day the rumor spread that the Allies were coming and that it would be only a matter of days before the war ended, that woman began to cry. She sat on the bunk crying. When I asked her what happened, she said that she didn't want the war to end. She didn't want to be free, she said, because then she would understand all that had happened to her."

"What does that have to do with us?" Natalia asked.

"I guess in a way the war hasn't ended for us yet. Maybe we don't want it to end for the same reason."

"Do you think we're scared?"

49

"Maybe we are," Lisa said. She paused. "I know nothing about you, Natalia. You never told me anything about yourself."

"You never asked."

"Do you suppose anyone else in your family survived?"

"My brother, maybe. He was young and healthy. He might have made it. I really expect—"

"Don't expect," Lisa interrupted. "If you don't expect anything, you won't get hurt."

Natalia looked at her as if she did not understand. "Not expect?" she said. "Then I might as well be dead. Then they might as well have killed me.... You never talked about yourself either. I asked you about Marek, and you wouldn't answer."

"Because," Lisa said, "sometimes I don't know anymore. Sometimes I don't believe he ever existed."

EIGHT

*T*he cleaned leg, a gauze square covering the wound, now rested between two oblong sand-filled sacks, which, even more than the cast, confined Lisa to one position. She envied Natalia's mobility. Having mastered the stairs, Natalia was out of the room most of the time. She discovered a lounge on the lower floor where visitors and convalescing patients would sit and where nurses would drop in for a chat.

From bits and pieces of conversation Natalia put together a picture of the surroundings. The town was small and quiet and of no special distinction. Located on a plain, it was not very picturesque. The soil was not fertile enough to be farmed, and the place had no heavy industry. An out-of-the-way town, it had escaped both the bombing and the fighting. The war casualties were brought in from places where the facilities were either destroyed or overcrowded. This small hospital was hardly equipped to handle those cases. Its medical staff consisted of old doctors like Luther, who had been retired, and Boesel, who had also stepped down, both of them recalled when the younger doctors were mobilized. Dr. Kamin had not yet completed her residency but was given the prerogatives and duties of a full-fledged physician. She was eyed by both the doctors and the nurses as an impostor, her medical approach considered unorthodox and radical.

Natalia had witnessed an argument between her and Dr. Boesel that, she believed, concerned Lisa.

"He must have suggested something," she reported later. "That made her angry, and she said that she would never agree to it."

"What makes you think they were talking about me?" Lisa asked.

"I heard your name," Natalia answered. "She said, 'By the way doctor, she has a name,' and then she said it."

Lisa tried to figure out how Dr. Boesel had referred to her—as the Jewess, the Inmate, the Foreigner, the Case of the Shattered Bone. But soon another question occupied her mind. She wondered what Dr. Boesel had suggested that made Dr. Kamin object so strongly.

She asked her about it when Dr. Kamin came for her daily visit.

"Just a difference of opinion," Dr. Kamin said. "Dr. Boesel and I often disagree. He is of the old school, and our approaches differ. In your case I would like to try something, a new drug that combats infection. I read about it. It's being used in the West. The results are spectacular."

Lisa imagined that the miracle drug, would magically re-arrange the molecules of her bone like a magnet pulling scattered metal particles together.

"It was really a purely academic discussion," Dr. Kamin went on. "The drug isn't available here; it is reserved for Allied soldiers only. We could contact the International Red Cross, but even there you must have the right connections, and I don't have them."

Lisa wanted to ask what Dr. Boesel's alternative had been, but Dr. Kamin had already risen to leave as Natalia, rustling a sheet of paper in one hand and waving a pencil like a baton in the other, walked in.

"What's that?" Lisa asked her.

"We're going to write a letter," Natalia replied.

"We are? To whom?"

"To the Jews in Leipzig."

Lisa tried to connect what she had just heard from Dr. Kamin and Natalia's sudden suggestion.

Natalia had already made herself comfortable on a chair she had pulled close to Lisa's bed. "Now," she said, "what language do we write it in?"

"In German, I suppose. After all, we're in Germany."

"*Your* German is better."

"But not my handwriting. My handwriting is illegible, and I don't know how to spell." She handed the pencil and paper to Lisa, who bent her good knee, propped a book against it, and placed the paper on top. "What shall we write?" she asked.

"First the heading. Should we say, '*Sehr geehrter*'?"

" 'Very esteemed'? We could. Too official, though."

" 'Dear Sirs'?"

"Very businesslike. It should be something more personal, and yet ... We'll think of something later." Lisa began to write, reading it out loud, as she went along. " 'For a long time we were cut off from any source of information. We accidentally heard over the radio—' "

"Wouldn't it be nicer if we said, 'over the waves,' " Natalia interrupted.

Lisa winced. "Oh, Natalia, that's horrible." She continued, " '... the news of the dedication of the synagogue in your city. We therefore assume the existence of a Jewish community in Leipzig. We appeal to you to help in ...' In what?" she said, turning to Natalia.

" '... in putting us in touch with the Red Cross or other organization that could be instrumental in obtaining proper medication as well as in locating possible survivors of our families.' " Lisa wrote Natalia's dictation.

" 'Hoping to hear from you, we remain respectfully ...' "

What's your last name?" Lisa said to Natalia. "I don't even know what your last name is."

"Berger."

" 'Natalia Berger, Lisa Unger-Rodwan,' " she concluded, signing both names. Then, without consulting Natalia, she wrote the salutation and handed the letter over to Natalia.

"To Our Jewish Brothers?" Natalia said, wrinkling her nose comically. "And to think that you objected to my—"

"I wanted to give it a personal touch. Besides," she admitted a bit bashfully, "as I wrote it, for a moment at least I meant it."

Natalia continued reading. "I still say 'over the waves' would be better. But that's not important. Now how will we send it?"

They thought for a moment, then looked at each other, and "Sasha," they exclaimed simultaneously and broke out laughing, like girls who considered uttering a word at the same time an omen for good luck.

But Sasha hadn't been seen or heard from ever since he had brought them the radio. They weren't even sure whether he was still stationed in town.

"I have an idea," Natalia exclaimed. "There's a woman down the hall whose sister works in the garrison kitchen. The next time she comes to visit, I'll ask her to look for him."

Lisa had her doubts. "Look for whom? Sasha? Do you realize how many Sashas there must be there? Any Russian soldier whose name isn't Misha or Vanya is a Sasha. As to the rest—his pockmarks, the crew cut, the metal-capped teeth—tens of them must fit that description, judging by any newspaper picture I've ever seen."

Lisa was not entirely wrong, but as it turned out, among all the closely cropped, pock-faced soldiers, only one bore the name of Sasha, and Natalia's efforts were rewarded when he wobbled into the room, a bottle sticking out of his pants pocket. He took it out before plopping across the width of Natalia's bed, his head against the wall, his legs outstretched. He took a big gulp, made a smacking sound of delight, wiped the lip of the bottle with the palm of his hand, and passed it to Natalia.

She hesitated, took a swallow, and handed the bottle over to Lisa.

Lisa brought it up to her lips and sipped. She did not care for the way it tasted and did not like the burning sensation in her throat, but she enjoyed the feeling of sudden camaraderie, as well as the conspiracy of illicit drinking.

The bottle made another round, then still another. Soon Sasha's arm was around Natalia's waist. She giggled and tried to free herself. Sasha, wrestling with her, pushed the table next to the bed and knocked a book down. It opened as it hit the floor, and a folded sheet of paper fell out.

Suddenly sobered, Natalia remembered her reason for summoning Sasha. She bent down and reached to pick up the note.

"Here," she said, handing it to Sasha.

"What's that?" he asked.

"A letter."

"For me?"

"No, not for you. You will get it to Leipzig for us."

Sasha knew about Leipzig, the big city that the Americans had besieged first and then, retreating, had left for the Red Army to take.

"Leipzig," he repeated. He made a prolonged hissing sound, then flung his arms up, and spreading them apart, "Boom," he said.

"Yes," Natalia said. "Lots of bombs fell there." Then, pointing to the letter, "I don't know the address. It's a synagogue. Probably the only one there, so it shouldn't be too hard to find."

55

Sasha didn't seem to understand.

"A synagogue," Natalia said again. "A church for Jews, *Yevrei*."

"Oh-h-h," Sasha said. "*Yevrei*." He made a short dismissing motion with his wrist. "*Yevrei kaput*, no more *yevrei*."

"That's not so," Natalia protested, shaking her head vehemently. She repeated what they had heard over the radio, her gesture, a smile, implying that she gratefully acknowledged his part in receiving the news.

When Sasha still remained unconvinced, Natalia pointed first at herself and then at Lisa, saying, "*Yevrei*, Jews."

Sasha's mouth fell open, his eyes moving from one to the other. His hands went up, the palms pressing against his cheeks, head swaying sideways, "*Kroshki, kroshenki moyi*," he wailed.

"What was that he called us?" Lisa wanted to know later.

"He called us his 'little ones,' " Natalia said.

Sasha's endearing expression, seemed to be well-chosen for Natalia, at least, or else the German woman whom he ransacked for her sake was enormous—for out of all the clothes he brought in the next day, only one dress looked as if it might fit her. It was of white, silky material with a satin sheen, deeply cut at the neck, and with a broad red sash at the waist.

Natalia chased Sasha out of the room, eager to put it on right away.

The dress looked awkward with the big, shapeless slippers, the neckline baring great hollows above the protruding collarbones. But Natalia's face was flushed with excitement, and her voice had a treble of laughter in it when she called Sasha back inside. She handed him a small mirror to hold for her, instructing him to move it up and down, as she admired herself in it inch by inch. There was so much loud talk and so much happy noise that Irmgard, passing by, stopped short and, looking aghast, clasped her hand against her mouth, holding back laughter. Catching Natalia's startled, offended look, she stammered, "It's not you ... it's the dress ... the official Hitler Youth Girls' dress. We wore it to dances." She turned on her heel and dashed out, her laughter resounding in the stillness of the corridor.

Natalia, at first dumbfounded, quickly regained her composure. She thought for a moment, then walked over to Sasha.

"Sashenka," she said, tilting her head, her voice coy, as if the dress brought out the dormant coquetry in her. Touching the Red Star on his uniform with the tip of her forefinger, she said "Let me have this."

Sasha covered the star protectively with his hand, then, "The devil with it," he mumbled, took it off, and handed it to her.

Natalia pinned the Red Star on the dress. It was heavy and weighed the thin material down. She adjusted the dress in the front, patted the skirt with both hands, and, without a word, walked out of the room.

Forewarned by Irmgard, lined up along the wall, other nurses and some of the patients seemed to be waiting for her.

She passed them, head up, looking ahead, her feet shuffling in the elephantine slippers, one leg dragging behind, and on the sunken chest, pinned to the official dress of the Hitler Youth Girls, the Red Star glittered.

Unlike Irmgard, the others did not find the sight humorous. Their eyes followed her with a mixture of horror, nostalgia, and indignation, or, to quote Natalia as she related it to Lisa later, they looked as if they were witnessing an act of sacrilege.

"Too bad Rosemarie isn't here anymore. I wish she could have seen it," Natalia said.

"Rosemarie?"

"The one who was on duty when we first got here."

Lisa looked at her blankly.

"I'm sorry," Natalia said. "I keep forgetting how little you remember of our first days here. Rosemarie ... a nice

name, sometimes names seem inappropriate, but this one fit
her perfectly. She was pert and blond, looked gentle but was
not. When she pulled the prison rags off me, I nearly
screamed. Then she moved over to you. You must have been
in awful pain because you moaned, and all the while the scissors hung on the tape down her waist. Finally, I couldn't
stand hearing you moan like that, and I said to her, 'Why
don't you take the scissors and cut it open?' She looked at
me as if I was out of my mind, and she said, 'And ruin it?
And what will she wear when she is ready to leave?' "

"I don't believe it. You made it up."

"I swear," Natalia said. "Then she folded the filthy tatters, ready to take them for storage, and I said, 'Don't
bother, just lead the way. They'll follow you. The lice will
carry them.' "

"You said *that*?"

"Not really," Natalia admitted. "I should have, but I
thought of it too late. Ever since then I've wished that I'd
said it. Now, at least, I know how it would have sounded if I
did."

"You're funny."

She marveled that something so vivid in Natalia's memory had never happened as far as she was concerned. And
in a way, it hadn't, since she had not consciously experienced it. This thought brought to mind the theory of the
world being just an illusion that disappeared with one's last
breath. She remembered how upset it used to make her just
to think about it. Like certain words, "infinite," for one.
You could count up to a million quadrillion and then add
one, and on and on, without an end. "Endless," was another
word. The universe was endless, she was taught. What did it
mean? She would imagine a sign stuck somewhere among
the stars, "Here is the end of the universe," but beyond the
sign, what? Exasperating, confusing thoughts.

*T*he nurses acted strangely that day.

Dorothea entered the room without as much as a "Good morning," and yanked the window shade so that it snapped and rolled up with a loud clatter. Suzanne's hands did not feel quite as gentle, and Irmgard did not show up at all. During the doctors' rounds, the whispers were even more hushed than usual, and they all seemed to leave in a great hurry.

"Something is going on," Natalia said and left to find out. She returned a while later.

"Irmgard is on the second floor," she informed Lisa.

"Was she transferred?" Lisa asked, thinking she would miss her cheerful "How are we today?" and the smile on her round, well-scrubbed face.

"She is there as a patient," Natalia said.

"What's wrong with her?"

"She had a miscarriage, or an abortion, depending on whose version you choose to believe."

"What?" Lisa propped herself up.

"Rumor has it she had been sleeping with the whole Russian garrison."

"Irmgard?" Lisa looked at Natalia incredulously. "Is she going to be all right?"

"I am sure she will," Natalia said. "She is young and as strong as a horse. Don't worry, she will be fine. She will find herself a husband and have a dozen children."

The last words triggered a recollection. *The kind doctor*, Lisa thought. She lay back and let the memory come.

The pond outside was covered with a layer of ice, and it wasn't much warmer inside unless they sat right next to the heater.

Dusk came early. They would argue over who should go into the bed first to make it warm for the other. Most of the time it was Lisa who would slip between the ice-cold sheets, her teeth chattering. They would lie in the dark room watching the glowing spirals of the electric heater before turning it off for the night.

"I swear," she said one morning, "I'm going to survive this war if for no other reason than to make love on a big, soft bed."

"As good a reason as any," Marek said. "Once I promised to build you a house, remember? What kind would you like?"

"Doesn't matter, as long as it is warm," Lisa said, shivering. "A fireplace in every room, preferably two."

She would get up feeling as tired as she had been before going to bed. She was constantly drowsy. She didn't say anything to Marek, and he wasn't aware of the fact that she would crawl back into bed right after he left for work and sleep most of the day, getting up shortly before his return. He didn't know that she hardly ate, that preparing food required great effort and that she couldn't stand the smell of it, and that the sight of raw meat revolted her to the point of nausea.

Then one day, as she got up, she staggered, overcome by a dizzy spell.

"What's the matter?" Marek asked.

"Nothing. My head felt funny for a second, and my stomach is queasy. Something I ate must have disagreed with me."

Marek looked at her closely. "Lisa," he said, "when was the last time you had your period?"

She thought a moment. "Last month. I don't remember. Why do you ask? You don't think . . . For heaven's sake, you were careful?"

"Of course I was."

"Then it's nothing. It must be the tension, the change of air and water . . . Besides, I was never regular."

But she promised herself to see a doctor.

She found out that of the five doctors in town, four were Jewish and gone. The one who remained lived at the other end of town. She took a horse-driven cab there.

There were two patients in the waiting room, an obviously pregnant woman and a youth with his arm in a sling. The room was untidy. Newspapers were scattered over the dusty tables, the curtains were wilted, and the green paint on the walls was peeling.

The examination room, she discovered, did not look sterile either.

"What's your complaint?" the doctor asked, sitting down.

"I am constantly tired," Lisa replied. "Listless, I think is the word. I have no appetite, I sleep too much."

"You could be anemic."

"Also," Lisa went on, "my period is late." Then she added quickly, as if fearing his disapproval, "But I was never very regular."

"We shall see in a moment."

She was glad to see him reach for rubber gloves. She hoped they were sterilized. He probed into her flesh.

"Hmm," he said. Then again, "Hmm." He straightened up. "Congratulations," he said, taking the gloves off.

61

"You don't mean . . ." Lisa said. "No, it's impossible, I thought . . . I had a lot of tension recently. . . ."

"You don't get pregnant from tension." When he looked at her, there was sympathy in his eyes.

"What's your problem? You are married, aren't you?"

"I am, but—"

"I know," the doctor said, "the war. It's not easy, but life goes on: people get married, people have children."

People, Lisa thought, but not them. They were not people anymore. They were prey.

"I can't have this baby."

"Why? You can tell me. Telling a doctor is like telling a priest."

"I have a serious reason."

"For an abortion? Is that an answer for a Catholic?"

"That's just it," Lisa said. "I am Catholic, and my husband is Greek Orthodox. We don't have a very stable marriage. There are problems."

"Abortion would be expensive."

"How expensive?"

"Seven hundred and fifty zlotys. I'll have to refer you to someone else."

Lisa was thinking. She couldn't tell Marek about it. There was no way for him to raise such a sum, unless he got involved in something illegal and dangerous, such as black-market trade or smuggling.

"It's out of the question," Lisa said. "We don't have that kind of money. We are refugees from the east."

"Then, what is left is to try to induce a miscarriage. That could be done in my office."

Lisa looked around. "Is it safe?"

"If you have any doubts . . . I didn't suggest anything."

"I don't have any doubts," Lisa said quickly. "I'm sorry if I sounded as if I had. It's my first experience, and—"

"It's not going to be pleasant," the doctor said. "Let me

warn you about that. I can't even give you a local anesthetic. We don't get the supplies anymore."

"I understand. What will your fee be for the ... treatment?"

"One hundred zlotys."

There were eighty zlotys she had managed to save in the drawstring bag she wore around her neck.

"I have eighty zlotys. That's all I have. I don't want my husband to know."

"That will be all right."

"When can you do it?" Lisa asked.

"Not now. I have two house calls to make." He checked his calendar. "How about the sixteenth? That will give you almost a week until the holiday, and by Christmas you will be as good as new."

"Let's make it the eighteenth," Lisa said. "It's a lucky day."

Soon she came to regret the delay, slight as it was. The dizziness and the nausea became worse each day, but that she rather welcomed, for it allowed her to consider her condition as a sickness caused by a foreign body that, like an ulcerous tumor, had to be removed.

It was the moments of relative comfort that became intolerable. Because then the doubts would rise, and the sweet and tormenting visions would take over: of a warm home, of Marek receiving the news of her pregnancy with delight, of a maternity hospital, of lacy peignoirs and baskets of flowers on the bedside table.

The doctor opened the door himself. There was no one waiting in the room, which seemed cleaner and more orderly than before. So did the examination room.

"Nippy, isn't it?" the doctor said, referring to the weather outside. He smiled reassuringly at her.

A rubber tube lay snarled among the instruments ar-

63

ranged evenly on a tray. The doctor picked up a medicine bottle, shook out two white pills and handed them over to Lisa.

"Take them," he said. "It will relax you."

He poured her a glass of water.

The water was lukewarm; the pills left a sour-tasting film on her tongue.

The doctor tinkered with something in a corner. The sound of a Chopin polonaise loudly filled the room.

"Just in case you scream," he said over the music and the noise of the running water as he began to scrub.

"I am not going to scream."

When he bent over her, she shut her eyes tightly and clenched her fists just the way she used to do when in a dentist's chair. The pain was so sharp that it had an almost anesthetic effect.

"It will be over in a moment," the doctor said.

When it was, she opened her eyes. She touched her face— it was covered with sweat. There was a taste of blood in her mouth. She must have bitten into her lip hard enough to cut it.

The doctor turned the music off.

"Brave girl. That's the first time I had to do it on two aspirins."

So that's what they were, Lisa thought.

"Rest for a while now. How do you feel?"

"My insides feel raw, as if there was something there."

"There is," the doctor said. "There is a catheter inserted into the womb. You will remove it once you start to bleed."

Lisa reached for the money.

"There is no charge," the doctor said.

She didn't understand.

"There were five of us in this town, five doctors. Now it's only me. I get all the business. I don't need your money."

He knows, Lisa thought suddenly. She looked at him.

64

There was no threat in his eyes, just compassion.

"How did you know? When?"

"When you said the eighteenth was a lucky day. As a student I had a Jewish friend, who was fascinated by the symbolism of cabalistic numerals. He explained their meaning to me. Eighteen stands for life, doesn't it?"

Lisa nodded.

"And where there is life, there is hope," he said. "You will have other children."

"Thank you, Doctor. Then, as if apologizing for her trembling voice, "I am not spoiled by human kindness."

"Come back in two weeks. Earlier, if need be."

He took a few more tablets from the bottle. "Here, take two at a time in case of discomfort."

"Discomfort," turned out to be a euphemism, for it felt as if a pneumatic pump was sucking her guts out. Soon after she got home she began to bleed.

She followed the doctor's instructions, then staggered into bed. "What's the matter?" Marek asked seeing her lying there. "What's wrong?"

"Nothing. I just got my period."

"Good," Marek said, hanging up his coat. "I was beginning to worry. Don't get up. I'll fix supper."

Lisa told him she had already eaten. He scrambled some eggs and buttered a piece of bread for himself.

"We can't sleep in one bed tonight," Lisa said. "I seem to be making up for lost time. I'm bleeding like a stuck pig."

Marek rinsed the dirty dishes, put them away.

"Do you know what I want once the war is over?" Lisa said.

"A house with two fireplaces in each room?"

"Before that," Lisa said. "A child."

"Nesting instinct," Marek said. "I read about that. Women get it when they have their period. It usually manifests itself by compulsive cleaning, which, by the way, this

65

place could use."

When she didn't smile, he gave her a closer look.

"Are you sure you're all right?"

"Of course I am. Don't be silly. This is not a sickness."

"You look absolutely green. How long does it usually take?"

"Three, four days. By next week I should be fine."

"I sure hope so. We've been invited to the Mikulskis for Christmas dinner."

"Do we have to go?"

"I ran out of excuses. It might look suspicious."

"I have no dress."

The perennial female excuse made him smile. "You don't need one. A skirt and blouse will do."

"Marek," she said, for it just occurred to her, "I don't know any carols."

"You will by Christmas. I will teach you. We'll start right now."

He began slowly, making her repeat the words after him, until she got them right. Then together softly, their arms around each other, they sang into the darkness of the room:

> Hush, little Jesus,
> Hush, hush, hush,
> And you, sweet Mother,
> Lull Him to sleep. . . .

On Christmas Eve Lisa presented herself to Marek after getting dressed and combing her hair, which she put in a single braid.

He examined her closely.

"Your hair," he said, "is no good pulled back like that. Makes your nose look long."

She let it fall loose. The braiding left it slightly wavy.

The Mikulskis lived in the middle of town, right off Main

66

Street. It was a long walk, but luckily a peasant, driving a horse-drawn sleigh, overcome by the Christmas spirit, gave them a ride part of the way.

The house was a gray, neglected building whose ornaments on the outside proclaimed the legend of past glory.

They walked one flight up, dusted the snow off their coats, and stamped their feet to shake it off their boots.

Marek rang the bell.

Mrs. Mikulski opened the door for them. She was a small woman with hair piled on top of her head, which made her seem taller. She had a flat, pancake face and a broad smile.

"Welcome, welcome. When a guest enters, God is right behind," she said and led them into the room. A modest-sized tree stood next to the window, its branches bending under the weight of glass ornaments, paper chains, and red apples.

In the middle of the room the table was set for eight. The Mikulskis were expecting more guests.

Misia, their six-year-old daughter, wouldn't leave Lisa alone until Mrs. Mikulski intervened.

"Misia, don't bother Mrs. Rodwanski," she said.

"It's all right," Lisa said.

Children somehow took to her, a fact that never ceased to amaze her.

Soon the other guests arrived: a couple, Mr. and Mrs. Hayda, she a corpulent blonde, he looking like a bulldog with bad teeth, and a rather handsome bachelor whom Mr. Mikulski introduced simply as Janusz.

They sat at the table, Lisa across from Marek and next to Janusz, whose calf, she realized after a while, was seeking hers under the table. She got up inconspicuously and asked Marek to change seats with her.

"Draft," she said for the benefit of the others, pointing at the window and adding that she was susceptible to colds.

Making her way to the other side of the table, she passed

67

by the china cabinet and stopped to comment on the beautiful dishes behind the glass door.

"They *are* lovely, aren't they?" Mrs. Mikulski said. "Julius wanted me to use them tonight, but they came from Jews, so I said no, not on the holiest of nights."

Lisa quickly looked around. No one seemed surprised or particularly interested. Marek's face was a blank. She sat down and, pointing at the plate setting in front of her, said these were lovely too.

Mr. Mikulski made the sign of the cross in the air, invoked the Lord, His Son, and the Holy Spirit, then he broke the wafer with his family and guests. They wished one another Merry Christmas.

Mrs. Mikulski brought in a platter with a glazed ham on it and put it in the middle of the table.

"Humble riches but joyfully shared," she said.

Mrs. Mikulski was fond of proverbs.

Lisa stuffed her mouth with food, even though she was not hungry, so that she wouldn't have to talk.

Mrs. Mikulski watched her with obvious pleasure.

"Eat with hearty appetite, my child. You are too skinny. You are a pretty little woman. There should be more of you."

After the meal, the table was pushed against the wall and they gathered around the Christmas tree and exchanged gifts.

Lisa and Marek gave tobacco to Mikulski and a bottle of toilet water to his wife. They got one present from their host: a crystal creamer, which, Lisa was sure, came from the same source as the dishes in the china cabinet.

Then it was time for singing carols.

Lisa joined in.

"Doesn't Mrs. Rodwanski sing beautifully, Mama?" Misia said.

"She certainly does," Mrs. Mikulski said. Then to Lisa,

68

"How about a solo?"

"Solo, solo!" they urged and clapped.

Lisa looked at Marek.

He nodded at her slightly.

"Go ahead, Lisa," he said, "sing."

She closed her eyes, blocking out the room with the Jewish china in the closet, Hayda and his portly wife, Janusz with the sleazy smile. And thinking of the child that hadn't been allowed to grow in her womb, that had trickled out of her in bloody blobs, she sang:

> Hush, little Jesus,
> Hush, hush, hush,
> And you, sweet Mother,
> Lull Him to sleep. . . .

When she finished, there was silence. Then they applauded loudly. Mrs. Mikulski dabbed at her eyes and said that she had never before heard it sung with such feeling.

*S*asha gave the letter to the commandant's chauffeur, who not only delivered it but brought back a reply. The envelope bore a rubber stamp reading "The Council of the Jewish Community, Leipzig." The same stamp was on the letterhead, giving it an official appearance.

"'Dear Friends,'" Natalia read aloud. "'We acknowledge receipt of your letter. We find it extremely difficult, if not impossible, to assist you from afar. You made no mention in your letter of the condition of your health, and the messenger could not provide us with more information. We can only promise that once you come here we shall do our best to help you. With the approaching New Year, please accept our best wishes. Sincerely . . .'"

The signature was illegible. Natalia put the letter down.

Lisa turned her head and looked at the window. Outside, the tree was covered with golden leaves. It was the beginning of September.

Soon after they received the reply from the Jewish Council, without any further communciation, a nun arrived with authorization to bring her and Natalia to the hospital in Leipzig. Sister Rosamunde had come by train, but seeing Lisa's condition, she found it impossible to take them back the same way, as the trains were crowded, filled with refugees from Poland and the Sudeten. There was no time to be lost, for the beds reserved for them by request of the Jewish Council would be occupied if their arrival were delayed.

The hospital's one ambulance had been requisitioned, and the only alternative was to seek help from the Russians. Sasha immediately came to mind, and Dr. Kamin herself went to look for him.

He arrived half an hour later in a jeep. Then everything happened very fast. There was nothing to pack; all they took was the radio, which, wrapped in a blanket, was carefully placed on the back seat. Natalia, wearing the Hitler Youth dress and a sweater that Dr. Kamin hastily threw over her shoulders, sat in front. Sister Rosamunde sat on the floor between the two seats.

Lisa looked at the hospital building. It was the first time she had seen it from the outside. It was small and white among the bare trees. She could recognize her window and the branch of her tree, and she felt as she had on her last day of high school, a sadness over leaving the place forever, even though she had never really been happy there.

The nurses gathered in the doorway to wave good-bye, and Dr. Kamin ran up with two large envelopes in her hand, containing the X rays, the case histories, and her own recommendations.

"This one," she said, pointing to Lisa as she handed the envelopes to Sister Rosamunde, "needs penicillin. Everything else has been tried."

It was the first time Lisa heard the word. It was like the name of an exotic plant printed on a sign and stuck into the ground at a botanical display.

Dr. Kamin called out something, cupping her hand around her mouth, trying to be heard over the noise of the motor as the jeep jerked forward. Sister Rosamunde held on to Lisa so she wouldn't roll off the seat.

Sasha drove like a madman, taking the sharp curves with

71

incredible speed, one hand on the wheel, the other around Natalia's shoulder. When he began to sing a song about a girl named Katyusha who went to a river bank when the apple and pear trees were in bloom, he clapped the beat with both hands, letting the jeep roll down the hill.

Sister Rosamunde shut her eyes and, holding on to Lisa with one hand, fingered the beads of her rosary with the other.

Lisa watched her silently. Her hair completely covered, must have been blond, judging from the blue of her eyes and from her milky complexion. Her name, adopted after she had taken her vows, seemed to have been chosen because of her mouth, shapely and full and the color of a rose petal. On her hand was a ring, declaring her to be a bride of Christ. Lisa wondered why a woman so young and pretty had chosen to be betrothed to a Jew tortured to death two thousand years ago. How did she reconcile the fact that Christ had been a Jew with Hitler's theories and their consequences? Was that the reason she had become a nun? Was it her answer, her protest, her hiding place?

Soon Natalia pointed out road signs of towns they had passed during the march. Riesa, Wurzen, familiar names. One of the signs, with an arrow pointing to the left, read "Dresden." Lisa thought of the body wrapped in bandages. She remembered how it bounced on the canvas stretcher and was glad when they bypassed the city.

They did not see much destruction when they approached Leipzig. The hospital was located on the outskirts of town. It was a huge three-wing complex, with a large empty square at the entrance, a parking lot before the cars were requisitioned. Natalia bid Sasha a tearful good-bye and Lisa made him promise to come and visit.

Two beds had been waiting for them since morning, and so was Fraulein Federdorfer of the Jewish Council. She had been there since the early afternoon. She greeted them when

72

they arrived in the evening and soon left. The room was spacious and dark; the window faced a gray building. The walls, painted green, were bare except for the big crucifix hanging next to the door.

All nurses here were nuns who came and went, their bodies hidden in habits as if in tents, their hair and part of their foreheads covered by coifs—they all looked alike. There was no tree, there were no shadows on the ceiling, no church bells tolling in the valley. There was nothing to hold on to. But there could be, the sudden comforting warmth, the short-lasting bliss, the feeling of something resembling love, for herself, for people, for life itself before melting into nothingness. There could be, if she handled it right.

A sister came in. This one looked different from the others because of her wire-rimmed glasses.

"The journey," Lisa said. "Yes, it must have been the discomfort of the trip, the shaking. I have pain. Oh, such pain . . ."

"I will give you something," the sister said, and came back after a while, a pill in one hand, a glass of water in the other.

"You don't seem to understand, Sister," Lisa said. She had to be careful now. "In the other hospital I was getting something, not a pill. What do you call it? An injection."

The sister looked at the chart. "Not for quite a while," she said.

"But the journey. That's what I'm trying to tell you. That terrible ride . . ."

"Do you want a pill or don't you?"

"I want to talk to a doctor."

"The doctor will be here first thing in the morning."

A short while later, Natalia returned from her exploratory expedition. "I'm not going to budge out of this room if I can help it," she said. "This is an orthopedic ward, and . . . well, I'd rather not tell you what I saw."

73

"Maybe it was a mistake coming here," Lisa said.

"Maybe, maybe not," Natalia said. "We're here. There's nothing we can do about it now."

Lisa finally fell into a state that was half-sleep, half-consciousness, but that brought neither peace nor rest.

The doctor came the next morning. Dr. Schultz was rather young, short, stocky, and dark-haired, with horn-rimmed glasses, and Lisa couldn't help thinking that if he had been in Poland during the war, he would have have had a hard time proving the purity of his race to some zealous collaborators.

"I'm sorry I couldn't come last night," he said. "I hear there was some problem."

"There was," Lisa said. "I was in pain, I mean real pain, and the sister, whatever her name is, brought me a pill. I have a shattered bone, Doctor, that doesn't heal. I have an infection, not a runny nose, and when I am in pain, it is not an aspirin that I need."

"When you are in pain," Dr. Schultz said. "But you weren't. You haven't been for quite a while now."

Lisa looked at him. He reminded her of someone. She tried to remember who it was, and then she knew: the bugler in her summer camp.

"There are other kinds of pain," she said.

"I know," the doctor said. "But for those pains, what you asked for doesn't help."

"How would you know?"

The doctor walked to the door and opened it. A strange knocking sound came from the outside. "Do you know what that is?" the doctor asked. "Crutches. Shall I describe some of the cases to you?"

Lisa resented being deprived of the uniqueness of her suffering, inflicted by *them*. "I'm not interested," she said. Then, after a moment, "Where were you during the war, Doctor?"

74

"At the front, where else?"

"Well, you could have been in a camp, for instance, doing 'research,' you know."

From behind the thick lenses, Dr. Schultz's eyes looked angrily at her. "Just because I refuse to meet your unreasonable demands, for your own good . . . I don't think that's fair."

"Let's not talk about fairness," Lisa said.

"I read Dr. Kamin's recommendations," the doctor said. "I agree with her. You will be getting penicillin."

"When?" Lisa asked.

"The Jewish Council got in touch with the International Red Cross. It shouldn't be long before they get it. You are a very special case; you have the privileges of Allied soldiers," he said and left.

atalia was getting ready for the Yom Kippur service. She had received a suit from Fraulein Federdorfer, the secretary of the Jewish Council, whom they had nicknamed the One-Woman Reception Committee, as it was she who had welcomed them to Leipzig two weeks earlier. The suit, though not new, was quite presentable with its flowered silk blouse, but Natalia insisted on wearing the Hitler Youth dress, sash and all, with the Red Star pinned onto it.

"It'll be something to tell my grandchildren about one day," she said jokingly, but Lisa suspected that Natalia enjoyed the sensation the dress always created and the look of confusion and disbelief on the faces of those she encountered.

Fraulein Federdorfer also brought a jar of jellied pork with which to break the fast, her apologetic smile indicating that it was not ignorance on her part but the scarcity of food that dictated her choice. The food situation in the city was even more critical than in the rural area they had come from. The hospital's supplies that had been plundered were never replaced, and in spite of Fraulein Federdorfer's occasional gifts and the fact that the third patient in the room—a toothless woman with a fractured hip—would leave bread crusts for them, they often felt the familiar pangs of hunger.

And so Natalia, in a wheelchair pushed by Sister Magdalene, one of the nuns on the hospital's nursing staff, was on her way to a Jewish temple for Yom Kippur services.

"I'll remember you in my prayers," Natalia said.

"Don't bother," Lisa answered. "I'll find a pipeline to God directly from my bed."

After Natalia had left, Lisa looked at the skimpy breakfast, still untouched. She reached for it, hesitated, then put it back in spite of the queasy feeling in her stomach. She wondered what made her do it. Refusing food in camp on that day was one thing. It was a demonstration, an act of defiance, proof of her humanity, a sign that she still had some freedom of choice. Now it made little sense. But now the thought occurred to her that in every corner of the world, wherever there were Jews, at that very moment they were united by the act of fasting. She decided that it was a matter of identification and solidarity and had little to do with religious belief.

She tried to remember how it had been at home on that day, but all she could think of was her father's hands stretched out in blessing over her head. She could see them, strong and dark and veined, and she could hear her mother's sigh as she lighted the memorial candles.

She had no candle to light, and she had never known the meaning of the prayer, so she just thought of them, of her father's hands that she suddenly remembered down to every detail, and the sound of her mother's voice. She thought of them, the memory painless, like a part of the body that is anesthetized.

Natalia came back late in the afternoon.

Lisa looked at her anxiously, waiting for her to talk. But Natalia sat on her bed, strangley silent.

"Now we can open the jar with the meat and have a feast," Lisa said. "I have been waiting for you."

They ate in silence.

77

Finally Lisa couldn't stand it any longer. "Tell me, I'm dying to know. How was the synagogue? Tell me."

"I don't want to talk about it," Natalia said. "Not right now. Tomorrow."

The next day, when Lisa woke up, Natalia was sitting on her bed.

"I'm leaving," Natalia said.

Lisa didn't understand right away.

"What do you mean, you're leaving? You can hardly walk. They had to wheel you to the synagogue."

"Only because there was no other way of getting there. It's on the other side of town."

"But you can't," Lisa said. "What about your lungs?"

There had been some talk of sending Natalia to the mountains in the West, Switzerland perhaps.

"No," Natalia said.

"But they said—"

"I know what they said. My lungs will have to take care of themselves."

"It has something to do with yesterday, your decision, doesn't it?"

"In a way."

"What happened yesterday?"

"Do you really want to know?"

"I really do."

"So I'll tell you. Nothing."

"What do you mean?"

"Just what I said. Nothing. It wasn't a synagogue, not the way we imagined it. Just a room on the second floor of an old building. A few rows of chairs and people—it's hard to say how many. Twenty, maybe even less. Most of them were old, people who used to live here and came back from I don't know where. From hiding, perhaps; I didn't ask. A few of our people, camp people, I mean. Mostly men, a few women. The men looked shabby. The women were well-

78

dressed. Some of them even had jewelry on. Anyway, remember how we imagined the dedication of the synagogue? People pouring in from all over? The great miracle of the temple, like in the time of the Maccabees? I asked about the dedication and, you know, nobody remembered it. Nobody even knew what I was talking about. I decided then and there that I had to leave. I don't know exactly why. I still don't understand it."

"The dream and the reality," Lisa said.

"Something like that. It made me think of what Dr. Kamin once said. Remember? About hiding in the hospital. Going to Switzerland, or any other place they might send me, would be hiding again. So I have to go and find out—"

"Whether or not your brother is alive?"

"That too, of course, but mostly about myself. About freedom, not how I've imagined it, but how it really is. I'm not going to postpone it, because if I do, I might never have the courage again."

"So you've decided to take the plunge."

"You might call it that," Natalia said. She smiled.

Lisa noticed for the first time that when Natalia smiled, she was pretty. "What's funny?" she asked.

"Something I just remembered," Natalia said. "When I was about fifteen, I was a very poor athlete. So I'd make up stories. In the summer I'd tell everyone what a terrific skier I was, and in the winter I'd brag about my swimming, hoping no one would remember it. Then, one summer, I was standing at the edge of the public pool and someone pushed me right into the deep end. I kicked my feet and splashed my hands as hard as I could until I got hold of someone, as if playfully, and I made it."

"Could you have made it alone?"

"I'll never know. Maybe, but it would have been harder."

"Yes," Lisa said, "it probably would have." She thought about Marek.

"I feel terrible about leaving you like this," Natalia said, "but the penicillin will be here any day, and—"

"Let's not make another mistake," Lisa said, "like the dedication of the temple. The big miracle—I don't even want to think about it anymore. No more hocus-pocus, abracadabra, a miracle. Don't worry about me. When do you think you'll be leaving?"

"Tomorrow," Natalia said.

"What?" exclaimed Lisa, propping herself up. "How? In that Hitler Youth dress of yours?"

"I spoke to Fraulein Federdorfer. It's all arranged."

And indeed, the next day Fraulein Federdorfer arrived, her role changed from welcoming to farewell committee, carrying a cardboard suitcase containing a basic wardrobe, not new but clean, a few hundred German marks, a free transportation pass, and her best wishes.

The official release from the hospital was all ready, together with a letter of recommendation to a lung specialist should Natalia change her mind. Natalia, wearing a tweed suit with a colorful blouse, the suitcase in her hand, looked just like anybody else going on a trip. Only her face was terribly pale.

"Well . . ." she said, coming closer to Lisa.

"I don't like good-byes," Lisa said. Suddenly she became aware that she had not said good-bye to her parents, that she had not looked back to see Marek climb into the truck that took him away, that she would never know whether he had looked at her, trying to tell her something with a gesture, with a last glance.

"I just wanted to . . ." Natalia said. "I don't quite know how to put it. We've been through a lot together and I feel as if you were . . . What I'm trying to say, I guess, is that . . . I learned to love you."

Love. It was just a word, it meant nothing. It evoked no feeling. Lisa had forgotten how love felt. But she knew all

80

about loneliness, and she knew that she would be lonely without Natalia. It was almost impossible to imagine Natalia not being there.

"I'll miss you," Lisa said. "I really will."

Natalia started toward the door.

Maybe it was because she had not said good-bye to them that people had never come back—her parents, Marek, Dr. Kamin, whom she was sure she would never see again.

"Natalia," she called, and there was fear in her voice.

Natalia turned at the threshold.

"Don't walk back in," Lisa said. "It's a bad omen. I just wanted to wish you luck, and, Natalia, I'll see you."

She looked at Natalia. She was not sure, because of the bad light in the room, but it seemed to her that Natalia was crying.

*N*atalia's bed had been changed and stood waiting, white and cold, like an empty, freshly painted room for the furniture to arrive. It reflectd in a way Lisa's own hollow chill inside, the loneliness tangible now, like a physical pain, like the spasm of hunger in an empty stomach.

The bed remained unoccupied for less than an hour. Then a new patient was brought in, just waking up from the anesthesia. The chart was put on the table between the two beds, just long enough for Lisa to have a quick, furtive glance. Margaretha Reichmann, age eighteen, amputation of the right toe, it read.

The girl in the bed did not look eighteen. She had a pretty face, with a small, upturned nose and high cheekbones. Her brown hair was cut short, the bangs covering her forehead. She had long, curly lashes and slightly irregular brows. Since her eyes were closed, Lisa couldn't tell their color. When she finally opened them, they turned out to be deep blue. She was waking up slowly. "I want my mother, I want my father," she moaned.

"They have been notified," Sister Rosamunde said. Turning to Lisa, "She tried to get on a crowded streetcar on her way to school," she explained. She got on the first step when the streetcar began moving. She lost her footing. Luckily for her, she was wearing wooden shoes. Her schoolbooks got scattered all over. That's how we got her name and address, from the labels on her books. We tried to reach her parents. It's hard since they have no phone. They live at the other end of the city."

The girl mumbled something, moaned, and fell back into sleep.

When she opened her eyes again, she noticed Lisa for the first time. "Who are you?" she asked.

"My name is Lisa."

"Mine is Margaretha, but nobody calls me that. They call me Rita. Do you know what happened to me?"

"It seems you were in a hurry to get to school. You fell off the streetcar. Nothing much happened. They made one of your toes shorter, that's all," Lisa said.

"I suppose I should be grateful," Rita said. "It could be worse."

"I'm sure it could."

"My toe . . . I wonder," Rita said after a while. "Do you think I'll be able to wear high heels? I know it's stupid to think about it now. I could have been killed, or terribly maimed, but you see, it's important to me because when you're all dressed up for something special, you look really clumsy in flat-heeled shoes. Don't you think so?"

"I'm really no expert on fashion," Lisa said.

"Neither am I, but it makes sense to me. Wouldn't you say so?"

Then she fell asleep, and when she woke up, she cried that she wanted to see a priest.

"Now, now," Lisa said. "You have sore toes but you're not dying. What do you need a priest for?"

"You don't understand. There's something I have to confess. What happened to me . . . I think God tried to warn me. . . ."

The request was repeated to Sister Rosamunde, and a

83

while later the priest arrived looking just the way Lisa imagined he would look. Tall and clad in black, he twisted his neck as if the clerical collar were too tight.

With a quick look at Lisa, he pulled the yellow curtain separating the two beds. Rita spoke in a barely audible whisper. Then, the priest mumbled something in a monotone and drew the curtain back. He turned to Lisa now. "And what is wrong with you, my child?" he asked.

The "my child" made her skin shrink until it felt like an elastic cutting painfully into her flesh. "I was shot," she said, her throat tight and suddenly filled with phlegm. Her voice came out hoarse and low.

The priest, holding with both hands a small black book, a cross imprinted in gold on it, made a step toward her.

"Don't bother," Lisa said. "I am a Jew."

The clerical collar seemed to get even tighter as the priest's neck got redder, his eyes bulging. "My poor child," he said, "suffering for no fault of your own, but for ancestral sins. Who can explain God's—"

Lisa propped herself up into a half-sitting position, one finger pointing at the door. "Out," she said, quietly first, then louder. "Out, out!" she screamed.

The priest, lifting the long cassock with one hand, holding the prayer book in the other, fled in haste.

Lisa fell back, breathing heavily. Her heart was pounding.

"What was the commotion all about?" Sister Rosamunde asked, entering the room.

Lisa waited for Rita to say something. But she didn't.

That night Lisa dreamed that the penicillin arrived in a jar just like the one with pickled pork. But it was used on Rita instead of her so that she would be able to wear high-heeled shoes. The priest sprinkled it all over her like holy water, while the nuns stood in a semicircle, chanting in unison.

Rita's parents came the next day. The news reached them

the evening before, and it took them three hours to get to the hospital from where they lived.

The middle-aged woman, who still showed traces of past beauty—Rita looked just like her—wore a tailored coat-dress. The buttonholes and hand stitching showed quality, details that wouldn't have escaped Lisa's own mother's eye. The man, tall, straight, and distinguished-looking, in a dark, slightly shiny business suit, had a walking cane with a silver handle curved in the shape of a hound's head.

They were the kind of people Lisa had known in what she thought of as her "previous life." They were just like her own aunts and uncles, whom she had been forced by her parents to visit at least twice a year.

The woman rushed to Rita's bed, bravely fighting tears. "*Mein Kind*," she kept repeating. "My child."

The man stood aside, leaning on the walking stick, his expression unchanged, except that his eyelids blinked.

The woman leaned over Rita, who put her arms around her neck and, pulling her closer, whispered into her ear. The woman looked at her husband and mouthed something soundlessly to him that must have concerned Lisa, for both of them cast uneasy glances at her.

After the woman got up and her husband took her place, she approached Lisa's bed. "Let me introduce myself," she said. My name is Frau Reichmann, and this"—a gesture at her husband—"is Professor Reichmann. We are from Breslau. We lost our home in the bombing."

"I'm sorry to hear that," Lisa said, not knowing what else to say.

"Well, we would have lost it anyway. It's part of Poland now. We are living with relatives here. Rita, our daughter . . . she was very lucky. We are grateful to God. She has told us about you." She stopped talking and came closer. "Fraulein . . .—a quick glance at the chart—"Fraulein Rodwanski," she said, rolling the *R* and pronouncing the *w* hard, "I wish there was something I could say to you."

"It's not necessary," Lisa said.

"I know," Frau Reichmann said. "Words. What are words? Nothing ... But still, I would like, I wish you could believe, that ..." Her arm drew an unfinished circle in the air. "We are quite ordinary, decent people; we never really approved—"

"I don't want you to get the wrong impression, Fraulein." Professor Reichmann interrupted, mispronounding Lisa's last name. "We were not in active opposition. We did nothing. ... I taught philosophy at the university. I thought one could keep them apart, Plato and politics. What my wife was trying to say is that inwardly we disagreed. Can you understand that?"

"I think so," Lisa said. "You whispered '*Schrecklich*'—'terrible'—very softly." She didn't know why she said it. Then, she remembered the little man in the shabby, worn-out brown coat who got lost on the deserted road, and who whispered "*Schrecklich*," as the columns of shivering camp inmates were led through the slush and cold of a January dawn. She had even mentioned it in a journal she kept. Whatever happened to it? It had been sewn into her clothing. She had given it to somebody, a woman. Suddenly she remembered it all. Only the woman had neither a face nor a name.

"I wish there was something we could do," Frau Reichmann said. "If there is anything ..."

Lisa wished they would leave her alone.

But they didn't. They came every day, and at the door they would separate. Even before greeting Rita, one of them would come to Lisa and sit on her bed. They would do this alternately, one day the woman, the next day the man. Whatever they brought for Rita, which was not much, a dish of grated carrots or a cold potato salad, they would bring the same for Lisa. They would put it next to her bed without a

86

word, and the next day they would pick up the empty dish, replacing it with a new one.

One day they brought two identical packages wrapped in tissue paper. Rita opened hers right away. "Oh," she said, "finally," taking out a nightgown, the kind Lisa remembered without which no bride's trousseau would be complete; there would be at least a dozen made of the finest silk, the yoke embroidered with delicate flowers and appliqué design. Lisa opened hers, the tissue paper rustling. Rita's was yellow, hers was blue. Otherwise, they were identical.

"If you prefer yellow . . ." Frau Reichmann said. "But we thought blue would be nicer for you."

"I like blue," Lisa said. "Thank you."

"It's not new, of course," Frau Reichmann said. "But I soaked it before I washed it, and I ironed it carefully. It really is clean."

After they left, Rita put hers on right away. "I can't stand this hospital gown. It's as stiff as armor. Aren't you going to put yours on?"

"Not now," Lisa said. "I'll wait for a special occasion, when there is something to celebrate."

"Where are all the terrible Germans?" Lisa asked.

That question came later and was directed at a man by the name of Jacob Rosenkranz, who, some time earlier, had made a sudden appearance. He had walked into the room carrying something that looked like a saleman's sample case, and stood there for a moment, his eyes wandering from Lisa to Rita.

Lisa looked at him. He was rather handsome, tall and dark-haired. His face still bore the fading tan of the past summer. He had good-natured hazel eyes, and when he smiled, he showed healthy white teeth. But still, there was something that made him unappealing to her. Perhaps it was his ears, which were fleshy and too large for his head.

It was she whom he sought, not Rita, for he walked straight toward her. Without a word, he put the large case on the table between the two beds and snapped it open. Inside there was an apple and a crescent roll. He took them out and put them on the edge of the bed, rather bashfully.

Lisa found it both funny and strange to carry a big case just for that. But after having a closer look at him, she understood the reason for it. A paper bag could spoil his image of elegance. Suddenly she became aware of what bothered her about him; it was the pretension. His suit did not fit, and its pattern was too bright. His tie was loud, and his polished shoes were too yellow. He wore a signet ring on his pinky and smelled too strongly of cologne. There was something very provincial about him.

"The roll is from yesterday. I hope you don't mind," he said, and blushed under the tan. "I heard about you from Fraulein Federdorfer, so I came." Then he introduced himself. His Polish was uneducated and had a typical small-town inflection.

"That was very decent of you," Lisa said.

Rosenkranz closed the case.

"Do you have a pocketknife?" Lisa asked.

He had one, inlaid with mother-of-pearl, of course. He opened it before handing it to her. Lisa cut the apple and the roll into two even parts, half for Rita and half for herself.

"She shares things with me too," she explained.

Rosenkranz folded the knife and put it in his pocket. "I'll come back again," he said.

And he did, the next day, wearing a different, equally loud suit. The sample case this time contained a whole loaf of bread, lard, and more fruit.

"Tell me," he said in a confidential whisper, "are they good to you here? Are you getting good care?"

"Oh, yes," Lisa said. "Everybody is very nice, and for the last three days I've been given penicillin."

88

"What's that?" Rosenkranz asked.

"It's a medicine. They call it a miracle drug. It was very hard to get. It's available only for Allied soldiers. But I got it through the International Red Cross. My leg wouldn't heal. I was—"

"I know all about it," Rosenkranz interrupted. "So you say they're good to you."

Lisa nodded.

He looked around the room. "This room is dreary," he said. "You should have a private room. Would you like that?"

A private room? She didn't know such a thing existed. Not in this terribly crowded hospital, where to be in a room with only three beds was already considered a privilege, one that she and Natalia had been given only through the intervention of the Jewish Council.

Back home, Lisa had seen only one hospital. It wasn't even called by that fear-evoking name but was referred to as a "clinic," a place where women went to have babies. It was a place where baskets of flowers were put outside the door for the night to be taken care of, like shoes in a better-class hotel, where the doctors wore business suits and the nurses were all elderly and called everyone "love."

Rita would be leaving any day now, Lisa thought, and there was no way to know who would occupy the bed next to her. The old woman with the broken hip had been in a coma for the last few days and, to quote Dr. Schultz's crude remark, "refused to die"; her snoring became so loud that Lisa would stuff her ears with cotton to dampen its sound in order to sleep.

It would be nice to have a room of her own, to keep the light on as long as she pleased and read, or listen to the radio whenever she wanted. And if ... *when* she started to walk, she would have space to move around in, without having to go outside and face all the horrible cases everyone kept talk-

89

ing about.

"I would like that very much," she said. "But how can it be arranged?"

Rosenkranz rubbed his thumb against his first two fingers.

"A bribe?"

"That's an ugly word. 'Grease the palm' sounds much better, and I have connections," he said without a pretense of modesty.

The "greasing" and the "connections" worked, for a few days later, after having said good-bye to Rita, she was wheeled out of the room. It happened during lunchtime, when the patients were inside, and she was glad not to encounter anyone in the corridor.

The private room exceeded her wildest expectations. It was not like a hospital room at all. The walls were covered with ivy-patterned paper. There was a bed with a headboard, a chest of drawers, an upholstered chintz armchair— all in maple—and drapes of a matching fabric on the window.

The window faced one in an apartment building. During the day Lisa could see nothing. But in the evening, when dusk fell and the lights went on, she could see through the sheer muslin curtains of the window what was going on inside the room. It was like being in a theater, looking at the stage after the curtain had gone up, yet still a sheer screen separated the viewers from the actors to create the effect of distance.

Just as she had waited for the bells in the other hospital, now she waited for the lights to go on there, to watch the misty silhouettes: the big, husky man coming in from work, the woman busily moving about, the lanky boy, and the girl with hair falling to her shoulders.

They would sit around the table, on which a low-hanging, fringed lamp cast a yellow light. The woman put a big steaming dish in the middle, and everyone began to spoon the food onto their plates at once.

A family . . .

It was on such an evening, when Rosenkranz had come to visit, that, pointing at the lighted window, Lisa had said, "They look like ordinary people. Where are all the terrible Germans?"

Those whom she had met were at worst stupid, like Dr. Boesel, the pompous baboon; some of the nurses, like the fool who had stored their things, whom Natalia told her about, and the idiot priest who came to see Rita. But the others were just people.

"Where are all the terrible Germans, you ask?" Rosenkranz said. "I'll tell you where." He walked to the window and with a gesture at the street said, "Out there. Every place, all over. Every one of them. You sit in a streetcar and you look at the faces and you wonder, *Who is he? What did he do during the war? Maybe he is the one who killed my father? Maybe he shot my sister?* You walk into a shop to get something. You take it, but you make sure not to touch their hands. They are all over, the murderers."

He stopped.

"Let me give you an example," he went on after a moment or two. "On one of my trips I stopped to visit two men from my hometown who I knew lived there. A young German woman was staying with them, Greta. A housekeeper, that's what they told me she was. Angelic-looking, blond, you know, the braids twisted around her head like a halo, wearing a dirndl, very pretty. We talked about the war, my friends and I, and about the people we knew who were killed, and how they were killed, and she would get all upset, Greta, I mean, and she would cry and swear she had known nothing. We decided to avoid the topic in her presence. A few weeks later I passed the town again and stopped to say hello, and Greta wasn't there anymore. So I asked about her

91

and was told that the police had come looking for her and had taken her away. She was in charge of women in a camp. They used to call her the Beast of Ravensbrück. She beat women to death with an iron-tipped whip. So there you are."

"If you know all that," Lisa said slowly after a horrified silence, "why are you staying here?"

"Why? I'll tell you why. Money. This is the place to make money fast. Leipzig was the fur center. So, I buy furs. I buy them for nothing—for cigarettes, for coffee. And Dresden is only a few kilometers away. It's completely destroyed now. It was famous for its china. You can still find a lot of it there. So I buy it, the old pieces. I have a big collection of old Dresden china. It's worth its weight in gold, or it will be. If I stay here for another year, I will be a rich man, a very rich man."

"Is that important to you?"

He looked at her surprised. "Of course it is. I have nobody, nobody in this whole world, not even a distant relative. Who would help me? And where would I go? Back to Poland? What for? To the West? Do you know what they have in the West? Camps. DP camps they call them. In English it means 'Camps for displaced persons.' I don't want to be a displaced person, and I will go to no camp. I avoided camps successfully all through the war. I survived in Germany," he continued, "Not far away from here, working as a farmhand."

"How did you manage it?"

"I tell you," Jacob said, "I come from the small town of Zbaszyn, right on the German border, where the Polish-born Jews were deported to as early as 1938. The stories they told. Horrible. People didn't believe them; some even said they made them all up to evoke sympathy. Somehow I did believe, and as soon as the Germans marched in, I got myself Aryan papers, good authentic papers of somebody who was killed in the war, and his military record too. As

92

soon as I realized that the Germans, unlike the Poles, could not recognize a Jew, I figured I would be safer in Germany. So, when they were recruiting farmers, I volunteered as an Aryan, as a Pole. How did I succeed? Call it luck, call it timing. Everything in life is luck and timing. It was at the very beginning of the war. With the Poles I was careful, I hardly spoke. They thought I was a moron, which suited me fine. Once in Germany, I was assigned to a small farm, the only foreigner there. From then on it was easy, except . . ."

"Except what?"

"The thoughts I had about what might happen back home. I worked hard so as not to think. I was a good worker. The farmer liked me. After the war, I told him I was a Jew. You should have seen the expression on his face. So I figure I'll stay here for a year, a year and a half, perhaps. Then I'll be free to go wherever I choose—America, maybe Palestine. Who knows?"

His visits became more frequent, his gifts more extravagant. He brought her candy and cigarettes and even a silver wristwatch with a yellowed face and a black leather strap.

She accepted his gifts with increasing reluctance.

He would also bring stories from the outside, usually about Germans who were caught and arrested for war crimes.

One day he came and sat down, strangely silent.

"What's the matter?" Lisa asked.

"It's a very upsetting story," Rosenkranz said. "I should really spare you this one."

"I don't get upset easily."

"But, it's so incredible, so hard to understand. It doesn't make any sense. That's what is so upsetting about it."

"Go ahead," Lisa said. "Now I'm really curious."

"A couple, a Jewish couple—I never knew them, just heard the story—a man and his wife, were smuggling across the border. Now, that in itself is not unusual. It was gold that they were smuggling, lots of it. They were caught and let go, but the gold was confiscated." He stopped.

"So?" Lisa said.

"So, they went home and killed themselves. Can you imagine that? After all they had been through, they killed themselves. Can you understand that? To live through the war and kill oneself because—"

"The straw that broke the camel's back," Lisa said, as though to herself.

"What does that mean?"

"I'm not exactly sure. It's just a saying, but there is something to it. They must have had many other reasons for not wanting to live. Maybe they survived and found out that their children were killed? Maybe they stayed alive at the expense of others? Maybe . . . maybe . . . they couldn't take freedom." She thought of Natalia. "But, I doubt that losing the money was the real reason. I remember a book I once read. It was set in France. It was about a woman who went through all kinds of tragedies and was very strong, and bore them all very bravely, and then, one day she slept late and got up, opened the front door to get the bottle of milk that had been delivered that morning only to find that the milk had gone sour. And then she killed herself because the milk was sour. That was the last thing she could take. There's a name for that, I don't remember what. But I do recall learning about it."

"You are so wise," Rosenkranz said with admiration in his voice. "And learned."

The next time he came, he brought her a ring. It was a gold ring with one garnet. Lisa refused it. She had had qualms about the watch too, but that was more impersonal, an instrument for measuring time; a ring had something symbolic about it.

"I can't accept it," she said. "Why don't you give it to another girl?"

"I want to tell you something," Rosenkranz said. "I've never told this to anybody. It's a little embarrassing. Do you promise not to laugh?"

"How can I promise if I don't know what it is? But don't worry, I rarely laugh."

And then Rosenkranz, blushing to the roots of his hair, blurted out, "I'm . . . a virgin."

Lisa bit her lips, holding back the laughter, not because of the fact itself but because she had never connected that word with a man . . . Holy Virgin, Jacob Rosenkranz.

"How come?" she asked, trying hard to keep a straight face.

"You see," Rosenkranz confessed, "before the war, I went out with nice girls, from the best families in town, really the cream of society. So, you know . . . I wouldn't dare . . . And then I came here as a non-Jew. So of course I couldn't . . ."

"Of course," Lisa said quickly, sparing him the need to go into further detail. "How about now?"

"Now? Well, there are very few Jewish girls here, and the ones who are here, I am ashamed to say, are not nice girls. They go out with Russians. And I want a nice girl, so that I could marry her. There are German girls and, of course, I could have them by the dozen, but I wouldn't touch a German girl."

"That's very consistent of you," Lisa said.

Rosenkranz looked at her. "You are very pretty," he said. "You could have your pick. You could marry any man you wanted. But . . . you don't know how things are going to be, your leg I mean. When it finally heals, it could be shorter or something."

"Thanks for the encouragement."

"I didn't mean it the way it came out, really. A pretty girl like you and smart, why would you bother with me? But, under the circumstances, I take the courage to ask you . . .

95

Will you marry me?"

"What?"

"Let's get married," Marek had said, as he held her enveloped in the folds of his coat.

She recalled the warmth, the sound of his voice, and how, after he assured her he had meant it, nothing had mattered anymore but the two of them. Even time seemed to have stopped; there was no before and no after, just that moment. . . .

"I know I'm not in your class," she heard Rosenkranz say, "but, I will be a rich man. I already am. And I will take good care of you, I promise."

Lisa shook her head. "I can't," she said. Then added, "It has nothing to do with you."

Rosenkranz, his pride injured, did not show up for a whole week.

In the meantime, medical tests were taken to see if and how Lisa reacted to penicillin. Her blood tests were encouraging, and the doctors came and tried to sit her up, her legs down. Her leg hung double-jointed, as if she had two knees.

When Rosenkranz finally showed up, she tried to repeat to him what the doctors had explained to her.

"The infection is slowly decreasing," she said, "but the bone looks like this." She took a pencil and drew two horizontal lines separated by a space. "These two parts have to meet, or as they put it, make contact. That will happen when the bone produces new cells, but that hasn't started yet."

"You have to have the best doctor," Rosenkranz said. "I heard of one, a professor, a specialist who comes from Berlin. I am going to talk to the doctors here. I will demand a consultation."

If Jacob Rosenkranz could produce a private room, Lisa had no doubt that he could produce a professor as well. Two days later the professor arrived, looking exactly as a professor should, gray beard and all. Dr. Schultz and the others accompanied him in respectful silence.

He looked at the leg, and the X rays. "I would suggest one more thing," he said. "I would inject penicillin right into the bone. What have you got to lose?"

Then they left, and only Dr. Schultz stayed. "He suggested that we inject penicillin straight into the bone," he said to Lisa, as if she had been temporarily deaf.

"Yes," she said. "After all, what have you got to lose?"

Just as the tree outside Lisa's window in the first hospital marked the passage of time, so the room across the street became an indicator of the changing seasons. She watched the dresses of the women being replaced by woolen suits, the men's windbreakers by heavier jackets, the raincoats by winter parkas.

Now that the days were short, the light in the window would go on as early as four o'clock, and Lisa spent long hours watching the people inside. Soon she became familiar with their ways and habits.

The older woman seemed to be home at all times; at least she was there when the light went on. Then, around four-thirty, the daughter would arrive and then the son, and by the time the man walked in, the table would be set and the steaming dish put in the middle of it.

After a while Lisa felt as if she knew them intimately. What she didn't know, she imagined. The woman seemed quite ordinary, the kind, though, who probably got hysterical at rallies and threw flowers at the marching soldiers. The daughter, most likely, had a white dress with a red sash still hanging in a closet, and in the spirit of "Strength Through Joy" had probably provided pleasure to the departing heroes. The son, too young to have been inducted sooner, could have been drafted in the last desperate move to mobilize sixteen-year-olds, and was lucky that the war had ended before he was sent to die.

The man ... He could be anybody. He could have been a soldier in occupied Poland, a member of the SS, a camp guard and, who knows, he could even have been the one who shot her.

Lisa spent her evenings looking through the window, but her days were busy with many things. It was Sister Rosamunde who first brought her a basket full of black stockings, asking her if she could mend them for her. "It might make your days go faster," she had said.

Lisa did not mind it. She could do it while listening to the radio. It was tuned to a station that played continuous music. She was not interested in the news.

She would thread the needle, find the hole, usually on the heel of the stocking, stretch it on a wooden darning device shaped like a mushroom, and holding on to the stem, she would run the thread in close vertical lines, then weave horizontally.

After a while she brought it to such perfection that her darning resembled fine embroidery and was shown and admired like a work of art. Soon other sisters supplied her with more work.

Then there were the books. It took her some time to get used to reading German. She started with an easy one, *Emil and the Detectives*, rereading it with nostalgia, smiling at passages that used to make her laugh out loud, still excited when the mean thief was about to be apprehended. She recalled how she had been unable to put the book down and had brought it to the dining table, and how only at her mother's stern look had she put it away. Next she struggled through *Buddenbrooks*, a gift from Dr. Kamin, the long family chronicle whose characters were so recognizable that she could easily give them the faces of her great-aunts, great-uncles, and cousins.

She started *The Magic Mountain* but put it away, for it made her think of Natalia, who should be in a place like Davos and who might be coughing her lungs out, wandering around in her ambiguous search. The book made Lisa worry about Natalia and miss her.

There were almost no visitors. Fraulein Federdorfer came to bid her a quick good-bye, for she was going to the West Zone of Germany. She was replaced by a man, Helmut Hirsch, who promised to see Lisa but somehow never did.

Rita had gone home, and while her parents assured Lisa that they would stay in touch, they never did. Lisa could not blame them. They lived very far away, and Rita needed all their attention. It would be a long time before she would be wearing high-heeled shoes again.

Jacob Rosenkranz's visits, after she had turned him down, became infrequent. When after a long absence he showed up, he confided to Lisa that he had met a girl. A nice girl she was too, he told her, from the best family, the cream of society of a small town not far from the one he came from.

Lisa said she was happy for him and expressed a wish to meet her.

"Really?" Rosenkranz seemed delighted. "You mean it?"

"Of course I mean it."

The next day he brought the girl over. Her name was Rachel. She was short and bosomy. Wisps of hair, pulled behind her ears, were fastened in a small ringlet in the back of her head with a pin. The rest fell in unruly curls down her shoulders. She wore the garnet ring that Lisa had refused. It was too small for her, and she wore it on her pinky, just like Jacob wore his. And once she started to talk, Lisa decided that they were truly meant for each other—even their names, Jacob and Rachel.

It soon became evident that the real purpose of the visit was to show Lisa off like a pet monkey.

"What did I tell you?" Rosenkranz said to Rachel, pointing at the books on the bedside table. "Cultured."

Then he told her, as he had probably done many times before, how he had first met Lisa when she was lying in the ward with no special care, and how it was he who had arranged for that private room and, what was most important, had summoned a specialist, the best man in the field, who had really performed a miracle.

For the miracle had happened. After only a few applications of the drug, the infection was arrested. The bone particles either got absorbed into the muscle or came out onto the surface to be removed easily, like wood splinters, with nothing more than local anesthesia.

The bone started producing new cells, and after four weeks, the X ray showed results exceeding everyone's expectations.

A few days later, Lisa was seated for a short while on the edge of her bed with her legs down. The leg felt numb, as if it had been asleep for a long time. She could sit in that position for only a few minutes at first. The time increased every day.

A week later, supported by two sisters, she stood up for the first time. It was a strange sensation. The blood seemed to run out of her head and down into her legs, where it changed into thousands of needles prickling into her flesh. She had no sense of balance and, after a short while, had to be put back in bed. This procedure was repeated for a few days, and a sister would come to massage her leg in order to restore circulation.

One day, Sister Rosamunde appeared, crutches in hand and a broad smile on her face.

"The big day has come," she announced. "We will take our first steps."

Lisa looked at the crutches. She thought of the man who had a kiosk at the corner of her street and a concession to sell tobacco because he was a war invalid. She thought of the clicking sound coming from the corridor that haunted her

100

through the closed door.

"Take them away," she said.

Sister Rosamunde looked at her, surprised.

"Take them away, I don't want them," Lisa shouted hysterically.

"But ..." Sister Rosamunde started, then walked out taking the crutches with her. In a few minutes she returned with Dr. Schultz.

"You are being unreasonable," Dr. Schultz said.

"Did I ever claim to be reasonable?"

"Your leg cannot possibly support the weight of your body. You'll only prolong the recovery."

"I am in no rush, Doctor. I have all the time in the world."

"A cane, at least," Dr. Schultz tried.

"No cane."

"You will never make it," he said.

"Just watch me."

She put her leg down, and slowly straightened up. Her hand got hold of the bedpost. She had her balance now. She looked around. She made the armchair her goal. Gritting her teeth, one hand clenched in a fist, she let go of the bed. She stretched out her arm, tapping for another support, the table. She made her first step. Then there was nothing but the wall to hold on to. The chair that had looked so close seemed to be moving farther and farther away. Another step, still another. She leaned forward. Her outstretched hand touched the arm of the chair. She sank into it. Her face was covered with cold sweat. She was breathing heavily, but there was a triumphant smile on her face.

"So?" she said.

"If you think your little performance was more aesthetic than walking with crutches, you are mistaken," Dr. Schultz said, but there was a trace of admiration in his voice.

For days Lisa made the chair her aim. Then the window,

then the door. She refused to go outside into the corridor, and made her trips only around the room. Then she would sit in the chair and wait for the lights in the window across the street to go on.

hat evening she felt particularly tired. She had done a lot of walking. Dusk came early. The sheer curtains had been removed from the window across the street, to be laundered, perhaps, and she could see the people with clarity for the first time. They walked in one after the other, like actors about to take the final bow. The man, as usual, was the last to arrive. He pointed at his dark jacket, which was covered with what looked like white snowflakes. He must have come from a northern suburb, where it was snowing. The woman helped him take the jacket off and carefully carried it out of the room.

Lisa thought that soon it would be Christmas time.

At the age of six, when she had her tonsils taken out, St. Nicholas had come to the hospital. It was not Christmas but on the eve of St. Nicholas's Day, December 6. He walked into the children's ward, red suit, white beard and whiskers, the belly sticking out, a sack over his shoulder. He distributed toys to the children that, as she learned later, had been provided by the parents. He had nothing for her, and all she got was a small chocolate bar that she couldn't even eat. The other children laughed at her. She felt cheated and humiliated.

At home there was a big gift-wrapped package waiting for

her. Her father explained to her that St. Nicholas did not exist, that it was the male attendant, with a false beard and a pillow stuck inside his trousers. But the explanation only piled disillusionment on top of her shame.

She wondered whether St. Nicholas would be making rounds on Christmas Day here and thought that in the hospital she came from, Dr. Boesel would make a perfect one. He wouldn't even need a pillow.

It had been a long day for her, and right after supper she decided to go to bed. She didn't even attempt to read. She switched off the night lamp and put on the radio. The lit dial gleamed in the dark room. She listened to the music and hoped for a restful sleep. Lately her nights had been crowded with disturbing dreams.

The door opened carefully, revealing the wings of the boat-shaped hats worn by nuns other than those tending the sick.

"Are you asleep?" a voice asked.

"Just resting," Lisa said.

"How are you?" the nun said, walking in. She wore a dark blue habit, a large cross dangling from her neck. "I am Sister Gertrude," she introduced herself. "The gatekeeper—there are so many I let in each day. They come and they go, it's hard to keep track. But somehow I remember you, and your friend too. I was happy to see she was well enough to leave. And how are *you* doing?"

"I am making progress," Lisa replied, trying to figure out what the purpose of this visit was.

As if reading her mind, Sister Gertrude said, "You're probably wondering why I am here. I brought you visitors. They came by car and after curfew too. I figured they must be important and that I better accompany them myself."

"And they asked for me?" Lisa said with surprise, for she couldn't think of anyone she knew who would enjoy such privileges.

"May they come in?"

Lisa thought she should perhaps put on the silk nightgown Rita's mother had given her, but the visit might not be worth the effort.

"Have them come in," she said.

The man walked in first. He was about thirty and tall. The well-cut officer's uniform emphasized his broad shoulders and narrow waist. His legs in breeches and military boots were long and straight. His chest was covered with medals, and when he got closer, Lisa recognized the insignia and the Polish eagle. Only the eagle looked different—something was missing. She tried to think what it was, but by then it was his face that drew her attention. It was a handsome face, weathered and tanned, with light blue eyes that seemed to grow darker when he smiled at her. She looked at him transfixed, and only after a while did she notice the woman. Younger than the man, slender, in a long, military-style coat, she was beautiful in a slightly melancholy way, the heavy-lidded eyes dark and large, the black shiny hair worn in a loose knot.

"Hello, Lisa," the man said.

He knew her name. Lisa looked at him questioningly.

"We came from Poland," the man said, "on official business. It somehow brought us to Helmut Hirsch. You do know Helmut Hirsch from the Council?"

"I heard about him," Lisa said.

"Anyway, when he heard we came from Krakow, he told us about you. We got here as soon as possible."

"From Krakow?" Lisa exclaimed. "That's my hometown. How is Krakow?"

"Undamaged, thank God," the man said.

"Undamaged is relative," the woman, silent until now, said. Her voice had a melodious intonation. Suddenly she seemed familiar.

"Do I know you?" Lisa asked.

105

"I don't think so. We live in Krakow, but originally we came from Lvov. It is Russia now."

"Lvov is Russia?" Lisa understood nothing.

"I don't think we introduced ourselves," the young woman said before Lisa had a chance to find out more. "I am Marta." Then motioning toward the man, "My husband, Adam Polanski."

Lisa looked from one to another, a bit confussed. "Are you . . ."

"Jewish?" the young woman finished for her. "I am, Adam is not."

They were still standing in the middle of the room.

"How rude of me," Lisa said. "Please, do sit down."

Adam pulled up a chair.

"May I?" Marta said, pointing at the foot of the bed.

"Please, do," Lisa said.

They both sat down. Marta on the bed, Adam on the chair next to it.

Lisa remembered something. "What happened to the eagle?" she said pointing. "It looks different, as if something was missing."

"It is," Adam said. "The crown is gone."

"Why?"

"Symbolic, I guess. It wouldn't befit the People's Republic."

"People's Republic?"

"What's with you, woman? Where have you been all this time?"

"Why don't you leave her alone?" Marta said.

"What is a People's Republic?" Lisa wanted to know.

"It means Poland is under the Russian boot now," Adam said.

"And Lvov is Russia?"

"Lvov and the whole eastern part. Instead, we got part of Prussia and Lower Silesia."

Lisa remembered that Rita's mother had told her that they couldn't go back to Breslau because it was in Polish hands now.

"That's where Breslau is," she said.

"You are catching on. Only it is called Wroclaw now. That whole area is referred to as the Wild West."

"Why?"

"For one, they resettled the peasants from the east there, gave them former German farms, much better than the ones they have left behind, all modern equipment and a big house to boot. But, you know the Polish peasant. He doesn't want it—doesn't know what to do with a tractor. He is used to his half-dead mare. And then—" Adam interrupted himself, his eyes suddenly focused on the framed plate bearing her name at the head of Lisa's bed.

"Rodwanski?" he said. "Helmuth Hirsch told us your name was Rodwan."

"It is," Lisa said. "We, my husband and I, added the 'ski' to it when we tried to pass as Aryans. When I was brought to the hospital, the war was still on. So I kept it. It was safer that way."

"Rodwanski," Adam repeated as if to himself, "Rodwanski. I have heard that name before. I am trying to remember where."

Lisa's heart stopped for a moment.

"Somebody, at a conference . . . Where was it? Near Breslau somewhere, the place was called Grünberg, I think. The name came up in connection with a position to be filled by someone already living there."

"What did he look like?" Lisa's voice came out choked.

"I have no idea," Adam said. "I never met him, just the name sounds familiar. I really don't remember. For all I know, I may be mistaken."

"You probably are," Lisa said. "For a moment I thought . . . well, I thought it might have been Marek, my husband.

107

Only he wouldn't call himself Rodwanski now. As I told you, the real name is Rodwan. I see no reason why he would use Rodwanski now."

"You would be surprised," Marta said.

"I got you upset," Adam said. "I am sorry. As I said, I could be completely mistaken. The name I might have heard could have sounded similar."

"Yes," Lisa said. "That's probably it."

Marta got up. "We'll be back tomorrow," she said, buttoning her coat. "First thing, early in the morning."

Lisa didn't try to stop them from leaving. She wanted to be alone

She lay back thinking. *No*, she said to herself, *it couldn't possibly be.* If Marek were alive, he wouldn't be in Silesia, he would be in Krakow. That's what they had agreed upon—should they be separated and survive, they would meet there. Had Marek been alive, he would be looking for her. He would have found her by now. Almost seven months had passed since the war ended. She would have at least heard from him . . . somehow. But what if he had searched for her, what would he have found out? That she had been shot and was last seen lying in a field, bleeding to death. She would have died if not for the farmer; it was safe to assume she had. If Marek encountered any of the women who were with her then, he would have heard just that—she was dead.

He would probably mourn her at first. And then . . . Two and a half years had passed since the time they were separated. They hadn't heard from each other. It is a long time, two and a half years. . . . He could have met somebody else. He could have even gotten married again. She remembered, "People cannot be all alone," Jacob Rosenkranz had once told her. "They get married after knowing each other for no more than a week sometimes. Just so they would not be alone." If Marek did . . . Her eyes were burning from tears she was unable to shed. She closed them hoping to fall

108

asleep, but she couldn't. She was lying, staring at the ceiling. She wished Natalia was there. Suddenly she missed her very much.

Lisa put on the silk nightgown and reached for the mirror. Her hair had grown longer, reaching her shoulders. Her face, usually pale, was almost transparent now, and her lips lacked color. Otherwise, she thought, she hadn't changed much. Except for her eyes. Her eyes were . . . She tried to come up with the right adjective and failed.

Adam and Marta had promised to be back first thing in the morning. She walked over to the armchair, sat down, and waited. As time passed without them showing up, she thought, *They won't come at all*, and she almost wished they wouldn't. They managed to unnerve her, especially Adam. All that talk . . . and the fact that they came from Krakow. She hadn't thought of Krakow in a long time. Now she couldn't stop.

She could see the city she grew up in, where the cobblestone streets shot out from the Main Square like a sunburst, cut by the parks, green in the summer, white with snow in the winter.

If Marek were alive, that's where he would be, in Krakow. It was irresponsible of that man, Adam, to upset her like that, just because it seemed to him he had heard the name, which was probably a common one, even though Marek and she had invented it. And then he wasn't sure it was the one he heard. Lisa's hand cut the air in a dismissing gesture.

A rattling sound came from the corridor—lunchtime. Sister Rosamunde walked in with a tray, and as she opened the door, Lisa caught a glimpse of Marta and Adam standing there, talking to Dr. Schultz. A short while later they walked in.

"I'd almost given up," Lisa said. She waited for them to

109

sit down, but they didn't. They seemed fretful and in a hurry.

"Sorry," Adam said. "We had some things to take care of. How long will it take you to get ready?"

"Ready for what?" Lisa said.

Marta pulled up the chair and sat down next to her. "We spoke to the doctor, what's his name, Schultz. He said he had no objection."

Lisa still didn't understand. "Objection to what?"

"To your coming with us."

"Where to?"

"You don't intend to stay here forever, do you?" Adam said, a note of impatience in his voice.

"But ..." Lisa stammered. "How can I? ... I'm not well. . . ."

"Dr. Schultz said you are. He said your treatment here had been completed. He is in the office right now signing the release."

It was so sudden; it wasn't fair to spring it on her like that.

"Dr. Schultz said," Adam went on, "that you don't belong in a hospital anymore, that it's time for you to go home."

"I have no home," Lisa said, and waited.

The words failed to bring forth the expected reaction. Both Adam and Marta remained unperturbed.

Lisa thought of Dr. Kamin: "Don't you want to get better? Don't you mind lying here? Sometimes I wonder about you?" Then of Natalia: "If I don't leave now, I might never have the courage again."

"You will stay with us," Marta said. "We have a large apartment. Adam's brother used to live with us. Last month he moved to Warsaw. You will have a room to yourself."

"Why are you doing this for me?"

"Stop asking silly questions," Adam said, "and get dressed."

"Dressed?"

"This nightgown is very pretty, but you don't expect to travel in it, or do you?"

"But, I have nothing. . . ."

"Oh, how stupid of me," Marta exclaimed. "Why didn't I think of it?"

"I could get clothes from the Council."

"There is no time for that," Adam said. "We have to leave right now; we are late as it is." Then, "I'll be right back," he said and rushed out of the room.

Lisa looked at Marta.

"I'm scared," Lisa said in a whisper.

"Of course you are."

"It's just that it came so suddenly. I didn't—"

"I know."

Adam returned, a black Persian-lamb coat over his arm.

"I bought it here for Marta," he said to Lisa. "Put it on, it's better than nothing." He helped her with it.

"A long silk nightgown, felt slippers, and a fur coat," Lisa said. "It makes for some unique outfit."

"It sure does," Adam laughed. "You are a sight. I wish I had a camera."

Sister Rosamunde appeared, pushing a wheelchair.

The air outside was clear and crisp. The car was parked in front.

Dr. Schultz came running, the tails of his open, white coat blowing in the wind.

"Just wanted to say good-bye," he said, catching his breath.

Lisa stretched her hand out. "Good-bye, Doctor," she said. "And thanks for everything."

Sister Rosamunde helped Lisa to the back of the car. "Have a safe trip," she said.

Adam sat behind the wheel, Marta next to him.

"Let's go," Adam said, and started the engine. It made a purring sound; the car jerked and lurched forward.

$\mathscr{A}$dam brought home a Christmas tree. It was a large spruce, and he had to summon Jan, the janitor, to help him with it. The two of them lowered and tilted the tree and maneuvered it through the door. Michalina, the part-time housekeeper, a middle-aged, stout, always angry woman, came out of the kitchen, wiping her hands on an apron, admonishing them to be careful.

Marta moved the low round table that stood between the windows on the north wall to make room for the tree. The ceiling was high enough for the tall tree; the room was large, with a sitting arrangement on one side, a dining table and chairs on the other. The window faced the park, the naked tree branches powdered with snow that had just begun to fall.

The apartment consisted of two more rooms: a bedroom, which in addition to the standard furniture contained an antique desk Marta had picked up in a junk store and refinished herself, and a combination study–guest room, simply furnished with a settee that opened to a bed. Bookshelves and framed prints adorned the walls. This was Lisa's room.

The kitchen, with a coal-burning stove and a wooden floor, was rather old-fashioned for a new house built shortly before the war in what was considered the outskirts of the

112

city. Apartments like this one were reserved for the privileged few now, and both Adam and Marta belonged to that category: Adam held a high position in the Ministry of the Interior, and Marta headed the Office of City Planning.

"Want to help me trim the tree?" Marta asked. The long dining table was covered with colorful glass ornaments, paper garlands, gold stars, and gilded angels.

"I'd love to," Lisa answered, and soon Marta was standing on a step chair, decorating the top branches, while Lisa, sitting on the floor, was putting streamers on the lower ones.

"I dreamed of a Christmas tree when I was a child," Lisa said. "My parents, of course, wouldn't allow it. I remember one Christmas—I couldn't have been more than eight then—I took the small potted evergreen from the living room into my room, decorated it with colorful cutouts, and hid it in the closet. My mother noticed it missing and looked for it all over. At night, when everybody was asleep, I put it back. I wanted a Christmas tree in the worst way until . . ." She paused, thinking of the Christmas eve, of the Mikulskis, her with her proverbs, him with his drinking, of the Jewish china in their closet, and of the way Marek's eyes had looked then.

"We always had a Christmas tree," Marta said, then told Lisa about her parents.

Her father was a doctor, a veterinarian, an unusual profession for a Jew. He would go out to the country and tend sick horses or deliver calves, more often than not bartering his services for butter and eggs or a bushel of fruits. He was a great patriot, her father, and fought in the First World War for Poland's independence. Her mother was an artist of sorts, famous for ingenious, dainty figurines she would fashion out of twigs, straw, and dried berries. They observed none of the Jewish holidays, her parents, but each year they would put up a tree, sparkling and richly decorated. "They

113

lived like Christians but died a Jewish death," Marta said. They died of typhus in the Lvov ghetto, where they knew no one and no one knew them, leaving Marta alone until the day Adam appeared.

Adam, by his own admission, was a "reformed anti-Semite." He would talk about it freely and with little remorse, as if it were an infectious disease he had contracted and had little to do with individual choice. He would remember a nursemaid who had threatened him with a Jew, who would take him whenever he misbehaved; he recalled his father's fist-pounding rage each time he felt he had been "Jewed" and his mother piously taking him to church, where the priest would talk about the infidels and the damnation of the Christ killers.

In grammar school he would gang up on the few Jewish boys, in high school he joined the National Democratic Party, and as a student at the university, he actively supported the classroom ghetto, forcing the Jewish students into the designated back seats.

It was during one of those excesses that he had first noticed Marta, who, after having refused to move, was roughed up by one of the students. Adam, his chivalry stronger than his political beliefs, had rushed to her rescue, pushing the assailant away.

He stood next to her throughout the lecture, making sure no harm would come to her, and then insisted on escorting her out. Marta had let him walk her as far as the main gate and then told him she would not be seen with him on the street if her life depended on it.

Adam, who had grown to believe himself irresistible to women, was angered and amused by her attitude and followed her all the way home. After that, he would stand in front of her house almost every day waiting for her to come out. He tried to call her, and when she refused to come to the phone, he wrote letters to her, alternately calling her his Jewish princess and a Jewish bitch, then gave up.

The war broke out, a ghetto was established. A year later, when rumors spread that it was going to be liquidated, he made his way in, found Marta already orphaned, smuggled her out, sheltered her throughout the war, himself becoming an underground hero, and married her when it was all over.

"When did you first realize you were in love with him?" Lisa asked.

"I guess I did from the very beginning," Marta said. Then added, "Sometimes it is hard loving him so much. Women do find him extremely attractive, you know, and he is not exactly immune to them either."

Lisa knew. She had noticed the way women looked at him and how he reacted to them. Once, after a party, she found Marta crying.

"He is always surrounded by women, and I feel threatened by each and every one of them."

Lisa laughed.

"What's so funny?"

"You paid me a compliment. Obviously you didn't fear my competition. You were the one who wanted me to come with you. It was your idea, wasn't it?"

"Oh," Marta said, "that's a whole different story. Yes, I did want you to come with us and it was my idea. I had a hard time convincing Adam it was the right thing to do. He feared the responsibility. But you were so forlorn, like a little girl . . . Yes, that was one of the reasons . . . I guess it also had something to do with my in-laws and, maybe, with myself?"

Lisa didn't understand. "Your in-laws? Aren't they nice to you?"

"Oh, yes, they are, and *so* polite. 'Please my *dear*, yes my dear, are you comfortable my dear' . . . and, you know, they never look me in the eye, never. And the way they measure their words when they talk to me, as if afraid a wrong word

115

might slip out. They avoid saying, 'Jew,' as if it were a dirty word. The last time I was there, somebody mentioned Einstein, and Adam's mother wanted to know—and then she almost said it—but at the last moment she caught herself and asked whether Einstein was an . . . Israelite. And I sit there with that smile I put on when I walk in, and take off only after I leave, until I feel every tooth in my mouth ache and my jaw gets so stiff I'm afraid it might crack if I unlock it. I look at other Jews with *their* eyes and I am ashamed of my own feelings. That's, I guess, why I needed you. To lay shame on them, to show what people like them could do to people like you. Can you understand that?"

"I think so," Lisa said, even though she wasn't quite sure she did.

Understanding came accompanied by a feeling of gladness. For the first time Lisa did not look at her guest status as an imposition, something she should apologize or be grateful for. It was she who was needed, to be turned into a symbol and be used by Marta against Adam's family, or perhaps against Adam himself.

She thought of him, the dashing Pole who fell in love with a proud Jewess, whom he protected and eventually rescued, then of Marta, who under the serene and almost sleepy facade harbored a passion ready to explode.

She thought of Marek and herself, the two of them against the world, holding on to each other for comfort, then of Marta again with the intolerance of a terminally ill patient listening to someone blessed with health complain about trivial matters.

The holidays came and went, and shortly after, Adam was sent to attend a conference in Peterswald, a town not far from Breslau. He returned after midnight and wakened Lisa from her first sleep. Marta must have woken up too, or else she had been waiting for him, for Lisa could hear her moving around the kitchen, then the two of them talking in the adjoining room.

"Did you find out anything?" Marta asked.

"Nothing," Adam said.

"The man who had mentioned him was not there?"

"I told you before, if I knew who it was, there would be no problem."

Lisa listened carefully.

"You don't have to raise your voice at me," Marta said. "I just thought that once you saw him, you might remember. How about the minutes? They do take minutes at those meetings."

"Sometimes they do, sometimes they don't. These are not parliamentary proceedings after all. Anyway, when the name came up, it was already after the meeting, and everybody was drunk by then, including me."

He was drunk, Lisa thought. She had seen Adam drunk once. He was his most charming self then, and so witty. But the next day he remembered nothing. It wasn't hard to guess what they were talking about. She wondered whether they would bring it up, then decided they wouldn't. They would probably wait for her to ask. If she hadn't until now, if she didn't try to find out more, it was because she was afraid of what she might learn. That night in the hospital, when Adam made a connection between the name she had been using and the one he believed he had heard, he had tossed her hope like a line to someone hanging from a cliff and she held on to it, knowing she would fall down into an abyss once she let go.

For a similar reason, she was reluctant to leave the house. The city she once had been happy in, the city she loved, was only a short streetcar ride away, yet she was horrified by the mere thought of confronting it again. And so, the winter coat and the fur-lined boots Adam and Marta had provided her with remained unused and seemed to reproach her each

117

time the closet was opened.

The next morning there was no mention of the meeting. Both Marta and Adam greeted her cheerfully and pointed at the window. It was snowing.

It had been a strange winter until then, usually cold but snowless, which was quite uncommon for this part of the country. This was the first sizable snowfall, and Adam and Marta were planning a skiing trip.

After they both left for work, Lisa sat at the window and looked out. The snow was coming down steadily and covered the footprints as soon as they were made. The street was white and very quiet; across, at the entrance to the small park, a squirrel sat in a tree on its bushy tail, nibbling on something held between its front paws. Children, their bright knit caps colorful splashes against the white snow, pulled sleds by a string, the sound of their laughter ringing in the quiet of the street.

The world outside looked pure, inviting, and happy.

Lisa opened the closet, hesitated a moment, took the soft warm boots out, slipped her feet into them, took the coat off the hanger, put it on, and draped Marta's shawl around her head.

"I'll be back in a little while," she told Michalina.

"When you do, take the boots off and leave them outside the door. Don't bring me any snow in here," Michalina said.

Lisa walked down the stairs, into the street. She stopped in front of the house and took a deep breath. The air was sharp and clear, just like the day Marek and she had met. The snow was coming down heavily. She stood there motionless, her face lifted, letting it set on her.

"Just standing here, turning into a snowman?" As if in a dream Marek's voice came back to her.

"I happen to like snow."

"In that case, let's go to the park. There is plenty there."

*   *   *

Her feet were ankle-deep in the white stuff. She made the first step carefully, testingly; the slippery crust did not form yet. She ventured another step, then still another, and lifting her feet high, wading through the snow like through water, she started toward the park.

"An hour ago it didn't even look like snow." That was she talking then.

And Marek, "Now that we have covered the subject of weather, what would you like to talk about?"

Longingly, painfully, she cried his name in her mind.

The happy noise of the children brought her back. She followed it and found herself at the top of a slope. The children, bellies on sleds, were sliding down the hill; a boy in a heavy blue sweater and a red stocking cap rolled down. He came back panting, covered with snow.

"Hey, miss," he said, looking at her. "Want to roll down with me? It's fun."

"Why not," Lisa said.

She lay on the snow, then followed the boy rolling down the hill.

"Hey," the boy called.

"Hey," she called back.

When she got up, her head felt light and dizzy, as if she were pleasantly drunk. She brushed off the coat; she had no gloves, and her hands were blue from the cold. She blew at them, her breath hanging like vapor in the air. She stamped her feet and laughed aloud.

"It felt good," she said to the boy. Then in her thoughts, *It feels good to be alive.*

Part Two

*I*t was the end of June when Marek went to look for Lisa. He pedaled the rusty bicycle he had found on the roadside to the town nearby, where after a long wait, he boarded a crowded train to Krakow.

Coming from the railroad station, through the familiar streets, was like moving in another dimension. The city, untouched by war, was disturbingly unchanged. The deserted streets and closed stores, the iron shutters down, merely gave it a festive air. He cut through the park, which smelled of flowers, where the girls in summer dresses walked arm in arm; the pensioners sat on the benches warming themselves in the sun; and at the exit, the children crowded around the balloon man and counted their pennies in front of the ice-cream cart.

As he approached the house where Lisa used to live, he stopped and instinctively looked up. On the third floor the curtain blown by the wind out of the open window flapped in the air like a flag.

"If it's an apartment you are looking for, sir," the janitor's wife said without recognizing him, "there is none. You can put your name on a waiting list if you wish." She opened the door and let him in.

The dingy quarters were crowded with furniture. The big

antique credenza looked familiar. Marek turned his eyes away.

"I am not interested in an apartment," he said. "I just want to know if any of the old tenants came back."

The expression on the woman's face changed from politeness to suspicion.

"Nobody came back," she said, looking closely at him. Then exclaimed, "Now I know who you are. My, you got skinny; you're Miss Lisa's boyfriend."

"I thought she might have been here," Marek said.

"Nobody came back." Then, as if feeling she should say more, she added, "They were such nice people, Mr. and Mrs. Unger. Good tenants too, and Miss Lisa always with a smile. What they left behind the Germans took, every bit of it." She followed Marek's eyes uneasily.

"I didn't come here to reclaim things."

He took out a pocket notebook, wrote down his name and address, and tore the page out.

"Should Miss Unger show up, will you please give her this." He handed the piece of paper to her, bade her goodbye, and left.

He had been wandering aimlessly for a long while when he came face to face with a haggard man with shorn hair, wearing ill-matched clothes.

They both stopped.

"One of ours?" Marek asked carefully and watched the stranger's face light up.

"Amhoo?" the man asked. Using the wartime code, "A Jew?"

"Amhoo," Marek said.

They shook hands.

"Where are you coming from?" the man asked.

"Lower Silesia."

"Any Jews there?"

"A few camps were liberated in that area. And here?"

124

"A handful," the man said. "They trickle in slowly."

"Is there a place where I could make inquiries to find out who did come back?"

"There is the Jewish Search Center," the man said. "St. Hedwig Street 10 or 12. Don't remember exactly. You can't miss it. There is a sign on the building. Do you know how to get there?"

"I'll find it."

Once he reached the street, he didn't have to look. On the sidewalk in front there was a group of people talking and gesticulating animatedly. He glanced at them and, recognizing no one, passed by them and entered the hallway. He walked through a courtyard and past still another group, then following an arrowed sign, he started up the winding staircase. The stairs squeaked. The door was heavy and he had to push hard.

He found himself in a narrow, crowded corridor, the walls covered with thumbtacked notices written in pencil, crayon, and ink. He tried to read them but couldn't, for his vision was blurred. He pushed another door. Behind a long table sat three women workers, and in front of it people waited in a triple line. Against the wall on a wooden bench sat a woman, holding a small child on her lap, and a young, dark-haired girl. He sat down in the middle. The atmosphere was much like that of a hospital waiting room, compelling one to talk in whispers.

When the line moved, he got up and stood at its end. In front of him was a short man with a shaved head, wearing a military jacket, the buttons removed, turning a cap in his hands, as the worker leafed through her papers.

She looked up after a while, her expression unchanged. "Presumed dead," she said.

The man stood there for another moment. He was still turning the cap in his hands. Then he nodded and said "Thank you" and nodded again. He put the cap on and

125

stepped out of the line.

"Next," the girl said.

Marek moved closer. He clutched the end of the table with both hands.

The girl looked up. "Yes," she said. Her hair was bleached, getting dark at the roots.

"Lisa Rodwan," Marek said, and waited.

"Rodwan, Rodwan," the girl mumbled to herself. Her index finger moved down a column of names. He watched it, thinking she must bite her nails.

She looked up again. "We have nothing under Rodwan," she said.

"Look under Unger," Marek said, "Lisa Unger. That's her maiden name."

The other woman clerk suddenly turned in her chair. "Did you say Lisa Unger?" she said. She was an aging woman. Her hair was harsh and graying, her skin had a yellowish pallor. Her green eyes, with silky lashes that seemed to have been put on her face by mistake, looked at him curiously. "Of course," she said getting up, "you must be Marek." Her dress, that hung loosely on her, was sliding down her hunched shoulders. "Come with me," she said.

An angry murmur rose from those waiting. The line shifted.

Marek followed her into the adjoining room with a desk covered with files. She offered him a chair and pulled one over for herself.

"So *you* are Marek," she said again. "Lisa spoke so often about you. Oh, forgive me," she said, stretching out her hand. "My name is Sabina. I knew Lisa."

Her use of the past tense stunned him and stopped his breathing for a second. Their eyes met. Sabina didn't say anything more. She just looked at him, then slowly shook her head.

Marek sat there, hunched forward, without moving.

"How?" he said finally.

"I'll tell you what I know," Sabina said. "I was with Lisa until the last moment, until we were marched out, that is. The camp was evacuated, pardon the euphemism, as the Allies were closing in. I won't go into details; I won't describe the march to you." She paused. "I don't really know what happened—whether Lisa tried to escape or hide or simply ran into the field to pick up a potato. I really don't know. I wasn't there when it happened."

"When what happened?" Marek managed to say.

"She was shot. I heard it from the others. As I told you before, I wasn't there. When I passed by a while later, she was already lying there."

"Was she—"

"No," she said. "I stopped by her. I spoke to her. She even answered me. She was conscious. She told me that in her pocket there was something for you, a diary. I took it." She got up, picked a folder out of a file, took out a soft-covered notebook, and handed it to Marek. "There was nothing I could do, you understand. A German guard chased me away."

Marek nodded. He reached for the notebook.

"A few feet from her, there was another woman lying face down, also hurt. I couldn't tell who she was."

Marek got up and started toward the door. He turned around. "When you left her, was she still alive?"

"There was nothing I could do," Sabina repeated. "I called to a farmer who was working across the road. I don't even know if he heard me. And even if he did, even if he went to her . . . Marek, she was very badly hurt."

He was already at the door when she called him back. She took a slip of paper out of the file and gave it to Marek. "Here are some names and addresses of women who were with her there, who saw . . . " she said. He folded it, put it in his pocket, and walked out of the room. He sank down on the bench. The woman with the child was gone, but the dark-haired girl was still there, sitting at the opposite end. Without getting up, she slid toward him.

"The news wasn't good?" she said. Not waiting for an answer, she bent over and tilted her head to look into his face. "You don't have the parents bad news look, or the brother or sister bad news look. Who was it? Your girl, your wife?"

He nodded.

"Oh," she said. "You see, I can tell. I've been here every-day since they opened this center. I sit right here and wait for a friend of mine. I could call him my husband, I guess. He was my husband, you see. Only we didn't have time to get married. We will, though, as soon as he comes back." She pulled the string of her sack bag and took out a roll. She tore it in half and offered Marek a piece. He waved her hand away. "They will be closing here soon," she said, looking at the clock on the wall. "There is a soup kitchen down in the yard. You can have some hot soup if you want to."

"I don't want any." Marek said.

"Do you live here?"

"No."

"Where are you going to sleep?"

"I don't know."

She got up. "Let's go," she said.

He rose and followed her, moving like a sleepwalker. They walked down the street and crossed the park. The pensioners were gone, as were the balloon man and the ice-cream vendor. The girl stopped at the pond. She crumbled the roll between her fingers and fed it to the ducks.

They walked into a wide street, then a narrow one, then one still narrower, and finally into an alley. There was a doorway again, another courtyard, and another squeaky staircase. The girl stopped in front of a door and opened it with a key. They walked into a kitchen, then into a room.

Marek looked around. He couldn't help being startled by

128

how lovely the room was. It had white lacquered furniture. A chest and a desk were pushed against the wall. In the corner was a bed covered with a sheer ruffled spread, and the window had curtains made out of the same transparent material.

"I got my room's furniture back," the girl was saying. "I went to the house where I used to live with my parents, and the people who live there now let me have it. They had no use for it. They even helped me get this place. Want to see something?" She walked over to the desk and pulled out a drawer. "My old math book," she said. "Isn't that something? Isn't it strange? Of all things, to find a math book." She stopped and mused.

Marek noticed a name on the cover: Miriam Lenz.

"Strange," she repeated. "And I didn't even like math." She put the book back and pushed the drawer in. "Sit down," she said.

He looked around. There was no chair in the room.

"Sit on the bed," she said. "It's all right." She went into the kitchen and came back carrying a plate with bread and cheese. She took a piece, he refused. He asked for a drink. She brought in a bottle and a glass. He poured himself a glassful, then another, and then still another. He fell back on the bed and closed his eyes.

When he woke up, she was sitting on the edge of the bed. "Move," she said. She pulled the cover from under him. "I don't like to sleep alone."

He moved all the way to the wall.

She looked at him. "No touching," she said warningly. She curled up next to him. "No touching," she repeated.

She reached for his arm, though, and put it under her head, using it as a pillow. She sighed a deep, soft sigh and was asleep.

Marek lay quietly without moving, feeling his arm slowly get numb. Turning carefully, he lifted her head with his free hand, pushed the pillow under it, and put her head down. Then he slid off the bed, opened the door cautiously, and walked out.

He spent the night sitting on a bench in the park, and in the morning he looked up the women whose names were on the list Sabina had given him. The story he heard from each of them was the same: Lisa had been shot, and when they saw her last, she was either dying or already dead. Only when he tried to pinpoint the exact location, their reports differed. He went back to the Center to check with Sabina.

When he got there, Miriam was sitting on the bench, talking to a young man. "Your news wasn't good," he heard her say. "I can tell. I come here everyday; I am waiting for a friend of mine."

Marek greeted her. She turned around and looked and didn't recognize him.

He walked out and went to the railroad station to wait for a train that would take him home.

Home was a small town in Lower Silesia, at the foot of the Eulen Mountains, ten kilometers from the camp he had been liberated from a few weeks before.

On that day he had stood in the back line of a triple-row square formation, waiting for the roll call. The sun had just risen and hung red and round, shining through the tree branches. The camp elders clustered together, talking in hushed voices. The commandant arrived unescorted, coming slowly down the hill.

As though in response to an order, the chief elder, a German Jew, started walking between the ranks, moving his arms up and down, as he counted the men, his lips moving in a mechanical whisper. Then, he walked to the middle of the square, where the commandant stood waiting. Straightening himself in a military fashion, heels together, chest forward, the elder reported to him.

130

Everyone stood at attention now. The commandant nodded absentmindedly, reached into his pocket, took out a penknife, and offered it to the chief. He stepped back, shaking his head. The commandant was saying something, waving the penknife in the air. The chief took another step backward, still shaking his head. The commandant raised his voice. The chief hesitated another moment, came closer, and reluctantly reached for the knife. The commandant extended his left arm, the forefinger of his right hand pointing at the sleeve.

"He wants him to cut the insignia off his sleeve." Roman Gold, standing next to Marek, gasped in disbelief. He was the one who had introduced him to the intricacies of camp life when Marek had first arrived there; they had remained friends ever since.

Marek stood on his toes and craned his neck, following with detached curiosity what seemed like a scene from a movie.

The camp chief removed the insignia and held it down in between his fingers. The sun rolled over the treetops. It was very quiet.

Then the commandant turned around. "Dismissed!" he bellowed.

Marek felt as if every part of his brain were unfolding to encompass what was happening.

No one moved. Only after a while did they dare to look at one another, uncertainly, from the corners of their eyes. Feet shuffled in place. The ranks remained unbroken as the inmates watched the German guards climb the trucks and leave.

After what seemed like a very long time, a cry broke out, following the word that the wires had been cut at the other end of the camp. Roman pulled Marek into a group that was running in that direction.

He stood awaiting his turn, watching those ahead of him

131

crawl out, one after the other. Then he too started out on hands and knees, the spikes sticking into his tatters, scratching his hands and face.

He had made it to the other side and turned around to look back just as someone, who had climbed the deserted watchtower and managed to dismantle the searchlight, was trying to push it down. It fell, hitting the pole on its way, and shattered in midair, the rays of the sun reflecting in thousands of flying crystals.

An ad-hoc committee was soon formed, headed by Pincus Horowitz, the oldest of them all, who in turn nominated Marek as one of his deputies. The purpose of the committee was to keep some semblance of order and to represent the others.

Freedom was at first considered a privilege that could be revoked. It was treated with disbelief and suspicion, and later approached with fearful caution. It was tasted carefully, like the food they found in the town, whose entire population had fled to the pine-covered mountains nearby. They had walked through the streets, deserted and unreal, like an abandoned stage set, frightened by the sound of their own footsteps. At nightfall they returned to the camp to sleep.

When the town's inhabitants slowly began to return, Pincus Horowitz called a meeting that was open to all and attended by most.

"The Germans are coming back," he began. "They are mostly women and children and the infirm. I am about to put down rules that won't make me very popular with some of you. Here they are. We need food, clothes on our backs, and a roof over our heads. Other than that, there will be no plundering, no pillaging, no abuse, and no molestation of women."

The response was a disapproving mutter.

"He wants us to be friends with them," someone shouted.

"There also will be no fraternization of any kind," Horowitz concluded. "You voted me in, you can vote me out. But, as long as I am in this position, that's what I expect of you."

The angry voices demanded an explanation.

"We are Jews," Pincus Horowitz said. "We live by the law; we don't take it in our own hands."

"Why are you so concerned about them?" they wanted to know.

"My concern is not for them, but for you—us," Horowitz promptly corrected himself. Then he went on, his voice patient, persuasive now. "In order to survive we all did things that under the circumstances were understandable and could be tolerated. But now we are free, and the sooner we learn to act according to certain standards, the better we will be able to resume a normal life."

"You are trying to deprive us of the right to revenge," the former chief elder exclaimed.

"I never understood the expression 'sweet revenge,' " Marek said caustically.

Everybody burst out laughing, for it was common knowledge that the elder had carried on with a German woman and was now living with her.

The tension broken, the meeting came to a close.

The slant-eyed Mongols from Kalmukia marched in, ragged and slovenly, resembling neither victors nor liberators and evoking more fear than exaltation. They preceded a unit of Politburo officers, clean-cut and well equipped, who, upon arrival in camp, were greeted as heroes. Persuasive propagandists, they appealed for help and cooperation, after having pointed out the danger of sabotage the highly industrialized area was exposed to.

The volunteers were divided in groups of ten, each one assigned a different function.

133

Marek, Roman, and eight others were given guns, a plant of precision instruments to guard, the same one Marek had worked in, and the owner's abandoned villa nearby for living quarters. They moved in and searched the villa for hidden dangers, then for hidden treasures. They found a packed larder, closets full of clothes, and wine and a barrel of pure alcohol in the cellar. A suspicious noise turned out to be an electric refrigerator and not, as they feared, a time bomb. They ate carefully, warning one another against overindulging. They washed and dressed in clean clothes but slept on the floor, being unaccustomed to the softness of the beds. After a while they were joined by others, and soon there were twenty of them living in the villa. They took turns guarding the plant, they ate, and when they got drunk on the pure spirits, they would line up crystal and fine china to practice target shooting in the garden.

It was hard to live up to Horowitz's high principle—the temptation was too great, the justification too easy. While incidents of harassment or mistreatment were rather rare, looting was rampant and went on with impunity.

Even Roman, who was the first one to applaud Horowitz at the meeting, soon came up with a brand-new motorcycle, which, following the lead of a youthful informer, he had found hidden in a haystack. It had been abandoned, he explained, and the youngster had been rewarded. Besides, with trains still out of commission, he felt it was as important as "clothes on one's back" or a "roof over one's head."

As soon as their stomachs had learned to keep food down, their bones became covered with flesh, and their feet could carry them, they began to set forth, one after another. No one discussed the purpose or destination, and no questions were asked. Everyone knew theirs was a journey in time rather than space, a voyage in search of the lost past. They would come back after a few days, after a week or two, and still no questions were asked, no consolation offered. Sometimes they didn't come back alone, but brought a brother, a relative, a friend. Without comment, others would cram together to make room for the new arrival. The lucky ones who brought them offered little explanation, acting discreetly and unobtrusively, the affluent in a pauper society, where ostentation would be in bad taste.

Paula, neither a friend nor relative, appeared out of nowhere one day, moved into the villa, and took over the duties of washing, cleaning, and preparing meals for all. A wisp of a girl, with shoulder-length blond hair, she looked more like a schoolgirl than someone who had managed to fool the informers and outwit the Gestapo while passing as an Aryan.

Roman followed her around, watching jealously that no other man would be near her. They were married within a month. The wedding took place in the garden of the German villa, the canopy made out of a tablecloth found among abandoned German possessions. The young, slender bride wore everything borrowed and nothing new. Horowitz administered the marriage vows, and Marek gave the bride away.

Marek began to work for the Central Bureau of Western Industries, an agency created to administer the former German plants. It was a position he neither sought nor bargained for, but like everything else since his liberation, it had just happened to him.

He was walking along the road when a car, approaching from the opposite direction, stopped in front of him. The driver wearing the uniform of a Polish officer leaned out and asked for directions to the town's square. Marek began to explain the complicated turns, when the officer interrupted. "Are you doing anything important now?" he asked. Marek, startled by the question and by the idea he could be taken for one going about urgent business, shook his head.

"How about hopping in and showing me the way?" the

officer said, opening the door.

"Why not?" Marek said with a shrug and got in. The officer introduced himself as Alex Lipski. A longtime Communist, he had spent the war years in Russia and unlike many others did not get disillusioned. He was sent to head the Bureau here. By the time they reached the square, he had asked Marek to work for him.

"Why not?" Marek replied in the same tone of voice.

The offer could not have come at a more opportune time. An engineer was about to arrive from Central Poland to take over the plant and the villa too. Marek secured a job in the Central Bureau for Roman as well; they were given a two-family house as part of the bargain.

Roman chose the ground-floor apartment, which left Marek with the one upstairs.

"You don't mind the smaller one, do you?" Roman asked. "After all, you are alone." Then, noticing the sudden change in Marek's face, he said with a note of apology, "I didn't mean it the way it came out."

"Forget it," Marek said, but he himself never really could, and things between the two of them were never the same again.

Marek officially retained the polonized name of Rodwanski and stayed in Peterswald. The bastardized territory, neither German nor Polish, suited his mood in its unreality, the prevailing chaos fitting his inner turmoil. He needed time to think before undertaking any further search for Lisa and welcomed the breathing space the arrangement had offered him.

His days were spent at work, his evenings in solitude, in spite of a standing invitation from Roman and Paula to join them for supper. He preferred to eat alone, a simple meal that Frau Huber—the German neighbor who came to work for him after he had saved her and her daughters from eviction—would leave for him to be warmed up. Then, he

136

would turn the radio on and, in semidarkness, listen to music or reread Lisa's diary, even though he knew it by heart.

A shell exploded in Hall B last night. When the day shift arrived for work this morning, the walls were still splattered with blood. I tried not to look at it but I couldn't help it. I thought of all the ways I could die in this place. I enumerated them in my mind. They make a long list. I thought of each possibility separately. I don't believe any of them. . . .

The first snow is falling. I look and I wonder whether it is snowing where Marek is now, and if it is, whether he is watching it thinking of me. . . .

For the first time today I realized what we must look like to someone from the outside. There was a man standing on the side of the road as we were marched to work this morning. A little man in a shabby coat. He stood there staring and when I passed him by, I could hear him whisper, "*Schrecklich*, terrible." If he had shouted it, he would be a hero. But he wasn't, so he just whispered. . . .

After lights-out, the women on the upper bunk were talking about Freedom. "When still in Freedom," they were saying, or "When in Freedom again." It sounded like a place, or an era of long ago, or far off in the future. These talks frighten me. I'm trying not to imagine Freedom. It always makes me think of Sunday, expected to compensate for a hard week— but I know it never does. There used to be songs about melancholy Sundays. I remember reading somewhere that the suicide rate is highest on Sundays. . . .

The wall in back of my bunk is covered with writing in Cyrillic. I had it read to me. It's the signature of someone named Natasha Pavlovna. I often think about her. I wonder where she is now and what happened to her. I feel close to her. I know why she scribbled her name all over the wall; for the same reason I keep this journal. . . .

The notebook was falling apart, the pages loose. Marek knew he should have it bound but was reluctant to part with it even for a short time.

137

arek threw himself into work with fervor, spending ten to twelve hours daily in the office, and attended every conference. It was during one such meeting that he encountered Srebrny. After the business part was over, they all moved to an adjoining room, where a bar had been set up. Drinking was an integral part of those meetings, something Marek participated in reluctantly at first but eventually learned to enjoy. He was quite high when a heavyset, middle-aged man, whose uniform was covered with medals, approached him, glass in hand. "Citizen Rodwanski," he said with a drunken lilt. "What's your real name? Because I . . ."—he looked around and lowering his voice to a whisper concluded—"I'm Silber from Warsaw."

Marek juggled the two names in his mind, quickly realizing they were one and the same, Srebrny being a verbatim translation into Polish. He looked closer at him. The fleshy face with baggy eyes suddenly appeared unmistakably Jewish. Still not sure, he gazed at him questioningly.

Srebrny nodded and started out of the room, motioning Marek to follow him. Once alone, Srebrny began to talk. At the beginning of the war he had crossed the Russian border, leaving his family behind. He joined the Red Army, was decorated for bravery, and advanced to the rank of major. After his return to Warsaw he found no one. "Wife, two children, two brothers, a sister," unfolding his fingers, Srebrny counted out his losses in a dispassionate tone of voice.

Marek, his tongue loosened by liquor, as if feeling he had to give something in return, told him about Lisa.

Srebrny listened attentively, shaking his head from time to time. "What makes you think she is still alive?" he asked.

Marek thought before answering. "I am not sure," he said finally. "It's just a feeling I have. . . . She made it to the very end. . . . It just doesn't seem conceivable, it wouldn't make sense." He looked at Srebrny, as if waiting for him to agree. Then, "Major," he said, "maybe it's presumptuous of me, but you are in a high position, and I thought perhaps, through your connections . . ." He looked at him imploringly.

Srebrny remained silent for a while, then said, "I'll try. I promise nothing, but I'll see what I can do."

"Thank you, Major, thank you very much," Marek said and later marked a date in a small, leather-bound notebook, reminding himself to get in touch with Srebrny in two weeks' time.

Before going upstairs, Marek stopped to tell Roman and Paula about the strange encounter. They both listened carefully but remained silent.

"So, what do you say?" Marek insisted.

"I think it was very nice of the major," Paula said noncommittally. "Want to stay for supper?"

"I'm not hungry." He was disappointed with their lack of response. "Enjoy your evening," he added and walked out.

After he closed the door Marek heard them talking and stopped to listen when Lisa's name was mentioned. Roman had said something that must have prompted Paula's question. "Why do you think he does it to himself?" she asked.

139

"Why does he insist she is alive?"

"Who knows?"

"It's crazy."

"Not to him," said Roman.

Marek started up the stairs, feeling angry both at Roman and Paula and at himself for taking them into his confidence. Even from Alex, tough and remote as he was, he would get a more understanding response he thought, and considered approaching him in the morning.

But when he arrived at work the next day, Alex was engaged in conversation with a high-ranking Russian officer, who seemed perturbed.

"Colonel Maloviak," he made the introduction, "Citizen Rodwanski." Then, "There seems to be some trouble," Alex said to Marek by way of explanation. "Dorski has been arrested."

"The engineer from Precision Instruments, the one who took over the villa?"

"The same one."

"What for?"

Maloviak hurried to answer the question. "He sold the entire stock. He even started dismantling the machines and intended to sell those too."

"No," Marek said and was about to burst out laughing when he looked at the colonel's bloated, humorless face and restrained himself.

"A new man arrived last night. He looked at the production blueprints. He couldn't read them. It seems no one can figure them out," Alex said.

"I understand you worked in that plant for a while," Maloviak interrupted, turning to Marek.

"Yes, I did, during the war. The plant requested twenty men from the camp, and I was one of them."

"Did you work on the assembly line?"

"Yes."

"Who was your foreman?" Maloviak asked.

"His name was Holland," Marek answered. "Otto Holland."

"Do you know where we might find him?"

"He was a local man. It shouldn't be hard. Did you try his home?"

"We did. He isn't there anymore. A family repatriated from the east is living there now. Holland was recently seen in this vicinity though."

"Do you think he is hiding?" Marek asked.

"Is there any reason for him to be hiding? How did he behave in the camp?"

"Rather decently," Marek answered. "He told me to mark my mess tin so he could tell which one was mine. I put the ace of spades on it, and he would pour extra-thick soup for me. He called me the Ace of Spades. He and I got along. He had a wife, considerably younger than he, and rumor had it—"

"I want you to locate him," Maloviak interrupted. "Alex says you are the only one who can do it."

"Why me?"

"You speak fluent German, and according to Alex, they trust you."

"I wonder how he got that idea," Marek said defensively, aware that it was true, that ever since he had prevented Frau Huber's eviction, the Germans were constantly coming to him with grievances.

"Why don't you ask around?" Maloviak said and got up, indicating that there was nothing further to discuss.

"You got me into a nice mess," Marek said to Alex after Maloviak had left.

"What mess?" Alex said. "What's the problem? Actually, you'll be doing Holland a favor. You'll be giving the man his job back."

"Suppose he doesn't want it?"

"I'm afraid he will have little choice in the matter." Alex's eyes looked angry now.

"All right," Marek said. "No need to get upset."

"I am not upset," Alex said. "I just don't like being dragged out of bed at six in the morning. Now, getting back to Holland . . ."

"I'll see what I can do," Marek said.

As a first step he decided to talk to the people who were living in Holland's home. It turned out to be a long walk. The evening sky was clear, and the jasmines and acacias scented the air.

The white shingled house, fenced in on a corner lot, was spacious and well kept. The lawn was watered and cut, and a gravel path led to the doorway. He walked down it, looked for the bell, couldn't find it, stood there a moment, and then knocked.

"Are you expecting anybody?" a woman's voice inside asked in Polish.

She opened the door. The woman was in her middle years and plain. At the table, a steaming plate in from of him, sat a man in shirt sleeves.

"I am sorry to disturb you at dinnertime," Marek said. "I am trying to locate someone who used to live here, Otto Holland. I thought perhaps you—"

"I told the colonel the other day"—the man didn't try to hide his annoyance—"I don't know who used to live here. I didn't try to find out. I never even heard the name before."

"I thought there might still be some papers, names, addresses."

"I cleaned the drawers out myself," the woman said. "I threw out everything that was of no use to us."

"In that case," Marek said, "I am sorry to have bothered you." He looked around the room once more, and on the opposite wall noticed a portrait of a woman. She was holding a

142

bunch of flowers, her face demurely hidden halfway in the bouquet. Marek recognized her as Holland's wife even though she wore her hair differently when she visited her husband in the plant. He wondered why Holland hadn't taken it along. He must have left in a hurry and the people had simply kept it. "Thank you just the same," Marek said, stepping back. The door closed. Marek sucked in the air deeply, exhaling it through pursed lips. Then he started back. He was disturbed. The scene reminded him of something. It took him a while to realize what it was.

Some time ago he had been sent to his hometown on official business. Between conferences, he walked through the streets and found himself in front of his house. He had not planned to go there. His feet had carried him, and suddenly, there it was. The street, the house, the hallway. He ran upstairs, taking the steps two at a time as he had always done. He rang the bell twice, his identification signal, without realizing that he had done so. A woman opened the door carefully, peering at him through the crack.

"What do you want?" she asked.

Marek didn't know what he wanted. "I used to live here," he said.

The woman's look betrayed fear and indignation.

"I know nothing," she said. "My husband is not at home. Come back when my husband is home." She was about to shut the door, but Marek already had his foot in it. He pushed it, throwing the woman against the wall, and walked in. He wandered through the rooms, feeling nothing. The smell was different. The few pieces of furniture that he recognized were rearranged and held no memories. The curtains were gone, and the beds were covered with different spreads. He walked back into the foyer. The woman was still there, in the corner between the entrance and the wall, her eyes following him fearfully. He stopped by the built-in closet, where his father used to keep his books. Marek knew the books weren't there anymore. He himself had crated them. He tried the knob, but the closet was locked.

"Open it," he ordered the woman.

The closet was filled with linen now, sheets and table-cloths arranged in even piles. Scalloped strips of paper lace, thumbtacked to the edges, adorned the shelves. Marek looked at the inside frame of the door. The pencil marks were smudged and faded but still discernible. His father would put him against the frame of the open door and mark his height with a pencil. The first mark was hardly a meter from the floor. He must have been eight when the last mark was made, for after that he would not allow it anymore. Marek closed the closet and started toward the door.

"Come back when my husband is home," the woman called after him.

"I might," Marek said.

He felt as if he were in the middle of a nightmare, in which the world had become a huge chessboard and the people, like pawns, were shifted from house to house, into different homes, into beds that had been molded by the shapes of others, dressed in garments that retained the form and scent of previous owners. Suddenly the clothes he was wearing seemed alive.

He had to get hold of himself, he thought. He hadn't been getting enough sleep lately; he had better go home and rest.

The next morning he went to Frau Huber's house. She lived only half a block from him, in one of the red brick buildings. He had never been there before, and Frau Huber was obviously startled to see him.

Frau Huber's daughter greeted him with a nod and a smile, then disappeared into the next room. She had her mother's heavy build and her dark, square, un-Germanic face.

The room bore witness to Frau Huber's domestic talents. There were doilies all over, throw pillows on the chairs, and sentiments embroidered in Gothic lettering adorning the walls. On a table, among potted plants, was a photograph of a man in a *Wehrmacht* uniform.

"Please, sit down." Frau Huber cleared her throat. Was everything satisfactory yesterday? she wanted to know. Had Herr Rodwanski found the house in order? Was the dinner all right?

"Fine, everything was just fine," Marek said absentmindedly, then came straight to the point.

"Do you know a Herr Holland?" he asked. "Otto Holland?"

Frau Huber thought for a moment, then shook her head. She was sure she had heard the name before, she said, but no, she never knew him.

Marek took a sealed pack of cigarettes out of his pocket and put it on the table. That seemed to ignite a spark of recollection.

"Was his wife's name Louise?" Frau Huber asked.

"I don't know," Marek said.

"I used to be in a women's organization with a Louise Holland. Not a political organization," she added quickly. "More like a knitting circle. We used to knit socks and sweaters for the soldiers on the Eastern Front."

"Ask around," Marek said, ignoring the explanation. "Whoever comes up with information will get two cartons of these"—he pointed at the cigarettes—"and two cans of American Crisco. And I will double it. You will get the same."

Frau Huber looked at him. "You are a very generous man, Herr Rodwanski," she said slowly.

Under his careful glance, Frau Huber's mouth stretched into a smile, but her eyes remained unchanged. In the adjoining room, the daughter, who must have been eavesdropping and had grown tired of it, tiptoed away from the closed door.

Marek left the apartment and walked out into the street.

145

From the garrison, in a plaintive chorus muted by the distance, came the singing of Russian soldiers.

The next day Frau Huber stopped by, her usual pleasant self. She had made inquiries and had come up with the address of a place where Holland might be living—his brother-in-law's farm, some thirty kilometers away.

Marek thanked her and watched her scoop up the reward. Since she was already there, he asked her to brew fresh coffee, and he drank it with a slice of bread and honey as he looked up the village on the map. It was at least thirty-five kilometers away. He went to Roman, asked to have his motorcycle for the day, rode with him to work, then took over and started on his way.

He enjoyed the ride, the speed, the feeling of motion, the wind against his face. He drove through the valley, the mountains on the horizon covered with all shades of green. He went down the main highway and then turned into a country road, the motorcycle jumping on the bumps, until the road ended abruptly. He stopped, checked the map again, and proceeded along a narrow path beaten across the wheat field.

He could see the red dome of a silo and, as he got closer, a farmhouse next to it. He stopped the motor a few yards away, got off, and walked toward it. He pinched his nostrils against the sharp smell of manure, of the potato peels rotting in the trough, walked by a chicken coop, by a doghouse, the chained old balding dog asleep in the sun, and on to the house. He knocked. There was no answer. He opened the heavy door carefully, then pushed it. The hinges creaked. He walked into a dark, spacious kitchen with no one there. The door leading to another room was ajar. Inside, across a long table, a man sat, his face hidden behind a newspaper. The paper came down. There, eyeglasses pushed up his forehead, was Holland. He pulled his eyeglasses down, and looked at Marek standing in the doorway.

146

"*Lieber Gott*," he whispered. "The Ace of Spades." His face flushed crimson, then the color drained away, leaving it ghostly pale. Both hands on the table, he pushed himself up and rose very slowly, then in even slower motion, without taking his eyes off Marek's face, he lifted his arms.

Marek looked at him perplexed and, only after a few seconds, understood the meaning of this gesture. He walked closer and stopped at the opposite end of the table.

"Herr Holland," he said, "I mean you no harm."

Holland's expression changed from fear to distrust. His arms slowly came down, his face gradually regained its color.

They eyed each other steadily. "Sit down," Marek said. "You don't have to stand."

Holland sat down. His eyes still on Marek, he motioned to a chair next to him.

Holland must have lost considerable weight. Never a big man, he now looked fragile. The balding head, the wire-rimmed glasses, the thin elongated features, gave him the appearance of a medieval monk.

"You really thought I came here to hurt you?" Marek said.

"Why shouldn't you?" Holland said with a shrug, then asked for a cigarette. Marek gave him one and lit it for him. Holland inhaled with pleasure. "I often wondered," he said, "how you were going to pay us back."

"It's really very complicated, Holland," Marek said. He noticed that unconsciously he had dropped the "Herr." "You were a kind man. You never hit anyone, you never even raised your voice. You gave me thick soup. It meant a great deal to me then."

"Ace of Spades—oh, forgive me, I don't know your name."

"Rodwan," Marek said.

"Herr Rodwan," Holland said, "if I gave you thick soup,

the next fellow got water."

Marek had never thought of it that way. Suddenly he felt like an accomplice. "Your job at Precision Instruments," he said abruptly, "you can have it back."

He expected at least a sign of appreciation, but Holland only shook his head. "I cannot accept it."

Marek remembered what Alex had said. "I'm afraid you haven't much choice in the matter."

"I suppose not," Holland said. "You can take me with you now, you can force me. I know I have no choice. I never seem to have much of a choice. Supervising the camp inmates wasn't my choice either. Circumstances, Herr Rodwan."

He reached for the cigarette butt, straightened it out, and tried to relight it. Marek shook a few cigarettes out of the pack and put them on the table. "Let me tell you something, Herr Rodwan," Holland said, lighting one. "It is easy to be caught in circumstances. Only the first step is hard, and suddenly it isn't up to you anymore. It sucks you in. You sink in like in quicksand."

"You don't have to satisfy my curiosity if you don't want to," Marek said, trying to change the subject, "but why don't you want the job now?"

"Why?" Holland repeated. "It's hard to explain, but I'll try. You see, I love my country. It's like loving a bad woman. You know she is sinful but still you can't help loving her, and you can't stand seeing her with anyone else. That's how I feel about staying here, my hometown overrun with strangers."

Holland's parallel prompted the next question. "Where is your wife?"

"In the West Zone of Germany. I'm suppose to meet her there. Everything has been arranged. Today my brother-in-law is down at the market with two hogs, trying to raise some money." He looked at Marek.

148

Marek looked away. Then he got up. He hesitated a moment, then said, "Tomorrow you'd better be out of here. You'd better be far away."

Holland opened his mouth, but before he could speak, Marek was out the door.

He walked to the motorcycle, got on the seat, pumped the pedal, started the engine, and rode off.

He rode back, trying to understand why he had acted the way he did, and in fighting the temptation to feel self-congratulatory and noble, he went to another extreme, accusing himself of unmanly softness. He stopped at a roadside inn, ordered a beer, and acted demonstratively rude toward the German bartender. But he failed to prove anything to himself and only added to his irritation. He drove around until the sun began to set. It was dark by the time he got back. He left the motorcycle in the driveway.

Paula was waiting for him in the open door. "I've just been talking to Alex," she said. "I called to see if you were there. He was worried too. Where have you been for so long?"

"It was farther than I thought," Marek said, walking in. "And then I drove around. I stopped for a beer." He sank into an armchair and stretched his legs out. "Get me a drink, Paula," he said.

Hearing his voice, Roman came in from the other room. Paula reappeared, a filled glass in her hand.

"How did it go?" Roman asked. "Did you find him?"

Marek emptied the glass and put it down on the floor next to the chair. "I found him," he said, "and I let him go."

"What do you mean, you let him go?"

"Just what I said. He told me he had arranged to go to the West Zone tomorrow and join his wife. I told him to go ahead."

Roman and Paula exchanged glances.

"Why?"

149

"I don't know."

"You lost your nerve or something?"

Marek thought a moment. "Maybe I did. I'm not sure anymore."

"I don't understand it," Roman said.

"I don't understand it myself," Marek said and got up.

"Please," Paula said, "don't go. Have something warm to eat."

Marek smiled and sat down. He spooned the soup she gave him in silence, trying to figure out what he was going to tell Alex.

It was easier than Marek anticipated.

"Holland wasn't there anymore," he told Alex the next day. "He left about a week ago to join his wife in the West."

Alex took the news in stride. Maloviak had returned to Warsaw, and Srebrny was pushing his own man for the position.

Getting Holland didn't seem so imperative anymore.

"Speaking of Srebrny," Marek said, looking at the calendar, "I'd better call him up. He promised to find out something for me."

"You'll have a chance to see him before then—there's a meeting at his place next Tuesday," Alex said, then added that Srebrny lived in the former residence of a German count with a woman young enough to be his daughter. Marek dismissed this as just another rumor.

When he arrived there a few days later, the place turned out to be indeed a mansion, hidden in the shadow of old trees, a fountain in front and a wide pebbled driveway leading to the front gate. It had been the dwelling of a Nazi district chief and of Count von Braunhoffer before him.

To his astonishment, Marek discovered the rumor to be true when a wide-hipped young woman, with frightened eyes and a shy smile, made a brief appearance.

The meeting took place in a huge room, with a dark parquet floor, a threadbare Oriental rug in the middle, oil paintings in ornate frames on the walls, faded drapes at the windows, and a chandelier hanging from the ceiling. Twenty men, representing every plant in the region, sat around a long table covered with green felt, listening to one report after another. They spoke of the new social structure, the class struggle, the Soviet allies. Marek sat, restraining a yawn, his eyes wandering from one face to another. When they reached the last one, at the very end of the table, he blinked and looked again. He looked at the thinning hair glued to the top of the scalp, at the pointed features, at the small quickly moving eyes. Mikulski, the foreman at the brewery, Smolka's friend.

Mikulski must have recognized him too, for he began to squirm and, as soon as the official part was over, got up and disappeared through the open door.

Marek pushed his way past the others and caught up with him. He put his hand on Mikulski's shoulder. He was shorter than Marek and it was enough to stretch out his arm; he did not have to raise it.

"Mikulski," Marek said. "How are you, Julius? It's been a long time."

The man turned around. "Holy Ghost," he said, feigning surprise.

"Just a ghost," Marek said with a choked laugh. "Small world, isn't it? So, tell me, Julius, how are things? No more brewery business for you?" His hand was weighing Mikulski down.

Mikulski moved his shoulder uneasily. "Oh, no," he said. "Not for some time. Ever since the Soviets marched in, back in January."

"So, what happened? Did Ivan take your job?"

Mikulski laughed nervously. "I came here. Better opportunities, you know."

"And the family, everybody all right?"

151

Mikulski nodded.

"Fine, everybody's fine."

"And our friend, still in the brewery?"

"Who?"

"Smolka, of course."

"I don't know," Mikulski said.

The pressure of Marek's hand on Mikulski's shoulder increased. He seemed to be pushing him down.

"What do you have to do with Smolka, anyway?" Mikulski said, looking at the door.

"Let's just say I have an unsettled account," Marek said.

"I know nothing," Mikulski said. "I did nothing to you. What do you want of me?"

"Where is Smolka?" Marek replied.

"Somewhere in Germany. That's all I know, honestly. He is a big shot. Lives in a palace, like this one."

From the envy in Mikulski's voice, Marek deduced he was telling the truth. He removed his hand. "I'll see you around, Mikulski," he said.

The others began to file out of the conference room, and Mikulski hurried to join them.

Marek, not ready to face anyone, walked in the opposite direction, out of the door leading to the garden. He headed toward the trees, whose arched branches formed a natural gazebo, and sat down on a stone bench in their shade.

He leaned back and closed his eyes.

He saw the police station, the dusty table, the investigator in the brown uniform, the armband with a swastika on his right sleeve. Lisa being brought in, walking as if in a trance.

The next day he saw her climb the truck that was to take her away. He tried to call to her, to tell her he loved her, that she should stay alive, at any cost, stay alive, but the guards pushed him with the butt of his rifle.

Smolka's face appeared as if in a film close-up, every detail magnified. He could see each freckle, each reddish stub-

152

ble, the beady eyes, the short pale lashes, the fishy mouth. And he could see himself, his fist pounding at that face again and again, harder and harder, until there was nothing left but a pulp.

Marek trembled and opened his eyes. He was horrified by the intensity of his hatred. He had not been aware that he was capable of such violence, even in his fantasies. It was like meeting someone he had never known existed, dwelling within himself.

His breath came in short, heavy gasps. He could feel his blood pulsating in his head. Resting his elbows on his knees, he slouched over and pressed both hands against his temples. Unexpectedly and with relief, he found the answer to a question that had been bothering him for several days. He knew now why he had let Holland go. He had let him go because he did not hate him. Nor did he hate Frau Huber, nor the other wretched Germans who had pleaded with him to intervene on their behalf. They meant nothing to him. It was only by straining his imagination that he could connect them with his personal agony. Only by making an intellectual effort was he able to produce anything even vaguely resembling the emotion that had made the blood run hot and that had in some dark and terrible way made him feel alive again.

He lifted his head and saw Alex standing in the doorway, looking for him. Alex beckoned to him and walked into the house. Marek rose and slowly started back after him.

They were all gathered in the parlor now, standing in small groups, talking animatedly. The old butler, a relic from the era of the last count, wearing a worn livery, carried drinks around, the glasses tinkling as the tray shook in his unsteady hands.

Srebrny jumped from one group to another, a smile here, a nod there, in the manner of a gracious host. Out of uniform for the day, wearing a dark suit, he looked small and

153

vulnerably Jewish.

Marek waited for an opportune moment, and as Srebrny was about to cross to the other end of the room, he stepped forward, blocking his way.

"Excuse me, Major, may I have a minute of your time?"

Srebrny looked at him. His eyes registered no immediate recognition.

"Rodwanski," Marek said helpfully. "Rodwan."

The major slapped his forehead with the palm of his hand. "Of course," he exclaimed. "Please forgive me. . . . All this commotion."

"It's all right," Marek said.

Srebrny glanced around. "Come," he said, "let's have some privacy."

Marek followed him into a room almost entirely taken up by a huge oak desk and two armchairs, one in back of the desk, the other in front, both upholstered in black cracking leather. A long narrow window overlooked the garden, and on the opposite wall hung a map of Eastern Europe.

Srebrny sat down behind the desk and motioned at the other chair. He folded his hands and rested them on top of the desk and eyed Marek curiously.

"So," he said, "here we meet again. The last time, I remember, we were both drinking. When I drink I say all kinds of things. Did I talk too much?"

Marek assured him that he didn't and noticed a look of relief on the major's face.

"Coming back to you," Srebrny said, "could you briefly repeat to me what you told me then about your wife?"

Marek did so. Srebrny listened, nodding.

"Don't think I forgot. I didn't. But things have been hectic since I last saw you, and rather complicated. Could you show me the place on the map where you were told it happened?"

Marek walked over to the map. "Here," he said, pointing.

154

Srebrny, now next to him, made a circle with a red pencil where Marek's finger pointed, then drew connecting lines to the points representing surrounding towns. He went back to the desk. "I'll tell you what we'll do," he said, leafing through his calendar.

But Marek's thoughts were preoccupied with something else right now. "Major," he interrupted nervously, "does the name Smolka mean anything to you?"

"No," Srebrny said, still turning the calendar pages.

"Waclaw Smolka, also called Wacek. I understand he is in Germany in a highly placed position."

"A friend of yours?" Srebrny asked. He didn't wait for an answer, for suddenly he found what he was looking for. "The fifteenth," he said. "On September the fifteenth two of my men are going to the East Zone of Germany to purchase industrial dyes. One is a chemist. He will be busy there. The other is going just to keep an eye on him. Security, you know. He can do some investigating, check the hospital lists. I'll let you know as soon as they come back." He got up.

"Thank you, Major," Marek said. "One more thing— about that man, if you could possibly find out . . ."

"Of course," Srebrny said and reached for a pencil. "What did you say his name was?"

"Smolka," Marek said and spelled it out for him.

Marek drove back with Alex, who was in a good mood and talkative. "Did I exaggerate about the place?" he said. "Did you ever see anything like that? Unbelievable."

Marek nodded.

"Srebrny seemed to take a special interest in you," Alex said.

"He did?"

"He certainly gave you a lot of his time and, oh, I meant to ask you, who was the mousy-looking guy you were talking to?"

"His name is Mikulski. I worked with him in the brew-

155

ery," Marek said and fell silent.

If Alex could be satisfied with only a partial answer, it was different with Paula. Distress seldom escaped her.

"What happened?" she exclaimed as soon as Marek walked in. "You look as if you had ran into the angel of death himself."

"Not quite," Marek said, "but almost." He told Roman and Paula about the meeting, about Mikulski, and how he found out about Smolka being a dignitary somewhere in the East Zone of Germany, and how finally he had asked Srebrny to get some more details.

"Why?" Roman asked.

Marek did not seem to understand the question. "To expose him, of course. I'll have him arrested as a collaborator and informer."

"Are you joking?" Roman said. "If they were to arrest every Pole who was guilty of denouncing a Jew, there would be no room in the jails for the bastards."

"He's right, you know," Paula said with a note of importance in her voice, for she considered herself an authority on the subject.

Roman made a clumsy effort to add something. The silence that followed was heavy with sudden awareness that they were living among foes who had greeted them upon their return with looks of hurt surprise and who considered their survival almost an act of impudence.

Roman and Paula began to talk, their words coming in a loud, fast succession, while Marek listened without attention, their voices beating at his mind, like surf breaking against a lonely shore.

A few days later Marek was sitting in Alex's office when the telephone rang. Alex answered it and, after listening for a while, turned to Marek. "Can you recall what the appropriation was for the textile industry in July?"

"Not offhand," Marek said. "I'll have to check it."

Alex covered the mouthpiece with his hand. "Srebrny is on the phone. He wants to talk to you when we're through."

Marek jumped up and reached for the receiver.

Alex held him back and continued the conversation. "Right. Yes, Major. Here he is." He handed the receiver over to Marek.

"Rodwanski?" Srebrny's voice came over muffled, and there was a buzzing sound in the background. "Can you hear me?"

"Yes," Marek said, "just barely."

"I can hardly hear you. Now listen. The news is not good."

Alex's face seemed to be moving farther and farther away, getting smaller as if seen through the wrong end of binoculars. Marek's "Yes?" was hardly audible.

"I can't hear you. There's that damned noise. The news—what I mean, it has nothing to do with you, or with Lisa. . . ."

The air imprisoned in Marek's chest came out in a loud wheeze. Alex's face moved closer, growing back to its normal size.

"What I meant to say was that there is no news at all. I don't know how to put it. It's really quite embarrassing. The two men on the trade mission, the chemist and the security man . . . you see, they never got there. The truck, the money, the provisions, they made off with them and got away to the West."

Marek burst into uncontrollable laughter. "Forgive me, Major, I don't mean to . . . but really, I can't . . . "

"It isn't funny. You wouldn't be laughing if you were in my position. Oh, yes, another thing. The man you asked me about, Smol . . . "

The voice faded away, the last syllable was lost in a prolonged deafening buzz. The connection was broken. Marek waited a moment, then put the phone down.

157

"What was that all about?" Alex wanted to know. "What did he say that was so funny?"

"Nothing really," Marek said. "Just a joke not worth repeating. Come to think of it, it wasn't funny at all."

Marek checked the figures concerning the distribution of oil and fuel to the various plants, prepared a graph, and the next day took it over to Alex.

Alex looked at it approvingly, admiring Marek's precision and detail. "Srebrny must need the report urgently," he said, reaching for the phone, "or else he wouldn't have asked me to call him at home." He dialed the operator, gave her the number, waited, and then, cursing, banged the receiver back on the cradle. "His line is dead," he said.

"It went dead yesterday in the middle of our conversation," Marek said. "You mean it's still not fixed?"

"Obviously not," Alex said. "How the hell am I going to get this to him?"

"I could take it over if you let me have your car, or—"

"Would you?" Alex interrupted. "Of course you can have the car and don't hurry back. Take the rest of the day off. It's lovely there this time of year."

Alex was right. The woods had begun to change colors, and the mountains in the mist looked like an artist's outline in a preliminary sketch.

Srebrny was glad to see him. He studied the chart carefully before putting it down on the desk. "Good work," he said.

"Draftman's training," Marek said and smiled.

"Is that what you studied?"

"Architecture."

"You did? The war must have interrupted your studies. Do you plan to go on?"

"I might. It all depends. I haven't given it much thought. It's too soon. There are other things ..." Marek looked at

158

Srebrny. "Major," he said, "yesterday, when we were interrupted, you tried to tell me something about Smolka."

Srebrny pushed the chair away from the desk and leaned backward. "Your interest in Smolka seems to be personal. What is it? He owes you money?"

"He owes me more than that," Marek said.

"I hate to pry, but couldn't you be more specific?"

Srebrny listened, tapping the pencil rhythmically against the desk top. When Marek finished, he dropped the pencil and looked at him. "You cannot so much as touch Smolka," he said.

"Why not?"

"Intelligence, NKVD. From what you just told me, he's still in the same line of business, he just changed bosses. You can't go to the security police—he *is* the security police."

"Major," Marek said. "Mr. Silber," he corrected himself, as if to remind Srebrny of the bond between them, "there is this other matter, concerning my wife. Since your first effort failed, could I . . . could you send me, or else could you get me a pass so that—"

"Forget it," Srebrny interrupted him. "That I'll never do. You wouldn't accomplish a thing. You're too involved. Besides, what's really on your mind? Say nothing." He stopped Marek before he had a chance to say anything. "I know what's going on inside your head. More than anything you want to get to Smolka. And do what? Kill him? Beat him up? I wouldn't advise it. You've had more than your share of jails and camps, haven't you? As far as your wife is concerned, I'm willing to help. Don't ask me why, but I respect your hunches. I believe in such things. I also believe in fortune-tellers, and I wouldn't be caught dead making a decision on the thirteenth. That's why I understand you and will try to help—up to a point. You want to give yourself time, fine. But then . . . Do you know my own story?" he asked suddenly.

159

"You told it to me," Marek said.

"I thought I did. Anyway, once I realized I wasn't going to kill myself—well, you met Tamara, my fiancée."

Marek nodded.

"I decided that if I am to live, I'm going to live and take what comes along. Career, power, politics, it's all right with me. Red, white, what's the difference—one devil, believe me. You follow me?"

"I think so."

"What I'm trying to say is, you've got to give yourself a time limit. Then, close the book and put it aside. Make a new beginning. Get yourself a woman, start planning, perhaps—"

Marek got up. "I think I'd better go, Major. I should be back at the office by now."

"Remember what I told you," Srebrny called after him. "And in case I don't see you, have a happy New Year."

"What?" Marek said, turning around.

"The Jewish New Year," Srebrny said.

"Oh," Marek said. "And you too. All the best."

$\mathcal{M}$arek did not know why the stranger decided to approach him and why he chose the inn to do so. By then, he was quite drunk, having mixed vodka with beer, and the stranger's face was liquid in front of his eyes. When it came into focus, it turned out to be weather-beaten, with pinched features, squinting eyes, and a gray, unkempt mustache. The man had the large hardened hands of a laborer, and his clothes were worn.

He pointed at the vacant chair, asking with this gesture Marek's permission to sit down. He did so after Marek nodded. That in itself was not unusual, since it was a local custom, but the inn was deserted at this time of day, and there was plenty of room at other tables.

Marek ignored the man until the stranger asked him to buy him a beer. Since he spoke German, Marek did not feel obliged to accommodate, but not wanting to refuse either, he resolved the dilemma by pushing his own untouched mug toward the man.

Lifting the mug only a little, the man's head went down, the mustache dipping in the foam of the beer. He took a few sips, wiped the mustache with the back of his hand, and looked at Marek, who had been watching silently.

"Thank you, Herr Rodwan," the stranger said. Then, in

answer to Marek's startled look, added, "I've heard good things about you. Otto Holland told me what you did for him. That's why I decided to speak to you."

"I don't know what you're talking about," Marek said.

"Don't worry, Herr Rodwan," the man said. "I'm a friend." The way Marek understood it, the stranger was trying to tell him that he was a friend of Holland's, until he explained further. "I was always a friend of Jews."

Marek gave him a suspicious look; he had learned to beware of such declarations.

The man leaned across the table, his face so close that Marek could smell the beer on his breath, and said in a low voice, "I have Jewish things."

Marek's eyes narrowed.

"Holy things," the stranger elaborated. "You see, for many years I was a custodian in a synagogue in Breslau. Then we were not allowed to work for the Jews anymore, and I had to quit. I came here. This is my hometown. Got myself a job as a caretaker at a cemetery. Must say, I liked the other job better. I didn't go to Breslau until I heard what was being done to the Jews there. Then I went. The old sexton was still there. He had removed all the holy things, the silver, the books, the scroll, the fringed shawls, you know, the kind they prayed in, and kept them in his home. But he knew that it was only a matter of time until he too would have to go. So he gave me the things and told me to take care of them. I brought everything over here and buried them in the cemetery. I figured no one would look there."

"Why are you telling me this?" Marek asked. "What is it you want? Money?"

"It's not the money," the man said. "Believe me . . . But now that you mention it . . . something, a little reward, I could use it."

"You'll get it," Marek said. He guessed that the man had waited until the Jewish New Year to have a better bargaining position. "What took you so long to come out with it?"

"I wasn't here. I went to the West Zone. I ran into Holland there, and he told me how you helped him. But life is hard there, no work, too many refugees. I'm an old man. I decided it wasn't for me. So I came back. I waited, hoping someone from Breslau might contact me. Someone might return. No one did."

"How can I get in touch with you?" Marek asked.

"I live in the caretaker's cottage, near the cemetery."

It seemed more like late autumn than mid-September. The day was foggy and cold, the rain coming down in uninterrupted streams. Later, the fog lifted and the rain diminished, but the clouds still hung low and threatening.

When they knocked on the cottage door, it was around four in the afternoon, but so dark that the caretaker lit a lantern before setting out for the graveyard. They followed him: Marek, Roman, and four others, including Pincus Horowitz, their elder. The caretaker led the way, swinging the lantern in one hand, the other holding a spade across his shoulder.

The cemetery was old. Most of the gravestones were sunk into the ground; covered with moss, they each bore a cross. The newer ones, shiny from the rain, towered over them. Most of these had a swastika next to the cross; some had no cross at all.

The caretaker walked along the cemetery wall. Between two solitary graves, one old and the other new, he measured his steps in length and width, and then stopped. He gave the lantern to Roman. In the quivering yellow light the gravestones cast uneven shadows.

The caretaker, both hands on the handle of the spade, stuck it into the ground. It slid easily into the earth softened by the rain. He began to dig, tossing spadefuls of dirt aside. The deeper he dug, the slower it went.

163

Forming a circle around him, the others stood, slouched forward, the flame of the lantern illuminating their faces, the wind rustling through the weeping willows.

The spade hit a stone; the caretaker's movements grew slower. Roman put the lantern down on the ground, darted forward, jerked the spade out of his hand, and took over.

The circle of men tightened, heedless of the mud splashing on their clothes and faces.

Roman stopped abruptly as the spade's blade resounded against metal. He tossed it aside, went down on his knees, and began to push the dirt away with his hands. Marek knelt on the other side doing the same, until a black, ironbound trunk came into sight.

It took both of them to lift it out, and two more had to support it, as they carried it out of the cemetery. They carried it like a coffin, the others following, a strange cortege, a funeral in reverse, bringing it from the world of the dead back into the world of the living.

In the caretaker's cottage they pried the trunk open. Wrapped individually in pieces of cloth, tarnished almost beyond recognition, out came the silver goblets, the candelabras, the crowns, the breastplates, moldy-smelling books, and finally, on the very bottom, wrapped in oilcloth, the Torah scroll.

They left, each carrying something, and headed for Roman's house, where the women waited.

The women took the silver into the kitchen and polished it, while in the other room the men first sorted the books and folded the prayer shawls, then finally approached the scroll resting on another table.

They looked at it fearfully, touching it lightly with the tips of their fingers.

Suddenly a question arose. Having been buried between a grave with a cross and another one with a swastika, was the Torah desecrated? Could it have become impure?

All eyes turned to Horowitz, who, being erudite in Jewish

164

matters, could draw up a marriage contract in the holy tongue and answer questions concerning ritual. He sat in silence rubbing his forehead with his fingers, and finally admitted a bit haltingly that he did not know the answer and would not hazard a guess. The matter was too serious; he must consult a recognized authority.

The authority, one whose judgment could be accepted without reservation, was the rabbi who had recently arrived from Russia. After spending the war years not far from the city of Irkutsk, he now made his home in Warsaw. Since Marek was instrumental in the recovery of the sacred objects, the honor of taking the scroll to the rabbi was given to him. He asked Roman to accompany him.

It was a long, complicated trip to Warsaw, since the trains were still running sporadically. They decided that the best way would be to go to Breslau, where they could get on the back of a lorry, a common mode of transportation.

They wrapped the scroll in an army blanket and took it along so that the rabbi could actually see it.

The back of the truck was already packed, and they were the last ones to climb on. The driver waved away the others, who muttered angrily.

Marek sat down on the end of the bench, holding the scroll on the floor, between his knees.

Most of the riders had come from Central Poland to the newly annexed territories on a pillaging expedition and were now returning home. Textiles, radios, and cameras were in greatest demand, but anything was welcome, from pieces of dismantled machinery to raw materials and incomplete china sets. One of the riders amused the rest with a story of how he had stolen and transported a larger-than-life statue of St. Anthony. The story was greeted with an outburst of gaiety, as everyone knew that St. Anthony was the patron saint who guarded against thieves and helped retrieve lost objects.

Most of the riders were men, but there were two young

women in military parkas who soon became the objects of jokes and propositions, which neither of them seemed to mind.

After a while, everyone opened bundles containing food, not only because mealtime neared, but mostly because eating on a trip made the traveling time pass faster.

The man across from Marek, a piece of brown paper on his lap like a napkin, was cutting sausage into small pieces with a pocketknife. He opened a bottle of beer, taking a gulp after each bite, all the while looking curiously at the blanket-wrapped scroll.

"What do you have there, citizen?" he asked. "Something we could do business with?"

"I'm afraid not," Marek said. "She's not for trading."

"She?"

"She was buried alive a long time ago. We just dug her out, didn't we, Roman?"

Roman looked alarmed. "My friend here," he said with an uneasy laugh, "has a weird sense of humor."

"I asked a civil question," the man said, offended, "and he gives me the creeps."

Stomachs full, lulled by the noise of the motor, the riders dozed off one by one, heads swaying as the truck jumped on the bumpy road.

The sun was setting. On the roadside a small boy was chasing cows off a pasture with a long twig. From the village came the distant sound of evening bells.

The riders, now awakened, resumed talking. Someone was telling the story of the most successful expedition yet—three brand new automobiles hidden in an abandoned garage. He did not fail to stress that the lucky bastard who came across them happened to be a Jew.

This loosened their tongues. "There are just too many of them left," he said. "Creeping out like vermin from all over. Hitler, mad as he was, had the right idea as far as *they* were concerned. Too bad he didn't finish the job."

Marek put on the blank expression he had learned to adopt in such situations, but his stomach churned. When he looked around, all the faces looked alike to him. They all looked like Smolka.

Luckily they were already on the outskirts of Warsaw. A few minutes later, the truck stopped. Roman and Marek were the first to jump off.

"Damn them," Marek said through his teeth. "Damn every one of them."

They walked into what used to be a street and was now nothing but a pile of rubble, the smell of burning still in the air. Every now and then a house stuck out of the debris, the paneless windows covered with boards.

In the narrow passages between the ruins, man-pulled rickshaws seemed to be the new and only means of transportation.

From a house, of which only the ground floor was left, a storefront had been turned into an impromptu café, from which came the sounds of music. Couples were dancing in the room filled with cigarette smoke.

In front of a bombed-out church, half a cross hanging from a steeple, a woman, her head covered with a kerchief whose corners crossed over her breast, in a hoarse chant called attention to her wares: yellow peas measured into paper cones and pretzels strung on a stick.

The new, shiny signs, proclaiming the alleys of rubble-streets, added an ironic touch. But they turned out to be of help in locating the place they were looking for.

It was the surviving wing of a house that had been severed in the middle. They entered the unlit hallway and began climbing the stairs. Roman struck a match. There was one door with a mezuzah nailed to its frame. He knocked. A short, stocky woman, her head covered in the manner of orthodox matrons, opened the door. After they had stated their

167

business, she let them in.

In a sparsely furnished room, at a heavy uncovered table, the rabbi sat spooning tea from a thick glass. He wore a shabby black caftan and a large black skullcap. He was an old man, with a gray beard and earlocks. A tangled net of thin, red veins covered his cheeks and nose. Only his high forehead was pallid and smooth.

"Rabbi," Roman said, stepping forward, "we have come to ask a question of you."

The rabbi stopped drinking, lifted his head, his eyes looking out sharply from under bushy brows.

"We come from far away, Rabbi."

"What is your question?" the rabbi said.

Marek stood silent, hugging the scroll wrapped in the army blanket.

"This is a Torah," Roman said, pointing to it. "It was hidden in a Christian cemetery, and now we wonder, since it was buried in unsanctified ground not only next to a cross but also next to a swastika, if it can still be considered holy, or is it impure?"

A faint smile appeared on the rabbi's face. His eyes blinked and looked at them softly. "Nothing," the rabbi said, "nothing, not even being buried among the Nazis, may their names be erased, can make it impure. Nothing can desecrate the Torah, unless . . ."—here the long, bony finger pointed upward—"unless something happened to the writing. If a word is missing, or a letter, or even a dot, then it shouldn't be used. Leave it here with me. I'll examine it."

Marek put the scroll on the table. They bade the rabbi good-bye and left.

On the street, Roman suddenly stopped. "Nothing can desecrate the Torah," he said and there was amazement in his voice, and marvel in his eyes, and Marek thought that he had never seen Roman's face look like that. He himself had little use for mysticism.

But when a few days later the rabbi's message reached them that not a word was missing and not a sign obliterated, Marek felt something like a shiver go down his spine.

Wrapped in a silk shroud, the silver ornaments glittering, the Torah looked forsaken, like an overdressed woman at a poorly attended party.

The hall chosen for the services, small as it was, seemed big and empty, the seats unoccupied except for the two first rows, for those present hardly exceeded the necessary quorum.

There was no blowing of the shofar, for no ram's horn had been found among the buried objects. Marek, whose memories of the holy days were closely connected with the sounding of the shofar, did not bother to come back the second day, for without it the service had little meaning for him.

But during the week between Rosh Hashanah and Yom Kippur, as the news of the holiday services spread, inquiries came in from all over the vicinity. Since there were more people expected than there were prayer books available, the memorial prayer was carefully copied on sheets of yellow paper. Pincus Horowitz succeeded in locating a ram's horn and had it brought over all the way from Lodz. Marek joined Roman and Paula for the meal preceding the fast, with all the traditional dishes of broth and fowl and carrots as sweet as candy.

They arrived just in time for the evening prayer. Marek stood in the back of the half-filled room, listening to the sorrowful chant of the Kol Nidre, a prayer composed by the Marranos, the forced converts during the Spanish inquisition, annuling all vows that they had taken.

Marek did not join the others in singing. He stood with his eyes closed tightly thinking of the way he had chosen to survive, asking forgiveness for having renounced his name, for having renounced his faith, for not crying enough, for forgetting too soon. It was forgiveness that he prayed for, for he did not feel worthy of asking for anything else.

He woke up after a night of heavy, confused dreams. He dreamed of Miriam, who was really Lisa, and who crept into his bed, warning him not to touch her. He got dressed, decided that Roman must have already left, and set forth for the place of worship.

The room was crowded, people standing in the back. Roman, noticing him, beckoned and pointed at the seat he had kept for him.

Picking up the yellow sheet with the memorial prayer from the table against the wall, Marek walked over and sat down next to Roman.

Pincus Horowitz, wrapped in a big prayer shawl, faced the congregation, holding the shofar in his hand. "Even though it is not in the tradition to blow the shofar before sundown on this day," he said, "under these unusual circumstances, to symbolize our freedom, we decided to sound it twice today." He put the ram's horn to the corner of his mouth, puffing his cheeks until a hoarse, broken sound filled the room.

Could it be Horowitz's lack of skill that made the shofar sound so plaintive, so weak? Where was the threatening thunder that had made him shudder and huddle next to his father, who would stretch out his arm and take him under the wing of his prayer shawl?

Before *Yizkor*, the memorial prayer for the dead, Marek would be led into the yard together with other children who were fortunate enough to have their parents alive, so that the angel of death might not orphan them. Happy to be out in the open, away from the morose atmosphere of the stuffy room, they would run and shout and chase one another, until the sexton with the wispy beard would come and wave his finger in warning.

Later in the day, his father would tell him to go and see his

170

mother. The women prayed separately, in a smaller room, sitting around a long table, dressed in silks and taffetas, bedecked with jewels. They would greet his entry with affected smiles. His mother, though only a small silver brooch adorned her dress, was the most beautiful of them all, and her eyes would light up with a real smile at seeing him.

They prayed from small black books without understanding the meaning of the Hebrew text, crying into lace handkerchiefs their private grief, their personal petitions.

Toward the evening he would go there again. The women, faint from fasting, would be passing smelling salts around. Now, the rouge gone from their faces, they all looked gray and shrunken. Only his mother was still beautiful.

Pincus Horowitz put the shofar down. The echo died away.

"Let us pray together," he said. "Thank you, Oh Lord, God of our fathers, for keeping us alive. . . ."

For keeping us alive, Marek thought, *for keeping* me *alive?* He glanced at the sheet of paper in his hand. The words seemed to scream at him. From the bottom of the page the word "killed" caught his eye.

"Remember the souls of all my relatives who were killed, who were murdered, who were slaughtered, who were burned, who were drowned, who were strangled—for Your Name's sake. . . ."

It was hard to believe that those words had been written centuries ago. He began to read the memorial prayer from its beginning.

"Remember oh Lord, the soul of my father, my teacher, who went to his rest. I hereby vow to be just, so that his soul may be included in the eternal cycle of life, together with the souls of Abraham, Isaac, and Jacob, Sarah, Rebecca, Rachel, and Leah, and other righteous ones who dwell in paradise. . . ."

"Remember Oh Lord, the soul of my . . . wife . . ." Hor-

171

rified, Marek stopped short.

He got up abruptly, dropping the yellow sheet on the floor, and started toward the door. All eyes turned toward him.

He pushed his way through the group standing near the doorway and ran out. On the street he stopped, hesitated, not knowing which way to turn, then he started toward his house.

In front of it, secured with a chain, was Roman's motorcycle. He broke the lock with his bare hands. He got on and started the motor. He was not aware where he drove, nor for how long.

There was a tavern. Marek got off the motorcycle and walked in. He sat at the bar, ordered a bottle of vodka, and drank.

Marek staggered out of the tavern. He approached the motorcycle but succeeded in mounting only on the third try. He pumped, started the engine, and drove down the highway that stretched in front of him, white and blurred. He knew that at one point he should make a turn into a road that cut through the woods.

By the time he got there, his head felt like a nest of buzzing insects and he could hardly see ahead. *Steady now*, he said to himself, braking.

He felt himself losing control of the bike. There was a loud thump, and the next thing he knew, the bike was lying on its side like a wounded animal, and he was thrown next to a tree on a soft bedding of fallen leaves. Fragments of glass from the broken headlights were scattered around.

If he had been thrown onto the hard ground instead of the leaves, he would have been dead, Marek thought. Then everyone would say that it was his punishment for getting drunk on Yom Kippur, his verdict sealed and promptly executed.

But he had been lucky. Nothing much seemed to have happened to him. The right sleeve of his jacket was torn, as was that of his shirt; they must have caught on the handlebar. After a while he noticed something red on the bark of the tree. He looked at his arm. It was scratched. The scratches were superficial, though many, and at one point there was a cut, probably caused by a piece of broken glass. The blood dripped down in dark red oblong drops.

Marek knew he could stop the bleeding easily by ripping off the shirt sleeve and tying it around the cut. But instead, he sat there letting his blood trickle down. It felt cleansing and relieving, like tears. He watched it, his head empty of thoughts, until the sun began to set. Then he ripped off his sleeve, tied it around the cut, and stopped the bleeding. Slowly, he got up.

He propped up the bike, trying to spare his injured arm, and, breathing heavily, pulled it back onto the road. He got on and tried to start it. The motor rumbled; nothing had happened to the engine. Only the front fender was bent.

His head suddenly cleared, Marek proceeded on his way.

Roman and Paula must have heard the sound of the approaching motorcycle, for they were waiting for him in the doorway.

"I busted your bike," Marek said before anyone had a chance to ask him anything. "I'll take it to the garage first thing tomorrow and have it fixed."

"Never mind the bike," Paula said. "Your arm," she exclaimed. "What happened?"

"Nothing much," Marek said. "Just scratches."

Paula pulled him inside and sat him down on a chair. She took off his jacket and tore the sleeve of his shirt off his arm. Then she brought a lamp closer to have a better look.

"It is only a scratch," she said. "And the cut doesn't look bad either. But it has to be cleaned." She brought in a basin filled with water, a cloth, and a bar of soap. She washed

Marek's arm carefully and dried it, patting it gently. Then she brought in iodine and, holding Marek's arm over the basin, poured it straight out of the bottle. The sting, sharp enough to stop his breath, was a strangely welcome sensation.

Marek appreciated their not asking him questions, not offering him food, though there was still some left on the table. He took off his shirt and tossed it next to his jacket. "You might as well throw it out," he said to Paula.

"Your best suit," Paula said.

"It's only a suit," Marek said. "It could be worse. I'm going upstairs." He got up.

"There is a letter for you there," Roman said. "It's on your night table."

Once inside, Marek switched the light on and picked up the envelope. It had block-printed letters on it and bore no return address. Holding it between his teeth, Marek tore it open with his right hand. The letter itself was written in Gothic, which was hard for him to decipher. "*Sehr geehrter Heer Rodwan*," it read. "I never had a chance to thank you for what you did for me, and I now take the opportunity to do so. For the last few weeks I have been in a small town on the Molde River, doing odd jobs to raise money for further journeys. I will be leaving tomorrow for my destination. Here is my permanent address . . ." Marek's eyes skipped over it. "Maybe some day I will be able to return your favor. Gratefully, O.H."

O.H. Otto Holland.

Marek folded the letter absentmindedly and put it in his pocket, pulled off his boots, turned out the light, and threw himself on the bed.

He lay with his hands, as was his habit, under his head. After a while, the injured arm began to hurt and he released it, letting it hang over the edge of the bed. He felt a chill, pulled the blanket from underneath him, and covered his

174

bare chest.

He thought back, trying to understand what had happened that day, for suddenly it was very important that he did.

He remembered walking into the room crowded with worshippers being unable to join them in the prayer of thanksgiving. He recited the memorial prayer instead and, without intending it, included Lisa among the dead. Then he stopped, horrified, knowing he just acknowledged her death; that very moment he had buried her. Then he ran out, got drunk, and had the accident. He wondered whether it was an accident, or was he trying to kill himself. If he did, he certainly did not try hard enough, since he walked away with nothing more than a few scratches.

He wrapped the blanket around himself, trying to fall asleep. He couldn't. He got up and turned the light on. Lisa's journal was on the night table. He picked it up. He opened the bureau drawer and buried it under a pile of neatly folded shirts. Then, unexpectedly, he reached for a suitcase, took a few shirts from the top, tossed them in, added a sweater, a change of underwear, and shut the suitcase.

He got dressed, stopped, looked around, then opened the door and walked out, suitcase in hand.

Part Three

EIGHTEEN

*T*hat the stars should be shining and the moon so bright, that the air should be so fragrant, he found surprising if not offensive.

A dog's bark coming from afar turned into a prolonged howl, then died away. The street was quiet but for the sound of his footsteps clicking rhythmically against the pavement. He transferred the suitcase to his left hand because his right arm had begun to ache. The dull, throbbing pain had a sudden sobering effect. He stopped at the crossroads, put the suitcase down, and waited until he heard the sound of an approaching car. He stepped off the curb and lifted his arm, palm upturned.

The car came to a sudden halt.

"Where to?" the driver asked in Russian, sticking his head out the window.

It was only then that Marek realized he had no idea where he wanted to go.

The car stopped in Breslau. He thanked the driver with a saluting gesture and got out.

In the cold light of the moon, the bombed-out city stood ghostlike and still, the windowless skeletons of burned-out houses pointing skyward.

The railroad station, only a short walk away, was crowded in spite of the late hour, people still waiting for a train long overdue. Marek waded through the scattered pieces of luggage until he found a spot to put his suitcase and sat down, hunched forward.

The Gothic lettering over the destroyed lounge spelled, WARTE ... , the rest of the sign charred and illegible. "Wait ..." he translated the word in his mind, thinking that was all he ever did—wait: for his father to get well, for his mother's letter, for the war to end, for Lisa. Now he was sitting here, waiting for the train to come, and beyond that he had nothing to wait for.

"Pardon me," a voice said. "Would you mind moving a bit?"

Marek did, making room for a man in military garb and a jockey cap. "Trains," the man said contemptuously. "You wait and you wait. I was expected in Grünberg at six; there isn't even a phone to let anyone know."

The name of the town hit a familiar cord. Grünberg was where Srebrny lived.

"Could have gotten there faster on foot," the man went on. "It's only one stop." He turned to Marek. "And you, where are you going?"

Marek thought for a moment. Then, "Grünberg," he said.

As soon as the train could be heard in the distance, those waiting reached for their belongings and with a loud commotion rushed to the end of the platform.

Preceded by a shrill whistle, the train pulled in and stopped with a screech. Pushing and shoving, the crowd charged ahead, and by the time Marek gained a foothold on the step, the door closed, the train lurched forward, heavily at first then picking up speed, leaving him hanging there, with the suitcase in one hand and the other holding fast to the railing, and the soot of the locomotive blowing into his face, blinding his eyes. He managed to stay there until the train stopped.

He jumped off, rubbed his eyes, and looked around. He left the station, and once he figured the direction to Srebrny's house, he began to walk.

After a while the house emerged, standing on top of a hill, half-hidden among the trees, the white columns shining in the early-morning sun. He walked up the driveway, stopped at the door, and reflected a second before reaching for the cast-iron knocker.

He expected the old butler and was surprised to see Srebrny open the door. Not fully dressed, the military breeches held up by suspenders, a paper napkin stuck in the neck of his shirt, Srebrny looked at him bewilderedly, then exclaimed, "What in the devil's name? . . . What are you doing here?"

"May I come in?" Marek said.

"Sure," Srebrny answered, opening the door wide. Then, "Tamara," he called. "Tamara!"

The young woman Marek remembered having met fleetingly appeared, wearing a long robe, her dark hair tied back with a ribbon.

"I think you two have met before," Srebrny said and led the way through the parlor to a glass-enclosed porch, where a table was set for breakfast. The smell of freshly brewed coffee reminded Marek that it was a long time since he had last eaten.

"Tamara, take him upstairs," Srebrny said. Then to Marek, "Go and wash up. I'll wait for you here."

In the bathroom mirror Marek discovered that his face was black with soot and his eyes bloodshot. He scrubbed his face repeatedly, then dried it, leaving dark traces on the clean towel.

On the breakfast table an additional place had been set. Tamara filled his cup with coffee and offered him rolls from

181

the basket. He took one, bit into it, and put it down, too tired to eat.

"Haven't slept in two days," he explained.

"I guessed that much," Srebrny said. He wiped his mouth with the paper napkin, crumpled it, and put it aside.

"I have to go now," he said, getting up. He reached for the uniform jacket, hanging on the back of his chair. "Get a good rest," he said to Marek. "Tamara will show you to the guest room. We shall talk later."

Marek woke up sprawled on top of a wide bed. He turned, opened his eyes, and staring at the ceiling, watched the shadows play over his head. The rays of the setting sun reflected in the window pane like a prism, casting a rainbow of colors across the dark parquet floor.

The room was small, most of the space taken up by the bed, a mahogany chest, and a washstand with a porcelain basin and a matching pitcher, a linen towel folded neatly on the marble top. The walls were covered with a faded rosebud-patterned paper, and a muslin curtain billowed in the evening breeze.

He moved to the edge of the bed and sat up, his feet on a braided throw rug, his head resting between the palms of his hands. He sat like that for a while, then got up slowly and walked to the washstand. He emptied the pitcher into the basin, splashed his face with cold water, then dabbed it with the towel. He took a clean shirt out of his suitcase, put it on, ran his fingers through his hair, and went downstairs.

In the drawing room, sunk in a deep armchair, Srebrny seemed to be waiting for him. He straightened himself up. "Come in," he said as soon as he spotted Marek at the open door. He pointed at a chair next to his.

Marek sat down.

"It's only five o'clock," Srebrny said. "We don't eat before seven. How about a drink?"

"A small one," Marek said. "Nothing strong."

"A brandy?"

"Brandy would be fine."

Srebrny got up, slid the cabinet door open, came out with a bottle and two glasses, and put them on a table between them. He was about to fill Marek's glass when he remembered. "You have hardly eaten anything today. You should not drink on an empty stomach." He reached for a small silver bell on the table.

The tinkling brought an aproned, middle-aged woman in.

"Frau," Srebrny said. No name, just "Frau." Then in German, "A snack, please."

The woman disappeared, then tiptoed back carrying a plate with small sandwiches. She put it down and withdrew unobtrusively.

"She and the old man came with the house," Srebrny said, as he watched Marek devour the canapés.

"The butler?" Marek said, only now realizing how hungry he was.

"You did meet him?" Srebrny said. "I use him only occasionally; makes me uncomfortable, as does all this," he motioned widely. "As you can guess, I did not exactly grow up in a palace." Marek finished eating and pushed the empty plate away.

"Major," he began.

"Skip the 'Major,' " Srebrny interrupted him, pouring brandy into the glasses. "Ignacy will do. That's my new name."

"What was the old one?"

"Isidor."

"What's wrong with 'Isidor'?"

"Nothing, I guess," Srebrny said. "Ignacy goes better with the decor," he said with a chuckle. "Don't you think so?"

Marek agreed.

"Your health." Srebrny lifted his glass and emptied it in one gulp.

"To you," Marek said and began to sip slowly.

"Now," Srebrny said, putting his glass down, "tell me what happened."

"I left."

"I figured as much. But why?"

Marek rubbed his forehead. "I don't know," he said. "An impulse, call it instinct, something I developed during the war. An ability to sense danger."

"What danger?" Srebrny exclaimed. "You were in no danger. You had a safe position, a comfortable home . . . "

"That was exactly the danger."

"I don't understand," Srebrny said.

"I should have started from the beginning. Lisa is dead."

Srebrny looked at him silently. then, "I am sorry," he said. "When? I mean when did you find out?"

"As you know, I found out a long time ago, only I didn't believe it."

"And now you do?"

"Now I do."

"I still fail to see the connection," Srebrny said.

Marek rolled the empty glass between the palms of his hands before putting it down. "It's hard to explain," he began. "I woke up in the middle of the night and sensed the . . . danger," he concluded for a lack of a better word.

"You still didn't tell me what danger."

"The danger of half-existence," Marek said, for suddenly it all became clear to him.

Srebrny looked at him without comprehending.

"I took the path of least resistance," Marek said.

"You talk in riddles. What do you mean?"

"What I mean," Marek said, "is that I took the easiest way out. I settled fifteen kilometers away from where I was liberated, I accepted a position I had no liking for, and I

184

waited. I have been in a perpetual state of waiting."

"For Lisa?"

"That was what I made myself believe. Once I realized Lisa was dead, suddenly there was nothing to wait for."

"And so you left. With a plan?"

"I had no plan. I hitchhiked as far as Breslau, I got on a train, and remembering your kindness—"

"Oh, nonsense. I did nothing," Srebrny said, motioning impatiently.

"I mean it. I really do. And now that I am here, I don't want to intrude, but could you put me up for a short while, until I clear my head?"

"No problem, Marek. The house is certainly big enough, and Tamara won't mind. By the way, how do you like Tamara?"

"She seems very nice."

"That she is. I know you must be wondering about us. Her being so young . . ."

Marek was about to deny when Srebrny stopped him with a gesture. "I will tell you, so you won't have to wonder. It is quite simple. I was alone and she was alone. It is no good to be alone, so we got together. That's much better, even if one is to be alone together. Follow me?"

"I suppose so."

"Now, coming back to you, I want you to call up Lipski in the office first thing tomorrow. Tell him you had to take off, a sudden emergency, make something up. I don't want you to burn any bridges."

Marek shrugged. "I will call him if you insist," he said. "As for bridges, this is a shaky one and it might collapse if I try to cross back over it."

"You should be a poet."

The next morning Marek called up Alex.

"Where the hell are you?" Lipski exclaimed as soon as he

185

recognized his voice.

"Something came up suddenly." Marek had his answer well rehearsed. "A personal matter. It couldn't wait."

"When will you be coming back?"

"I don't know."

"Roman just left here. He seemed worried about you."

"Tell him not to worry. I'm all right. And yes, the pay that is coming to me, give it to him, will you? Tell him it's for the bike."

"What bike?"

"He will know."

"Where are you?" Lipski asked again.

"With friends," Marek said and hung up.

Tamara, who entered the room just in time to catch the tail end of the conversation, looked at him with a smile. Her full face with irregular features could hardly be considered beautiful, except when she smiled. She managed to do so without moving her mouth, merely curling her lips softly, the upper one overlapping, her eyes wide open like those of a surprised child.

"I promised the major I would call my boss," Marek explained. "I hope you don't mind my using the phone, or my imposing on you for that matter."

"You are not imposing. How about breakfast?"

Srebrny must have left already, for Tamara set the table for the two of them.

"Do you like buttermilk pancakes?"

"Love them."

Tamara walked toward the kitchen, and soon the clatter of dishes could be heard, followed by the sound of an eggbeater and the sweet smell of sizzling butter. She reappeared a while later, pancakes piled on a platter in one hand, a steaming pot of coffee in the other.

Marek rose to help her.

She handed the platter over to him and poured a cup of

coffee for herself.

"Aren't you eating?" Marek asked.

She took one. "Just to keep you company. I already had breakfast."

"You shouldn't have bothered just for me."

"No bother. I welcome the chance to do something. I love to cook. I would do without all the help if it were up to me, but Igor wouldn't hear of it. He means well, I guess. . . ."

"Igor?"

"I prefer to call him that. I find 'Ignacy' too long and a bit pretentious. 'Igor' is what he was called in Russia."

"Were you in Russia during the war? Is that where the two of you met?"

"No," Tamara said so vehemently that Marek wondered what it was he said that might have upset her.

"I was not in Russia during the war," Tamara said, this time softly. "More pancakes?"

"They are too good to refuse," Marek said and held up his plate, hoping that by pleasing her he would bring back the smile that would chase away the dark shadow that had just invaded her eyes.

"Igor and I are getting married," Tamara said, putting the remaining pancakes on his plate. "Did he tell you?"

"He mentioned that you were engaged when I first saw you here at the last conference."

"I remember that conference. All those people . . . The way they looked at me, as if I were . . . You know what I mean. Just because Igor is older. They probably thought I stayed with him because I like living like this, this . . . monstrosity of a house, or because of his position. Do you think so too?"

"Why should I? The major, Igor, is a good man."

"The best," Tamara said fervently, "one that can be trusted. Especially when he cares. He does care about you," she added. "You can trust him. Do you?"

"I wouldn't be here if I didn't."

"So he is older than I," Tamara said. "So what? I would not get involved with a young man. I feel good with Igor. I feel safe and comfortable. I know that I don't deprive him of anything."

"Deprive him?"

"He was married before. And he had children. Did he tell you?"

"Yes. He told me."

"I thought so. He had a family, and he doesn't want a new one. So, I know he doesn't mind. . . ."

"Doesn't mind what?"

"My being barren."

Marek looked at her. With wide hips and large breasts she seemed to have been put on this earth for the sole purpose of motherhood.

"I thought he might have told you about that too," Tamara said, as she noticed his bewilderment.

"He did not." Being the only child of parents who had been past their prime when he was born, he said, "Doctors can be mistaken, you know."

Tamara laughed a short, choked laugh, then got up abruptly and without a word began to clear the table.

Later in the day, when Srebrny came back, Marek told him he had spoken with Lipski.

"So I heard. Tamara told me. She also told me you and she had talked. What did you two talk about?"

"Nothing much. She told me you plan to get married."

"She seemed upset. Did you ask her any questions?"

Marek began to feel uncomfortable. "What questions?"

"Did you ask her where she was during the war?"

"Just if she met you in Russia."

"She didn't tell you where she was or what was done to her?"

Marek assured him she didn't and watched Srebrny sigh with relief.

188

*I*f his father's death was within the realm of normalcy, thus acceptable both intellectually and emotionally, and his mother's still incomprehensible, defying any imagination, so Lisa's fate fell somewhere in between. The vividly graphic picture he had envisioned stayed with him every waking hour and haunted his sleep. He wished to rid himself of it, yet kept bringing it back by conscious effort. Not wanting to know, wanting to know more, he wavered between acceptance and denial.

He waited for a chance to talk to Srebrny alone and welcomed the first opportunity to do so. "Major," he began, sipping a drink Srebrny had poured for him, "I have meant to ask you—"

Srebrny stopped him in mid-sentence. "I've told you to forget the 'Major.' "

"All right," Marek said, still not enough at ease to call him by any of his first names. "What I meant to ask you was . . . You must have seen a lot of military action in your time. Didn't you?"

"I sure did," Srebrny said. He refilled his glass, settled himself comfortably, obviously eager to share his combat experiences. "Did you ever heard of the battle of Smolensk?"

Marek nodded.

"I was in it."

"You were?"

"That was some battle," Srebrny said. "It's a miracle I came out of it alive."

"Were you ever wounded?"

"I was very lucky. Quite a few times. I came that close"—his thumb and forefinger an inch apart indicated how close—"to being blown up."

"By a bomb?"

"A bomb, a grenade, a mine, you name it. I wasn't one to duck danger," he said, not without bravado.

"I never thought you were. You didn't earn all these for ducking," Marek said, pointing at all the medals and ribbons on Srebrny's uniform. "You must have been in a lot of close-range fighting."

"You bet."

"When one is wounded," Marek proceeded cautiously now, "let's say badly shot but not immediately killed, how does one . . . how long does it take . . ."

If he hoped to sound only dispassionately interested, he did not succeed, or Srebrny had more insight than Marek gave him credit for, for he looked at him intently and said, "Don't. It's no good this way. . . . Stop thinking about it."

"I don't seem to be able to stop," Marek said, surprised at the plaintive tone that had crept into his voice, and even more at the fact that he could bring himself to say it at all.

Tamara came back from what Srebrny earlier referred to as "a woman's errand," happily animated, a package in hand. She tore the brown paper wrapper open, took out a dress of sheer blue wool, and held it up for them to admire.

"Nice color," Marek said.

"Igor got the material and the dressmaker did a real good job."

"It's beautiful," Srebrny said. "Why don't you try it on?"

"Oh, no. That would mean bad luck."

190

She gathered the paper and the dress, excused herself, and went upstairs.

"That is to be her wedding dress." Srebrny said. "We'll be getting married next month."

"Congratulations," Marek said.

"We want to keep it quiet. No party, no guests, just two witnesses. How would you like to be one?"

"I would consider it an honor but who knows where I will be then?"

"It's the first time for Tamara," Srebrny said, ignoring Marek's last remark. "She wants a real rabbi; it's important to her. It took me a while to locate one. He will be coming all the way from Lodz. You are from Lodz, aren't you? Perhaps you've heard of him, Rabbi Feldman, Moshe Feldman. Sound familiar?"

"I had little to do with rabbis."

"Did you ever go back to Lodz?"

"Once."

"And?"

"And nothing. It was strange." He paused to remember. "Very strange. The city was the same, yet different. It was like one of those dreams. . . . Did you ever dream you were in a place that was familiar and unknown at the same time?"

"Not really," Srebrny said, "but I know what you mean."

"I went to my house," Marek went on. "I rang the bell, a woman opened the door. I literally forced my way in. The way she looked at me . . . If she had a dog, she would have probably set it loose on me."

"Probably," Srebrny said. "Such things have happened, and worse. I interrupted you. Sorry. Go on."

"I walked through the rooms," Marek continued, "with the same feeling of unreality, looking . . . I don't know what I was looking for. Nothing concrete, a familiar smell perhaps . . . something. Anyway, whatever I was looking for, I did not find. As I was leaving, the woman said some-

191

thing to me. What it was I don't remember anymore."

"Did you ever go back again?"

"I didn't," Marek said.

"I am not surprised."

"What I said before about dogs being set loose ... whatever you meant by 'worse,' do you know it to be true?"

Srebrny nodded.

"And knowing it you don't mind?"

"The high position? Being on top?"

"Both," Marek said.

"Being on top means being in control," Srebrny said.

"For how long?"

"Who knows? I can't worry about it now. I managed to glue my life together. It wasn't easy, but I did. Should I fall apart again ... " He unfolded his arms in a gesture of resignation. "But enough about me. Now back to you. Did you family have property in Lodz, a business perhaps?"

"My father owned a big textile mill before the war," Marek said, "It's nationalized now."

"The Rodwan Brothers. Of course!" Srebrny exclaimed.

"You've heard of it?"

"I was in a related business. Anybody connected with textiles knew about Rodwan Brothers."

Marek thought his father would have been pleased to hear that. He himself was, in a way.

"How much do you know about the business?"

"Not much," Marek said. "I worked there for two summers before the war."

"That's enough. I could pull a few strings and put you in charge there. Would you like that?"

Marek shook his head.

"Don't answer me now, think about it."

"I don't have to think about it, and I can give you my answer now. I appreciate your offer, I really do. But living in Lodz ... How could I? There is nothing left for me there. It

192

would be like trying to walk backward."

"You ran away from the present and you want no part of the past. What do you want?"

"A future."

What it was he expected out of the future he did not know anymore. He was like a traveler who, after having made one wrong turn, had lost all sense of direction and, wandering aimlessly, had forgotten what he had hoped to find at journey's end.

For a long time a vision of a home to be shared with Lisa would come to mind. He managed to conjure it up again, only it was different now, isolated and bolted shut to keep the world out. Still, it was like coming upon a familiar landmark that made it possible to find one's bearings.

The more he thought, the more convinced he was that he should not remain here, in this land, where he was viewed with suspicion and resentment, where he felt as if he should apologize for staying alive, where he walked on rubble, haunted by the ghosts of the past.

"The other day you asked me what it was I wanted," he said to Srebrny. "I think I have the answer. I want to get out."

"Out of where?"

"Out of this country. I want a new start, where one can walk down the street without looking over one's shoulder, where cities are not in ruins, where the countryside is safe, where one shops in well-stocked stores instead of ransacking other people's homes."

"That leaves out most of Europe," Srebrny said, "with the exception of Sweden and Switzerland, both of which are next to impossible to get into. America would fit your poetic description, but it has a quota system and the waiting list is a mile long. Do you have any relatives there?"

"I don't think I have relatives there or any other place," Marek said. "My grandparents on both sides arrived in this country from Odessa at the turn of the century. They did not have many children. Ours was a small family, not a clan."

"I see," Srebrny said. He sat there pensively, then got up. "Come with me. I want to show you something."

Marek followed him into the study. Srebrny closed the door and locked it. He sat down behind the desk, Marek in front, facing the wall with the map of Eastern Europe on it. Marek thought of the day when he first met Srebrny who had offered him help and was overcome by a sudden feeling of gratitude.

"You've always been kind to me," he said warmly.

"Don't talk nonsense," Srebrny said. He took a bunch of keys out of his pocket, found a small one, and stooped to fit it in. Before turning the lock, he lifted his head to look at Marek.

"How is your spirit of adventure?"

"When I was younger, I considered myself quite adventurous," Marek said.

"Younger? Don't make me laugh. How old are you?"

"Twenty-four."

"Now I am laughing," Srebrny said and he did.

"What I was trying to say was that I have had enough adventures to last me awhile."

Srebrny unlocked the drawer, pulled it out, took a rolled-up sheet of paper, and placed it on top of the desk. He unrolled it carefully with one hand, the other holding it down at the edge so it would not snap back.

"Here," he said, "take a look."

Marek bent over what looked like a mimeographed poster. "Jews," the big black letters read. "Don't be led astray by false promises. It is time to leave the country of your oppression. Come and join us. Long live the Jewish Homeland! Long live Palestine!" It was signed "Operation Escape."

"Where did this come from?"

"From a kibbutz," Srebrny said.

194

"A what?"

"That's what they call it, the boys and girls who live there. After the liberation, they got together and squatted on an abandoned German farm, about twenty kilometers south of here. They live there in a collective of sorts that they prefer to call a kibbutz. It was the Hebrew term that got the authorities curious about them. The other day I put on civilian clothes and went there to find out what it was all about."

"So, that's where you went," Marek said. "Did you go there in an official capacity?"

"I found about fifty young people there," Srebrny went on without answering. "They were mostly between sixteen and twenty, with a few older men, approximately your age." He laughed a short laugh. "I also found a pile of these"—he motioned at the poster—"ready to be distributed."

"And?" Marek said.

"I took this one with me and told them to destroy the rest. Stupid, reckless kids." He shook his head.

"Are you going to report it?"

"Who do you take me for?" Srebrny exclaimed with indignation.

"Sorry. I didn't mean it the way it sounded. But you must admit you are in a delicate position. What do you think about it all, anyway?"

"What do I think? I say a blessing on their heads. They must be more careful, that's all. I told them as much."

"Why then did you take this one?" Marek said, pointing at the poster.

"I took it with you in mind. I had a hunch that sooner or later you would come to me, just as you did, saying you wanted to get out. I thought if you do, here is your chance. Interested?"

"I would have to know more," Marek said hesitantly. "What is Operation Escape?"

"I will tell you what I found out. It seems to be a well-or-

195

ganized movement with a network reaching all parts of Europe. They have guides stationed at certain border points who help small groups cross into Czechoslovakia, from there to Austria, Italy, and France. The ultimate goal is Palestine."

"Who is behind this operation?" Marek asked. "Where does the money come from?"

"I didn't ask. Frankly, I don't want to know. It's better this way. As long as I am in charge here they are safe. Should anything happen to me . . ."

"You're putting your position in jeopardy. Why?"

Srebrny shrugged, "Call it ethnic solidarity," he said only half jokingly.

If Srebrny's disclosure had left Marek only mildly interested at first, it must have stimulated his fancy, for after a while he caught himself thinking about it with ambiguous feelings. The loner in him dismissed any form of group living or venture, while the daredevil welcomed the intrigue and the clandestine operation. Even though in the past he had not been idealistically inclined, a sympathetic outsider rather than an involved activist, he was ready to accept the premise behind the Zionist reasoning. His interest stirred, he approached Srebrny for further information.

"You are full of surprises," Srebrny said, shaking his head with amazement. "What made you decide?"

"I decided nothing. I just thought it might be worth investigating."

"Before we go any further," Srebrny said, "there are a few things I would like to clear up with you."

"Go ahead."

"First of all, in case I gave you the impression I wanted you out of my house for some reason, I want you to know it is not so."

"I never thought it was."

"Good. If I didn't stress strongly enough all the difficulties, or possible consequences, I am doing so now."

"I am pretty much aware of the pitfalls."

"Now I am coming to the most important point." Srebrny scrutinized Marek. "I never forgot the look on your face when you told me about that man, the informer . . . "

"Smolka?" Marek said. The mere mention of the name caused the blood to rush to his head and blind his eyes.

"You looked as if you could tear him apart?"

"I probably would. There is no way of knowing what I would do if I ever saw him again."

"That's why you've got to promise me—" Srebrny said, but Marek would not let him finish.

"I can't," he said. "I respect you much too much to make you a promise I might not be able to keep. All I can say is I won't go out of my way to find him."

"That's good enough for me." Srebrny said.

"How do I get in touch with the kibbutz?" Marek asked.

"Now I can tell you," Srebrny said. "I would gladly drive you there myself, but I don't think I should, for obvious reasons. Take a bicycle—you will find one in the garage. Make sure to check the tires for air. I don't know how long it has been since it was used. Now . . . Got a pencil?"

Marek handed him one.

"First you go to the middle of town," Srebrny explained, as he was drawing a map on a piece of paper. "At the square turn right and proceed down the road until you hit a fork. Continue going straight. After a while, to your left, you will see a barn. Make a turn there. You will find yourself on a dirt road. Go past the barn. You will see the living quarters, small barracklike houses. In the middle there will be a bigger one, painted white. Go in there and ask for Shimon. He is the one I spoke to. Tell him Silber sent you."

"Silber?"

Srebrny smiled. "I figured that they might trust a Silber more than they would a Srebrny," he said. "Tell him you are my friend."

𝒮himon was a stocky man in his mid-twenties, broad-shouldered, with curly black hair and blue eyes that looked at Marek sharply, sizing him up. "What do I call you?" he asked.

"My name is Rodwan, Marek Rodwan."

"Where are you from?"

"Lodz."

"Where were you during the war?"

"In the ghetto for a short while. Then I passed as an Aryan until I was caught and sent to a camp. I was there until the end of the war. I was liberated not far from here."

"Who can vouch for you besides Silber?"

"The men who were in the camp with me," Marek said. "But then who can vouch for *them*?"

"You are right," Shimon said and smiled. "Did you belong to any youth organization within the Zionist movement before the war?"

"I am afraid not. I was never a joiner."

"What made you change your attitude now?"

"I am not sure my attitude *has* changed. I am not opting for Palestine, at least not yet. My objective is to get out of here."

"I appreciate your honesty," Shimon said. He leafed

through some papers piled up on the table, before asking, "How many?"

Marek did not understand the question.

"How many people in your group?" Shimon repeated impatiently.

"There is no group, just me."

"Only you? No one else? You mean to say you have no attachments, no obligations?"

"None whatsoever," Marek said. Then, "I do have a couple of friends," he added, thinking of Roman and Paula, "but I would rather go myself, at first. Then we shall see."

Shimon gave him a long, thoughtful look.

"Do you speak any foreign languages?" he asked.

"I am fluent in German," Marek said. "My French is, well, high-school French, and I managed to pick up enough Russian to get by."

"That's perfect"

"What is?"

"Tell you in a moment," Shimon said. "First let me explain the situation. Here are your choices: We can help you cross the border to Czechoslovakia. We can also get you into Austria, Italy, or West Germany. After that we can part company, if that's what you want. You will be on your own from then on. You might choose to remain in any of those places or enter a DP camp, register for a visa to America, Canada, Australia, whatever your preference may be, or decide you want to get rich quick and engage in black marketing. The other possibility would be to stay with the group, get to France or Italy, and wait for a boat to take you to Palestine. The wait might be long and hard, the trip even harder, if you get there at all. And don't expect a luxury liner either. The third and the last possibility would be working for us for a while. We have been waiting for someone like you."

"What is so special about me?"

199

"You are not tied down to anyone or bound to any place. You look healthy. Are you?"

"As far as I know, I am."

"You speak all the languages we need," Shimon went on, "and, what's most important, you don't look Jewish."

Marek had been told that before. Usually it was meant as a compliment. The way Shimon said it, it was merely a statement of fact.

"What will be expected of me?"

"You will go to the French Zone and stay near the crossing point, for a certain length of time, a few months, half a year perhaps."

"Doing what?"

"Your function would be to befriend the local people, gain their trust, receive new groups as they arrive, find shelter for them, and see them through until the time they are ready to move on. Would you consider that?"

"I cannot give you an answer right away. I have to think about it. How soon do you have to know?"

"The sooner the better."

Marek gave Srebrny a detailed account of the meeting, his voice getting more spirited as he went on.

"If nothing else, he did manage to get you excited," Srebrny noted.

"Excited? I don't know. Impressed might be a better word."

"Did you give him an answer?"

"Not yet. There are still matters I would like clarified. Also, I wanted to hear your opinion."

"My opinion doesn't really matter. So rather than voicing it, I will ask you one basic question. Why are you considering Shimon's offer at all?"

"Why?" Marek shrugged. "Why not? If I accept it, I will accomplish what I set out to do in the first place, namely, leave here. I'll gain time to explore all the alternatives, and while doing it, I will be of some use."

"Or, it could be just another postponement."

"It could," Marek agreed, after reflecting a moment. "But even if I am just buying myself more time, so what? Postponement or not, I will make a step forward, and who knows, I might get really caught up in all that" —he paused, then concluded— "which would be nice."

"It is a far cry from your tranquil dream," Srebrny said.

"The dream will wait. It is good to have a dream waiting."

Srebrny smiled. "Nothing happened to your spirit of adventure after all. It seems very much alive," he said.

Shimon was pleased to see Marek again and didn't try to hide it. "Frankly, I didn't think you would be coming back," he said. "I am glad you did. Now that you have thought it over, what did you decide?"

"Before I make a commitment, I need some additional information."

"Ask, and I will answer if I can."

"You never told me who is behind this operation," Marek said.

"We are getting our directives from Palestine. We cooperate closely with the Hagganah, the underground defense force. The Jewish Brigade, a military unit within the British Army, is also involved. The headquarters of our movement, known as Beriha, are in Paris, with branches all over Europe and emissaries at every collecting point. You will meet one of them, a Palestinian Jew by the name of Tzvi. You will be getting instructions from him."

"Other than smuggling people across the borders, what else does Beriha do?"

"Everything," Shimon said, "from providing food and clothes to vessels and refurbished icebreakers."

201

"How do they get the ships?"

"Mostly from Italian and French sources."

"Incredible," Marek said. "Where does the money come from?"

"Money? Call it conscience money. The Jews who were snug and comfortable while you and I were in a camp now have the need to expiate their guilt so they give money. Anything else you want to know?"

"You mentioned different borders and various crossing points. Where do I fit in?"

Shimon took a large map of Western Europe and spread it on top of the table. "Here," he pointed, "the French Zone, that's where we want you."

Marek bent over to look at the map. Next to the spot covered by Shimon's finger was a dot bigger than others, as were the letters that read "Freiburg."

The name of the town sounded familiar. He had heard it before, then suddenly remembering, he reached into his pocket for his wallet and took out a letter. He unfolded it, his eyes skiping the lines until he found what he was looking for. "Here is my permanent address," he read. "Ludwigstrasse 4, Freiburg."

"I thought so," he said, looking up at Shimon. "I know somebody who lives in Freiburg."

"You do?" Shimon seemed interested. "Who is it?"

"A German."

"A German? Where do you know him from?"

"He was a *Meister* in a factory I was assigned to while in the camp."

"Why does he write to you?"

"He and I . . . Well, he was a decent fellow."

"How decent?"

"Decent."

"Do you trust him?"

Marek thought before answering.

"I think I do, but I don't want to take any responsibility."

"The responsibility won't be yours. If we decide he could be of use to you, we shall check him out first."

"When do I leave?" Marek asked.

"Tomorrow."

"Tomorrow?"

"Too soon?"

"No," Marek said, "It's just . . ." He thought of Srebrny and Tamara, suddenly saddened.

"Do I come here?"

"No," Shimon said. "Be at the northwest corner of Garden Street, eight o'clock in the evening. Somebody will be waiting for you there."

Marek stretched out his hand.

"Not yet," Shimon said. He walked to the corner, took out a khaki knapsack from a large cardboard box, and tossed it across the room for Marek to catch.

"Here, take it. Pack a change of underwear, a heavy sweater, rain gear, if you have any. That's all. Don't make it too heavy."

Now it was Shimon who stretched out his hand. Marek shook it.

"Thanks," he said.

"Good luck," said Shimon.

"What?" Tamara exclaimed, when Marek, in Srebrny's absence, informed her that he was planning to leave the next day. "Can't you wait until after the wedding?"

"I can't," Marek said.

"Who is going to give me away?" Tamara said in a complaining voice. She stood with her back to him, suddenly very small against the frame of the huge window, and when she turned around, her eyes were filled with tears.

"Now, now . . ." Marek said, now knowing what else to say, the honor Tamara had planned for him as unexpected as

203

her disappointment.

"I'll have to think of someone else to do it," Tamara said. "It's a bad omen. One is not supposed to—"

"To what?"

"To make changes in wedding arrangements at the last moment. It's bad luck."

"Don't be silly."

"I am very superstitious. I know it's silly, but that's the way I am. Besides"—she managed a meager smile—"I got used to having you around."

"Me?" Marek said, pointing at himself and grimacing self-mockingly. "I can't imagine why. I was an impossible houseguest for almost a month, I did nothing but mope. I slept late, I was never on time for breakfast. Why, I hardly spoke to you."

"I didn't mind," Tamara said. "I'm not a big talker myself. Usually when I am around people, I feel like crawling into a hole. I didn't feel that way with you." She paused as if wondering why she didn't. "Maybe because you reminded me of my brother," she went on. "Not that you look like him. Not at all, but he was like you in a way. Silent, moody, but inside . . . I know that inside you must be—"

"I am no bargain, I assure you," Marek interrupted her, "inside or otherwise."

"I don't like when people suddenly disappear from my life," Tamara said. "It gets me upset."

"What is this all about?" asked Srebrny, who had just walked in. "What are the long faces for?" He began to unbutton his jacket absently, his eyes wandering from Tamara to Marek then back to her.

"He is not going to stay for the wedding," Tamara said. "He is leaving tomorrow."

"Is that true?" Srebrny said, turning to Marek.

Marek nodded.

Srebrny took his jacket off, hung it on the back of the

204

chair, and slumped in. "What a day," he said. "Tamarenka, bring me a drink."

"For you too?" Tamara looked at Marek.

After he had refused, she brought in one glass filled with gold, transparent liquid that shimmered.

Srebrny emptied the glass in one gulp and put it down. Propping his hands on the arms of the chair, he got up slowly and heavily, as if very tired.

"Come," he said to Marek, motioning toward the study with his head. Then to Tamara, "Excuse me."

She nodded.

Srebrny closed the door, walked toward the desk, and took the seat behind it. "Now," he said. "Let's have it."

"Well," Marek began, sitting down. "Here is the story. The operation is not to be believed. They collaborate with—"

Srebrny held up his hand. "I told you before, I don't want to know."

"All right. Just let me say the whole thing is amazing."

"Where do they want you to go?"

"To the French Zone in Germany. I speak both French and German. It seems I could be of use there. Now this you've got to hear; you're not going to believe it. Remember Otto Holland?"

"Who is Otto Holland?"

"The former *Meister* of Precision Instruments, the one Maloviak wanted back after the Polish engineer was arrested."

"Now I remember," Srebrny said. "What about him?"

"He lives there. Not far from where I am going to be."

"How do you know?"

"I got a letter from him."

"You are in correspondence with a German?"

"I didn't say I was. He sent me one note with his address."

"Why?"

"It's a long story. I don't want to get into it now. But isn't it a coincidence?"

Srebrny agreed. He pulled out a drawer, took out a billfold, and held it across the desk. "Here," he said. "Take it."

Marek raised his hand in a defensive gesture and shook his head. "I can't," he said. "It's a lot of money. I won't—"

"You can and you will," Srebrny said. "You never know. You might need it. If not, give it to the cause."

"Why are you doing this?" Marek asked.

"It might turn out to be the best investment I ever made," Srebrny said. "Weren't you the one to point out to me that I could fall from a mountaintop. So, just in case . . . I think of it as an insurance policy. Anyway, don't worry, there's plenty more where this came from."

Marek ripped the lining of his jacket open at the bottom and spread the paper bills flatly and evenly between the silk-like material and the soft inner padding, making sure they didn't bulge or rustle. All he had to to do now was to sew the seam. He thought of asking Tamara, then decided against it, suspecting that Srebrny would not like her to know the extent of his involvement. He had to get the thread and needle from her though.

"You need to have some sewing done?" Tamara asked. "I'll be glad to do it."

"It's just a loose button," Marek said. "I can do it."

"Suit yourself," Tamara said. She fumbled in the sewing basket. "What color thread?" she asked.

The jacket was salt-and-pepper tweed, with a solid brown lining.

"Brown would be fine," Marek said.

Tamara found a spool of brown thread and handed it over to him, the needle stuck in the thread.

In his room, Marek put the jacket down inside out and be-

206

gan to sew the lining with small stitches, smoothing the material with his hand as he went on. He finished, put the needle through the loop, making a knot, and bit the thread off. He counted the money he had put aside and placed it in his wallet. He opened his suit case and transferred the few articles of clothing into his knapsack, making sure to keep the sweater on top. His boots were sturdy, new but broken in, and comfortable. He lifted the knapsack. It weighed hardly anything.

He sat down on the edge of the bed and looked at his watch. It was three in the afternoon. The day had dragged on. He was becoming impatient, increasingly jittery, and at times overcome by doubts. He had been comfortable here; Srebrny and Tamara made him feel at home. He discovered to his surprise that he was reluctant to leave. He regretted that he would miss the wedding and wished he at least had something to give them to show that he cared. He remembered a sign, displayed in the window of a run-down wooden building he had passed at Market Square that read BOOK-BINDING DONE HERE. He realized the sign could be an old one, the workshop abandoned, the owner gone, but should it be open, there was a good chance he could find something there. He decided it was worth a try. If nothing else, he would kill an hour or two.

He pedaled into town. He found the house without difficulty, got off the bike, and propped it against the side of the building. He tried the door; it wasn't locked. The hallway was dark, as was the staircase.

"Anyone here?" Marek called in German.

"One moment," a man's voice answered. "Let me put the light on."

The naked bulb lit the hallway sufficiently for Marek to find his way.

"Right here," the man's voice came from behind the closed door.

Marek turned the knob and stopped short. He sniffed, closed his eyes, then sniffed again. The smell was disturbingly familiar; it reminded him of something—he did not know of what. Then it came back to him—the closet filled with his father's books.

"Come in," the man said.

Marek opened his eyes and looked around. There were tables alongside the walls with books piled up on them. On a smaller one a rusty tin can with glue stood next to a gas burner.

"What is it you wish, sir?" the man asked.

He was old and stooped, with a mane of white hair, his face yellowish and crinkled like parchment.

"I would like to buy a book," Marek said. "What I have in mind is a leather-bound volume. I need it for a wedding gift."

"I am not in the bookselling business," the man said, "I am a bookbinder."

"I realize that, I just thought—"

"But then," the man interrupted, "I do have a few books that no one ever claimed. Let me see."

He walked to one of the long tables and came back carrying a huge, heavy volume with an ornate clasp. "This is a Bible," he said, putting it down. "It is very old. It also has lovely woodcuts. It would be priceless, if not for the fact that there are quite a few of them. It is rarity as well as age that makes a book valuable."

Marek had learned to stay away from objects that were big and heavy and not easily transportable.

"It's both, the Old and New Testaments," the man said.

"Don't you have just the Old one?" Marek asked. The man looked at him curiously. "I am afraid not." he said. "But wait a moment." He bent down, rummaged in a cardboard box under the table, and came up with a small book with gilt pages, bound in faded brown leather.

"This is the Book of Psalms," the man said straightening up. "Care to look at it?"

Marek turned the page, trying to figure out the Roman numerals. "It is old," the man assured him. "The end of the eighteenth century and rarer than the Bible. Look inside. See how the page starts? The first letters were handwritten by a monk who was famous for his artwork. I think this would make a most appropriate gift."

"How much?" Marek asked.

"You want to pay with money?" the man said, both surprised and disappointed. "What can I get for money? You can have it for three cartons of cigarettes."

"I don't have any," Marek said. "I will give you enough money so you can buy five."

"They won't sell it to me, sir," the man said sadly.

"Too bad then," Marek said. "I have no time to look for cigarettes."

"There is a bar just three short blocks away, sir," the man said. "You could get some there. I would be glad to show you the way."

"Let's go," Marek said. He got on the bike and pedaled slowly, following the man. He left him and the bike a few steps away from the bar and walked in. After a while he came out with four cartons of Lucky Strikes.

"Didn't you say five cartons before, sir?" the man said.

"You asked for three and I'm giving you four. Fair enough?"

"Fair enough. Thank you, sir," the man said.

The book was small enough to fit into his inner breast-pocket. Marek touched his foreheard with two fingers in a salute, mounted the bike, and started back.

He got into the house unnoticed. He tiptoed upstairs and softly closed the door. He reached for a pencil and a piece of paper.

"Dear Friends," he wrote. "This is your wedding present.

It is also my way of saying thank you and so long, I will never forget you. May the future be good to you. Marek."

He put the note on the chest of drawers, weighing it down with the book.

The sun began to set. He decided to leave before Srebrny's return and wait in the bar until eight. He didn't want to see Tamara either. He dreaded farewells; there was something final about saying good-bye.

He put the jacket on and buttoned it. He picked up his knapsack, which he later fastened to the back of the bike in front of the house. He adjusted the seat, climbed on, and rode off without looking back.

TWENTY-ONE

"*L*isa," Marta called, storming into the room. "Lisa!"

"Here," Lisa called back.

"Your boots are outside." Marta held the front door open, her gloved fingers pointing at them accusingly.

"Michalina told me to leave them there," Lisa said, exchanging a winking look with Adam, who had come back together with Marta and stood there grinning.

"You know very well what I mean," Marta said. "You went out for the *first* time, *alone* in the *snow*. You could have slipped, you could have—"

"You are acting like a Jewish mother," Lisa interrupted.

"Isn't she?" Adam said. "Glad you noticed. I was about to comment, but I didn't dare. As you must know by now, Marta has her sensitivities."

"Oh, be serious," Marta said angrily. "Such foolishness! She wouldn't so much as stick her nose out of the house when I asked her, then all of a sudden she goes out alone in five centimeters-deep snow, couldn't wait until we got home."

"Nothing happened," Lisa said. "I came back in one piece."

A while later, when they sat down to supper, Lisa looked up from her plate and said, "It was because of the snow that

211

I went out."

"Oh?" Marta said. In the light of the lowered pulley lamp, her face had a tawny pallor and her eyes seemed even darker.

"We met on a day like this, Marek and I. The park was so quiet, so white," Lisa said dreamily, then resumed in a matter-of-fact voice. "After you left, I put the boots and the coat on, borrowed your shawl, Marta, and went out. I was careful, I assure you. I tested the ground before I took the first step to make sure it wasn't slippery. But the snow was as soft as fine sand on a beach."

"Where did you go?" Adam asked.

"Just across the street to the park. The children were sleighing down the slope, laughing and shouting. My mother used to call it a happy noise, the kind of noise children make while playing. I stood there watching them for a while, then followed a little boy rolling down the hill."

"You *are* crazy," Marta said.

"I got up," Lisa went on, disregarding the remark. "The snow glittered in the sun, the air was frosty and clear, and I got this joyous feeling. I felt ..." She looked at them, her eyes aglow. "When I came back, I sat in my room thinking. I said to myself, *Natalia was right.*" She deduced from the expression on their faces that she had never mentioned Natalia to them before. "We were in the hospital together and in the camp before that," she said. "Natalia was shot too, but not injured very badly. She had a theory about 'taking the plunge.'"

"A plunge into what?" Marta asked.

"Into life, I guess," Lisa said, quickly adding. "I will try to explain. Take me—I always depended on someone. First on my parents, then on Marek, then I was in the camp, then in the hospital, then you came along. I never had any responsibility for my own life."

Marta opened her mouth to say something, then thought

212

better of it.

"So I decided to 'take the plunge,' as Natalia would put it." She stopped and turned to Adam. "You have some information about Marek, an idea where he might be. You told me that much. I never asked you any more questions. Now I am." She finished and looked at him, waiting.

"I wish I had something concrete to tell you," Adam said. "I tried to follow it up, I did ask around. Nobody seemed to remember. Lower Silesia is a transient territory. Every time I'm there I encounter new people. They come and go, no one stays there permanently." He pondered, then said, "Suppose Marek did survive the camp and was strong enough to move around, where do you think he would go?"

"To Krakow," Lisa said without hesitation.

"Not home to Lodz?"

Lisa shook her head. "He had no reason to go there. He would come here, to Krakow, and go to ..." She paused, trying to think where. "My house," she concluded decisively.

"Who is still there?"

"Probably just the janitor and his wife."

"One should go and check with them."

"I could do that," Marta said.

"No," Lisa said. "I will."

"Then I'll come with you," Marta said.

Lisa shook her head and said, "This is one trip I have to make alone."

The next morning Adam and Marta put her in the back of a horse-drawn sleigh, acting as if she were going on a long journey.

"Take care," Adam said.

Marta removed the harsh gray blanket from the front seat and put in on Lisa's lap. "It's windy," she said. "You could catch a cold." Then to Adam, "Did you give her enough money?"

Lisa thought money was another thing she would have to worry about from now on, as she felt her pocket for the rolled notes Adam had squeezed into her hand.

The driver smacked his lips, pulled the reins, and, "*Vio!*" he called loudly, "*Vio!*" The horse neighed and the sleigh jerked, then slid smoothly down the street, bells jingling.

When the bugler's taps sounded from the top of the church tower, Lisa realized: there was the city. She looked without seeing, her heart pounding so hard that she put her hand over her chest as if to hold it in. At the corner of her street she told the driver to stop. She got out. "How much?" she asked.

"Three hundred zlotys."

"What?" she exclaimed.

When she took the money out of her pocket, she realized that the bills were all in one-hundred-zloty denominations. The money was either worth nothing, or perhaps new ones had not been printed yet and a hundred simply stood for one. She did not understand such matters. It was one more thing she would have to learn about.

She counted three bills, handed them over to the driver, and began to walk. She passed by the apothecary, the glass jars and the copper mortar still in the window. She pushed the door open and peered in. A new man stood behind the counter. "Where is Mr. Patulski?" she asked.

"Mr. Patulski died in the war," the man said.

Lisa said she was sorry and closed the door.

There was the tobacconist's where she used to pick up her father's paper on Saturdays, paid for a day before, so no money would change hands on the Sabbath. The store was empty of merchandise. The owner's wife, busy arranging the few magazines on the shelf, paid her no attention.

The school-supply store was closed. She was approaching her home. Lisa slowed down. She stopped in front and gasped for breath, her heart beating wildly. She closed her

214

eyes and stood there waiting for it to calm down. Then she walked into the hallway and knocked on the janitor's door.

"Who is there?" a man's voice asked.

"It's me, Stanislaw, Lisa."

The janitor opened the door, looked at her with disbelief then gasped, "Jesus Maria, it's you."

"How are you, Stanislaw?" Lisa asked, her voice trembling, and walked in. The smell of cooking cabbage hit her nostrils. Stanislaw wiped the seat of a chair with the back of his hand and offered it to her.

Lisa shook her head.

"Anything I can do for you?" Stanislaw asked.

"Has anyone been here asking for me?" The question came out in a whisper, and she had to repeat it.

"I don't think so, but wait." He opened the door wide and "Yulka!" he called.

"What are you hollering for?" Yulka, his wife, said, walking in, a broom made out of twigs in her hand.

"Look who is here," Stanislaw said.

She put the broom down and stared at Lisa agape. "Sweet Mother of God," she said, "it's Lisa."

"Didn't someone come by here looking for her sometime ago?" Stanislaw asked.

Yulka nodded. "The young man, what's his name. That boyfriend of yours."

"We got married," Lisa managed to whisper. The room began to spin in front of her eyes. Her hand groped for the chair. She found it and sat down.

"Are you all right, miss?" Yulka asked. "Can I give you something? A cup of coffee?"

Lisa shook her head.

"So the two of you got married," Yulka said. "That's nice."

"When was he here?" Lisa asked.

"Let me see now," Yulka said, her finger drilling into her

215

cheek as she was trying to remember. "It was on a warm day, warm but not hot. It must have been the end of spring or early summer."

"Did he say where he was living? Where he could be found?"

"He wrote something on a piece of paper," Yulka said. "But it was such a long time ago, who would have thought ..." Then, "It was a very small piece of paper," she added, as if that would explain her misplacing it or throwing it away.

Lisa sat there for a while saying nothing, then got up.

"Can I find a sleigh around here?" she asked.

They said the stand was down the block, at the intersection.

Marta opened the door, an unspoken question in her eyes. She watched as Lisa took off her coat looking around as if wondering where to put it. "I stayed home," she said. "I wanted to be here when you came back."

Swept by a warm wave of gratefulness, Lisa began to cry. She sat down on a couch, coat in hand, and cried silently, the tears suddenly released, flowing in an uninterrupted stream.

Marta sat next to Lisa, put her arms around her, and held her close.

Lisa raised her face, her eyes red and moist, and stammered between sobs, "He was there ... He ..."

Marta turned her head and looked at her incredulously, "Why are you bawling then?" she said, and she too burst into tears.

They sat, holding on to each other, crying.

Marta was the first one to stop. "Where is he?" she asked.

"They don't know," Lisa said, wiping the tears with her wrist.

"He was there a long time ago, in June I think. He left a written message. They threw it away."

"What?" Marta cried out.

Lisa looked at her helplessly. "What do I do now?" she said. "Where do I begin to look?"

"Take it easy," Marta said, "take it easy. We will think of something, I promise."

In the afternoon the telephone rang.

"Hello," Marta said, picking up the receiver. "Yes, a while ago. . . . They don't know. . . . Just as I said, they don't know. . . . She is fine, a little weepy but fine." There was a pause as she listened, her head nodding. She reached for a pad next to the phone and wrote something down. She glanced at her watch. "Now it's too late," she said. She listened again. "See you in a little while," she said and hung up.

"That was Adam," she informed Lisa, as though she hadn't guessed that much. "He went to the Red Cross. They told him to get in touch with"—she glanced at the pad—"the Jewish Search Center on St. Hedwig Street. They would be closed now. Anyway, you've had enough for one day."

*T*here were only a few waiting in the large room, dark in spite of the sunny day: a shabbily dressed woman, a man in a Russian-style parka, and a thin, slightly built adolescent boy stood lined up in front of a desk, four more sat on a bench looking anxious and sad. Lisa, who expected the place to be crowded and bustling with activity, felt suddenly let down.

The woman clerk, her dark hair with reddish-blond ends, showing traces of past bleaching, must have noticed her distress. "You seem confused," she said as Lisa approached the desk.

"It's so empty here," Lisa said. "Not at all the way I imagined it."

"You should have seen the place a few months back. There were three of us working here and we could hardly keep up. Now it is only me and one other girl part-time. The first wave passed. Now mostly repatriates from Russia come here," she said, obviously not taking Lisa for one. "They had no idea what to expect. Sometimes it is so pathetic—" She interrupted herself. "But I am sure you didn't come here to chat."

"I don't mind." Lisa had welcomed the delay. "My name is Rodwan," she said.

218

The young woman looked at her with sudden interest. "No," she said after a while. "It cannot be, not *Lisa* Rodwan? My God," she said, after Lisa said she was. "My God, if only Sabina were here now."

"Who is Sabina?" Lisa asked.

"You don't know Sabina? She had your notebook; you gave it to her. She spoke of you so much that it seems I have known you for a long time." She stretched her hand across the desk. "Helena Bloch," she introduced herself.

"Where is Sabina?" Lisa asked. The name still failed to bring forth a face.

"In Germany. She works for UNRRA, the United Nations Relief and Rehabilitation Administration."

"What happened to the notebook?"

"Marek took it," Helena said.

Lisa leaned against the desk. It took her a while to ask the next question. "When was he here?"

"Oh," Helena said, "a long time ago. In June, when we first opened the Center. Sabina told him about you."

"What did she tell him?"

"I don't know exactly, but judging by the way he looked, nothing encouraging. He seemed quite distraught when he left."

"Do you have his address?"

"Let me see," Helena said. "I am sure Sabina wrote it down." She went through the file drawer and came up with a folder. "Here it is," she said. "Rodwan Marek, also known as Rodwanski, Peterswald—that's Lower Silesia"—she added by way of explanation—"Birch Lane 9. There is even a phone number here, 104-44."

"Could you do me a favor," Lisa said, surprised at the calm in her voice, "and call the number for me? I will reimburse you for the call."

"I'll be happy to try," Helena said. "I hope the call will go through. It's sometimes hard to get a connection." She dialed the operator. "104-44," she said, "Peterswald, Lower Silesia." She waited, frowned listening, then hung up. "There is a funny buzz. I think it would be better to try after five. You might get through then."

Lisa thanked her and turned, about to leave, when Helena called her back.

"I found something in the file," she said. She handed her an envelope. It bore her name. In the upper left-hand corner was the name N. Berger.

Lisa waited until she was out in the street before tearing it open. "Dear Lisa," she read. "I hope this will reach you somehow. I often think about you. I am fine. I haven't mastered the strokes yet, but I've learned to float. I miss you, Natalia."

As she put the letter back into the envelope Lisa realized she had been missing Natalia too.

In the evening Adam placed the call. "I'm getting a weird sound," he said and tried again. "Operator," he said, "104-44 in Peterswald. All I get is a strange signal. Would you please try it?" He waited, then "Disconnected" he said. He hung up and looked at Lisa. "Now what?" he asked.

"I am going there," Lisa said in a determined voice.

Adam arranged a ride for her with dignitaries' wives going home, in an official car driven by a German chauffeur. As it turned out, they had been to Krakow to be fitted for new wardrobes in Madame Kaleska's renowned fashion salon. Lisa could hardly believe their conversation.

"I gave her an old dress," one of them was saying, "and she turned it into a creation."

"She is the best," another one agreed. "She made a little suit for me, simple but elegant. The jacket was pulling a bit in the back, I hardly noticed it, but, you know Madame Kaleska, the perfectionist. She insisted I should leave it with her to be fixed."

"I got a fur jacket through her," the third one told the others, "a silver fox. How about you, dear?" she turned to Lisa, "You sit here so quietly."

"I came from Leipzig wearing a fur coat," Lisa said.

"Really," the women exclaimed. Their astonishment duly recorded, they went on chatting among themselves.

The driver let them out one by one at their respective destinations, carrying their packages as each of them waved and blew kisses to those still in the car.

After a while there was only Lisa left. It was getting dark when the car turned into a quiet well-paved street and stopped in front of a red brick house. The driver held the door open for her. Lisa stepped out of the car, looked around, then walked inside.

There were two doorbells in the hall. "Gold," read the nameplate next to one; the other was empty. Lisa rang.

The door opened a crack at first, then wider.

"What can I do for you?" a girl asked. She was slightly built, with shoulder-length blond hair.

"I am looking for Marek Rodwan," Lisa said.

The girl said nothing at first, then asked hesitantly, "Who are you?"

"I am Lisa."

The girl threw the door wide open and stood there dumbfounded. "His wife?" she said finally.

"I've come a long way ..." Lisa said.

"Forgive me," the girl stammered. "Come in, please do.... Forgive me, it's just ... it's hard to believe." She let Lisa in and closed the door. "Sit down," she said and began to pace, wringing her hands as she did, talking unceasingly. "Roman is not going to believe it, he will be here any minute now. He is my husband, I am Paula ... Paula Gold, Roman's wife. We and Marek, we were like family. We—"

Lisa was about to interrupt her when a man of medium height in his twenties appeared in the open door, looking at her curiously.

221

Paula ran toward him. "Roman," she cried, "can you imagine? This is Lisa."

Roman walked in and sank into a chair without taking his jacket off. "Marek's Lisa?" he said.

Liking the way it sounded, Lisa smiled and nodded.

"I think I need a drink," Roman said.

"Me too," said Paula. "How about you?" she asked Lisa.

"No," Lisa said, "thank you." She watched Paula fill the glasses and waited for them to finish drinking.

"Who would have believed it," Roman said.

"Marek did," Paula said to Lisa. "He believed all the time that you were alive somewhere."

"We couldn't understand it, no one could," Roman said. "I know Marek resented it. I think that was the reason for the estrangement."

"Roman and Marek, they were like brothers," Paula said. "They stuck together in the camp and after the liberation too. Marek arranged our wedding; he gave me away. They worked together."

"He got me my job," Roman said. "We shared this house."

"Where is he?" Lisa finally managed to get a word in.

"He is gone," Roman said. "He left. He sneaked out like a thief in the night, without as much as leaving a word."

"He did send you a message, through Alex," Paula said to Roman. "He asked him to give you the money."

"Who needed his money?" Roman said.

"Forgive me," Lisa said, "I cannot make sense out of anything you are saying."

"I am sorry," Paula said. "It's because it came as such a surprise. . . . We are so excited. I will try to tell you." Then she began, "As I told you, we were very close to Marek. When he came back from Krakow, after he found out . . . well, when he heard that you'd been left for dead, he was like a changed man. How many times did I ask him to stay

222

for supper?" She turned to Roman, as if taking him for a witness. "Did he ever stay? Never. He almost became a recluse. He would work ten, twelve hours, then would come home and lock himself upstairs. He became so, so . . . disinterested."

"Except for the one time when we dug the things out, remember?" Roman said.

"What things?"

"From the synagogue," Paula said. "They were buried in a cemetery here. It was Marek who found out about it. We dug them out just in time for the high holidays. We held services here. Marek was so involved in the preparations. Then, on Yom Kippur, in the middle of the prayers, for no good reason, he stormed out. We got home, he wasn't there and Roman's motorcycle was gone. Marek came back in the evening, his suit in shreds, his arm badly scratched. He was in an accident, he told us, and the headlights on the bike were broken, and a fender bent. I said never mind the bike and took care of his cut, cleaned it and all. He said he was tired and went upstairs. When we got up in the morning, he was gone."

"Have you heard from him since?"

"He called up Alex, his boss," Paula said. "He said he had to leave because of a sudden emergency. He asked Alex to give his wages to Roman. For the bike, he told him. He also said we shouldn't worry."

"Did he say where he was calling from?"

"All he said was he was with friends."

"Who were his friends?" Lisa asked.

"I always thought we were," Roman said.

"We have no idea," Paula said. "As I told you, he'd kept to himself lately." She stopped. Then, "Roman," she said, as if she just thought of something, "what was the name of the colonel, or was he a major, the one Marek claimed was Jewish, who had promised to help him? . . . Remember?"

223

"You mean Srebrny?"

"Yes, him."

"I heard he got arrested."

"He?" Paula seemed surprised. "Such an important man. What for?"

"Withholding information, or something like that," Roman said. "At least that's the rumor. Anyway, he isn't in Grünberg anymore."

There was a knock at the door. A German woman came to return the keys. "Thank you, Frau Huber," Lisa said and closed the door.

"She was Marek's housekeeper, Lisa," Paula said to her. "She still comes in to dust from time to time. We keep the apartment, just in case." She held the keys in her hand. "Would you like to see it?"

"What for?"

$\mathcal{M}$arta and Adam tiptoed around Lisa, watchful of every word. Lisa had been acting strangely ever since she returned from her trip. She spent most of the time in her room, ate little, and talked even less.

To get her out of that state, but expecting no concrete results, Marta suggested putting a notice in a personal column. They composed one and sent copies to every major newspaper.

For days after Lisa would sit next to the telephone staring at it as if trying to hypnotize it to ring, jumping up each time it did.

When the notices failed to bring a response, they decided all avenues had been explored, that trying anything more would be, as Adam put it, "chasing the wind in the field," and that there was nothing left to do but wait.

Soon Lisa discovered she was not very good at waiting and that patience was not one of her virtues. Now that she knew Marek was alive she agonized over each moment of inaction, frustrated by her own helplessness, and when not sure anymore what Marek was really like, she became afraid that she was in love with someone she had invented.

She was also bothered by the thought she might be a financial burden to Adam and Marta. Ever since she had

225

learned how worthless money had become, she realized they were far from rich and that the privileges they enjoyed were not only the result of hard work but of compromising and following the party line, with which they often disagreed.

Now that winter was over and traveling was less of a problem, she decided the time had come for her to earn her own keep.

"I would like to get a job," she announced one day. "It's not good to just sit around and wait."

"You are right about that," Adam said.

"What kind of a job?" Marta asked.

Suddenly it dawned on Lisa that she had no skills to speak of. "I am afraid there is very little I *can* do," she said.

"What about office work?" Adam asked.

"I don't even know how to type," Lisa said.

Marta sat there thinking. "How good are you with children?" she asked.

"I like them," Lisa said, "and I believe they like me. Why?"

"I'll tell you in the evening," Marta said.

"How does the idea of working in a day-care center strike you?" Marta asked as they sat around the table, then elaborated. "It is a service every large factory provides for women workers with preschool children, a place where they leave them in the morning and pick them up after work. The money isn't too great, but you might find the work rewarding."

"I think I would like it very much," Lisa said.

Most children in the center were between two to five years of age; the infants were kept separately. Lisa loved her work, and the children responded to her affectionately. Even though she tried not to play favorites, she couldn't help preferring some over others. Yurek Rakowski, a sad little boy with golden hair and big brown eyes, stole her heart. He

226

must have been a sickly child, for his mother, Irena, a blond, soft-spoken woman, would worry and check on him frequently.

One day Lisa was busy putting the toys and books into the cubicles on the wall after all the children had left when Irena Rakowski walked in.

"Why didn't you bring Yurek in today?" Lisa asked. "Is he sick?"

"I've got to talk to you." Irena Rakowski sat down on one of the little tables. "Miss Rodwan." She looked at Lisa.

"Mrs." Lisa corrected her.

"Mrs. Rodwan, are you ... Jewish?"

Lisa winced. "And if I am?"

"Nothing," Irena Rakowski said, "so am I. I am sure you must have known it all along."

"I had no idea."

"My real name is Bernstein. Rakowski is the name we assumed to pass as Poles, my husband and I. We got married just before the war, and Yurek was born a year later. When we saw what was coming, we left him with a Christian woman. It was just before he turned two. Shortly after, my husband was found out and shot. Am I bothering you, Mrs. Rodwan?"

Lisa assured her she wasn't.

"When the war was over, the woman we had left Yurek with was unwilling to give him up. What was even worse, he did not want to come with me. Have you noticed how he clings to me each morning? That's how he clung to her. He called her 'Mama.' I can't begin to tell you how it made me feel." She sighed. "When I got him back, I vowed that my child would not go through what I had to. His name was going to remain Rakowski, and he was never to know that he was a Jew. There was little doubt in my mind that that was the right thing to do. Until last week." She fell silent.

"What happened last week?" Lisa said in a soft voice.

227

"I was about to go shopping. The neighbors' boys, they are older than mine, eleven and eight, were playing outside. Yurek wanted to stay and play with them and I let him. When I returned, he was all excited. 'Mommy, Mommy,' he cried out, 'Guess what we saw. We saw a little Yid. We threw stones at him.' My heart just stopped, Mrs. Rodwan. Something like that I did not foresee. That was more than I bargained for. That was more than I could bear. I am leaving, Mrs. Rodwan, I am going to take my child and get out of here."

"Where to?" Lisa asked. "How?"

"There is an organization, it is called Beriha. They help Jews cross the border."

That was the first time Lisa heard of Operation Escape.

When Lisa repeated the story at the dinner table, she noticed Marta's eyes grow dark with anger. To avoid them, Adam turned to Lisa.

"Do you think Marek would get mixed up with anything like that like that Bri ... Operation Escape?" he asked.

Lisa shrugged. "I don't know. How should I know?" she said, thinking how hard it was for her to connect the Marek she had known to the one described by Roman and Paula. "People change."

Marta sat there without saying a word.

"What's with you?" Lisa asked her later.

"Nothing," Marta said. "It's the story.... It was so upsetting."

As Marta had warned her, the work in the center, gratifying as it was, paid badly, and money was still very much a problem. Lisa insisted on turning her paycheck over to Adam and Marta, which deprived her of the possibility of leaving should she so decide. In search of a solution Lisa thought of the silver her father had hidden in her uncles's house. The candelabra and the tea set had been sold before, but the cutlery and the few ornamental pieces still left must

228

have been worth something. She decided to recover them.

"I won't let you as much as go near the place," Marta said when Lisa told her about her intention to do it.

"Here she goes playing the Jewish mother again," Lisa said.

"This time she is right," Adam said. "There were some ugly incidents. I will take care of it. Just tell me where it is."

"In the basement of the house my uncle lived in." Lisa said and gave him the address.

"You will have to be more specific," Adam said.

"What do you mean?"

"You don't expect me to dig up the whole basement?"

"It wasn't buried," Lisa said, suddenly remembering. "They took some bricks out of the wall and put the things inside."

"Which wall? Try to remember."

"I am trying," Lisa said. Then, "Is there such a thing as a gas clock?" she asked uncertainly.

"You mean a gas meter?"

"That's it," Lisa exclaimed. "That's where it is. Inside the wall next to the gas meter."

"I will get it out for you," Adam promised.

"How?" Marta wanted to know.

"Give me time," Adam said. "I will think of something."

"Should you get it out," Lisa said, "don't bring it here. Try to sell it for me. Will you?"

"Wouldn't you like to keep something?" Marta asked. "A small thing for a memento?"

"I don't like mementos," Lisa said.

A few days later Adam came home in an unusually good mood, laughing and joking. He rubbed his hands, obviously very pleased with himself, and announced he had gotten the silver out. "It was a scream," he told them. "You're not going to believe it." Then he told them how he and Henryk, his

229

co-worker, had done it. "I took Henryk along because he is handy with tools. Speaking of tools, we carried them elegantly, in executive briefcases. We went to the house and found the janitor. We had it all planned ahead of time. There was a gas leak, Henryk told him. 'What gas leak?' the janitor asked. 'Can't you smell it? You will be charged with negligence,' Henryk screamed. I said we were city inspectors, flashed a stamped piece of paper in front of his nose, and asked how to get to the basement. He offered to take us there, but Henryk said there was danger of an explosion. I was afraid he might have gone too far, but the janitor was either too dumb or too scared to ask questions.

"We went down, found the place, removed the bricks, took the silver out, and put the bricks back. We left the tools there, divided the silver between the two briefcases, and beat it."

"Where is it?" Marta asked.

"I left it to be sold on consignment."

"Thank you," Lisa said.

Marta had shown good judgment when she objected to Lisa's having anything to do with recovering the hidden things. A few days later an old man who tried to reclaim his valuables was killed. It was not an isolated incident. Hardly a day would pass without an "excess" or "act of hooliganism," as the press would call it: a Jewish cemetery was desecrated, the few Jews who had returned were chased out of a nearby town by hostile neighbors, a synagogue was burned down.

News of such incidents would appear on the back pages of the newspapers, somewhere in a corner, spiced with a due amount of indignation and a reminder that anti-Semitism was outlawed by constitutional amendment. The notices could easily escape the eyes of all readers except those whom they concerned most—remnants of the Jewish community. But even they would skip over them without dwelling on

230

them too long, and they never discussed them openly. Like one just recovering from a near-fatal illness, they refused to accept the recurrence of symptoms or the possibility of a relapse.

But what happened in Kielce, a town in southeast central Poland, could not be hushed up or ignored. The story appeared on the front page of the morning paper in bold, red headlines, calling what happened there "a massacre and a pogrom." Out of the twenty-five thousand Jews who had lived there before the war, two hundred had come back. Most returned after having spent the war years in Russia. Some, like moles, had dug their way out of the bunkers in the surrounding forests. A few others were survivors of camps.

The first edition, carrying the news, gave no details of what happened, nor did it indicate how many were killed or wounded. But soon an "Extra" appeared on the streets. It revealed that an ancient myth of ritual murder had been revived when a little girl disappeared from her home. Between the time she was discovered missing and the time she was found wandering on the outskirts of the town, a mob had gathered, armed with axes, chopping knives, and hunting rifles, killing forty-two Jews and injuring many more.

The papers could not find sufficiently strong words of condemnation. They called it a mass murder, the blackest page in Poland's recent history, a brand of Cain. The prime minister declared that he was going to attend the funeral of the victims.

The day the news broke, Tadeusz, Adam's older brother, arrived from Warsaw and stopped by for a visit. In a way he was even handsomer than Adam. He was tall and carried himself very straight. The perfectly fitting blue-gray uniform of an air force officer deepened the color of his eyes, and the graying mustache added dignity to his appearance. He had been a flyer during the war after having studied aeronautics in Paris, and he combined the gallantry of a Polish nobleman with the suavity of one who spent part of his life in Western capitals.

The paper with the red headline lay folded on the table. Tadeusz bent over Marta's hand and brushed his lips against it. Marta pulled it back. He looked at Lisa and, after an introduction, graced her hand too. Marta went into the kitchen and came back carrying a plate with bits of sausage, a bottle of vodka, and drinking glasses and put them down without a word. Adam and Tadeusz drank and only after three rounds began to talk.

"Barbarians," Adam said. "In this day and age. After such a war to believe in ritual murder . . ."

"Ugly, isn't it," Tadeusz said. "Such things simply don't exist anymore."

"What do you mean, 'anymore'?" Marta asked.

"I mean now. *Entre nous*, you've got to admit those things did happen. Why, our maternal grandmother—"

"Tadeusz," Adam said warningly, "shut up!"

"No," Marta said, her eyes burning. "Go on. What about your grandmother?"

"Well, she used to tell us that when she was a little girl, a bearded Jew got hold of her in a barn, covered her with a featherbed, and—"

"I don't know what she was doing under the featherbed or with whom, but I can assure you no one was after her blood for matzos."

"Well—" Tadeusz started.

"Shut up," Adam said again, this time louder, his face red.

Marta got up and walked out of the room, slamming the door so hard that the glasses clanked on the table.

There was a moment of silence. Tadeusz rose. "I came to discuss something with you," he said, "but I see that I chose the wrong time. I might stop by tomorrow in the office."

After he left, Marta came back into the room.

"He was drunk," Adam said. "He did not know what he was saying."

"Forgive them for they know not what they do?" Marta said. "You know what, Adam? That's your tradition, not mine. Like turning the other cheek. Your tradition also, yours and your family's." She stood there, her hands on the frame of the chair.

"You have all the right to be mad at Tadeusz," Adam said, "but leave the rest of my family out of it."

"Screw your whole family," Marta said, the obscenity sounding strange coming from her.

"If you think talking like a drunken peasant becomes you, you are mistaken," Adam said, trying hard to control his voice. "You better cut it out, Marta, it's not your style, you know."

"Not my style? And what is my style? The Jewish style perhaps? What did you used to call me? Your proud Jewish princess, your dark Madonna. . . . Is that what I am supposed to be? You tell me, Adam."

"You are upset to the point of hysteria," Adam said.

"Upset? I will show you how upset I am. I am getting the hell out of here."

"Good idea," Adam said. "Go out, air your head, but take an umbrella. It looks like rain."

"I don't think I made myself clear," Marta said. "What I mean is I am leaving this damned country."

Adam looked at her. "How can we?" he said. "You can't ask that of me. I have my roots here."

"Did I say anything about you? I understand. . . . Roots, country, family. You still don't seem to get it. I am leaving you, Adam."

Adam looked around incredulously as if only now he began to understand. "You are not being fair," he said. "You can't make me responsible for my countrymen or for my

233

family or even for my foolhardy youth. I know I haven't always been an exemplary husband, but that will change. I won't as much as look at another woman, I swear."

"That is not the issue," Marta said.

"I think it is, partially at least. It seems you were just waiting for an opening to get back at me. Can't say I blame you. You want to leave? All right. You'll leave but not like that. We will leave together. Just give me time. One month is all I am asking for."

He walked over and gently removed her hands from the chair and turned her around to face him. "I love you," he said.

She looked at him for a long time. Then, "One month," she said with a warning in her voice. "Not a day longer."

$\mathcal{M}$arek decided to take a day off. He had been working hard lately, spending most of the time in a nearby village. More people were arriving now that the weather had improved and the days had grown longer.

He would wait for them in an old wooden farmhouse, which served both as a shelter and a distribution point. He couldn't tell anymore how many had passed through since he had been there, or what they looked like. Fatigued and frightened, they would all ask the same questions, with the same mixture of anticipation and anxiety, and after a while they melted into one faceless mass.

He would go down the list at first looking for familiar names, hoping Paula and Roman might be among the arrivals, then he gave up. He often thought about them though with a sense of guilt for failing them, for leaving the way he had, for not staying in touch. He wondered what had happened to the once-strong friendship, when and why they grew apart. He remembered how close they used to be in the camp, Roman and he, how inseparable they were afterward, and how their relationship had changed once Roman got married. It had little to do with Paula. It wasn't anyone's fault really. They simply didn't feel comfortable with each other anymore, Roman most of the time apologetic, Marek more often than not feeling like an intruder. He wished things had worked out differently between them; he would not be so lonely now.

He had learned the difference between being alone and being lonely. Being alone was an option he chose, while loneliness was a sorrowful state of mind that had nothing to do with choice.

Here he didn't have any friends. He admired Tzvi, the man he had been working with, for his resilience and courage, but found him brusque and hard to become friends with. Ben Rubin, the other emissary, was a sullen, busy man, obsessed with the mission. After months of close cooperation, his relationship with both of them was an impersonal and businesslike as the day they met.

The six months Marek had committed himself to were coming to an end. Soon he would have to decide whether to stay or move on. But not today. Today he was going to rest, take a hike in the country perhaps.

The countryside around Freiburg was that of awesome beauty, with tree-covered mountains, bucolic valleys, lakes and brooks, the picturesque villages untouched by war. The city itself was mostly destroyed; the cathedral, dating back many centuries, with filigree towers and a tall spire, had miraculously escaped the bombings, as did the archways and statues of Hapsburg rulers.

When he was not working, Marek would stay at Hildegard's Gasthaus, where he occupied a comfortable room, the wide bed covered with a quilted calico spread, the window adorned by matching curtains facing a quiet, cobblestone street. Originally called Zum Löwen, it had been renamed for the present owner, Frau Hildegard Bruckhaus, who was Louise Holland's sister and Otto Holland's sister-in-law.

Otto Holland was the one who waited for him when he first arrived. He looked younger than Marek remembered. His face had lost its ascetic look, either because he had put

236

some weight back on or because he had replaced the old-fashioned spectacles with horn-rimmed glasses. Wearing laced boots, a heavy plaid jacket, and a cap with a peak, he could easily be taken for a mountain-climbing tourist.

"It makes me happy to welcome you here, Herr Rodwan," he greeted Marek.

"How are you, Holland?" Marek said, significantly, if without intent, using the last name only, even though Holland had just addressed him respectfully as "Herr."

"Your friends send their greetings," Holland said, using the agreed-upon code. "You are to come with me." Then, "I hope you don't mind the means of transportation," he added, pointing at the beat-up motorcycle with a sidecar. "It's only a short ride away."

Louise Holland welcomed Marek like a long-lost relative and introduced him to her sister as "Otto's friend, the one who enabled him to come here," while Frau Bruckhaus stood there smiling and nodding.

She was a plain-looking woman of nondescript age with a passion for clocks. There were clocks all over the house: grandfather clocks, cuckoo clocks, mantelpiece clocks, new ones, and antiques that would chime in unison or out of step, separately.

Marek did not mind the chiming as much as the constant ticking, annoying as obtrusive insects.

It wasn't until the next day, when he found himself alone with Holland in the downstairs parlor with the framed petit-point landscapes on the wall, the clocks ticking away, that Marek confronted him.

"Why did you get involved?" he asked.

"I was contacted," Holland said—Marek did not have to ask by whom—"and I was happy to oblige, especially after I heard you were coming here. I never forgot your kindness, Herr Rodwan."

Marek accepted the praise reluctantly.

"I hope you found the accomodations comfortable," Holland said, then told him the guesthouse had been in the family for three generations now. Hildegard, widowed during the war, hoped he would stay and help out. But running a guesthouse was not exactly what Holland would consider "man's work." Besides, business was slow now: not many tourists were interested in the bombed-out city. "Other than your room and two more rooms reserved for Herr Zahavi"—Zahavi was Tzvi's last name—"and Herr Rubin, the Gasthaus stands empty most of the time," Holland told him, adding that he had planned to go to the industrial Saar region, hoping to find work there. "I was about to leave," he said, "when Herr Zahavi approached me."

"There can't be much money in it for you," Marek said carefully, not sure how freely he could talk. "I hope that you didn't change your plans because you felt obliged, that you are not doing it for me."

"I am grateful to you, Herr Rodwan," Holland said, "very grateful, but it is not for you that I am doing it, or for the money. It is for myself."

Marek looked at him. "How is that?" he asked.

"Shortly after I arrived here I saw a movie. My God, the way I put it, you might think it was some kind of entertainment, Zarah Leander or Leni Riefenstahl. It was not that kind of a movie. We were forced, it was compulsory, Herr Rodwan, to view films of concentration camps. It was horrible, just horrible ... the children ..." He paused, cleared his throat, then went on. "People couldn't stand it. They turned their heads away so as not to look. I *made* myself look, I looked and I prayed, I prayed and I looked. I thanked God; I realized how good he had been to me. It was only by chance that I was just a *Meister* in a factory, I could have been running such a camp instead. I could easily—"

"No, you wouldn't," Marek interrupted him, "not you."

"Not me? How do you know, Herr Rodwan? I don't

238

know, I guess I will never know. It is the not knowing that keeps me awake at night and the knowing that I will never know. But I am not making sense."

"Holland," Marek said, "back in Poland I was questioned about you. They wanted to know what kind of man you were. All I could tell them was that you were decent. You are a decent man, Holland."

"Decent? I wonder . . . I just wasn't put to the test."

Marek walked to the window and opened it wide. The air outside was fragrant and crisp, perfect weather for a walk in the mountains.

He got his hiking boots out of the closet, put them on, and sat down to lace them when there was a knock on the door.

"Come in," Marek said.

Ben Rubin entered, newspaper in hand, looking as if he had just gotten out of bed, the graying hair in unkempt tufts, the furrowed face crumpled. Only his blazing eyes were wide awake. "Did you hear the news?" he asked, stepping in.

"I just got up," Marek said. "Why?"

"*Your* Poland," Ben said. A native of Austria, he had lived in Palestine for some time. He slapped the paper with the back of his hand and gave it to Marek. "Here," he said, "read it."

Marek's eyes skimmed the headline, there it was: FORTY-TWO KILLED IN POLAND. It must have been a fire, or a train derailment, he thought, and went on reading.

"Forty-two Jews were killed in Kielce as a result of a 'blood libel.' The government in Warsaw voiced strong condemnation and expressed regrets. The prime minister . . ." He stopped and dropped the paper on the floor. He looked at it blankly. Then, "The bastards," he said through his teeth, "the damn bastards."

"There will be a run on the borders now," Ben said, but

239

Marek paid him no attention. He bent down, tied the shoelaces, straightened himself up, and said, his mind suddenly made up, "I am going back to Poland."

"That's insane," Ben said.

"I have left friends in Peterswald. I have to get them out."

"Forget it, you can't leave now," Ben said. "We expect increased traffic, and your replacement won't be here until the end of the month."

Marek got up, walked over to Ben, and faced him. "Do I have your permission, or do I leave without it."

Ben eyed him steadily for a long time. "It is important to you," he said finally, making it sound like a statement rather than a question.

"Extremely important," Marek said.

Ben glanced at his watch, then looked at Marek. "In that case, be ready in half an hour. I will drive you to Strasbourg. There should be a train heading for the east from there today."

Marek arrived in Breslau the next day. He walked down the streets, the rubble swept into piles now, to where the trucks stood.

"Which one to Peterswald?" he asked loudly.

"Here!" a driver called, leaning out the window.

Marek walked over and climbed on.

The lorry stopped in front of the old Rathaus, now the party headquarters. Marek jumped down, brushed off his pants, dusty from the ride in an open vehicle, and headed toward Birch Lane. Only when he reached the house and stopped there, panting, did he realize that he had been running all the way there. He waited to catch his breath, then walked in and rang the bell. No one answered. Roman must be at work, Marek thought, and for a moment contemplated going there, then decided against it. He would rather wait here until Paula came back than risk running into Alex. He

240

sat down on the steps of the staircase, leaned against the banister, closed his eyes, and before he knew it, dozed off. When he woke up, he looked at his watch; over an hour had passed.

He got out and began to walk aimlessly. He stopped at Frau Huber's house, went inside, and knocked on the door.

"Herr Rodwanski," Frau Huber exclaimed, looking genuinely pleased. "What a surprise. Welcome back." She invited him in. "Trude," she called, "look who is here. You remember Herr Rodwanski."

"Good morning, Herr Rodwanski," Trude said in her mother's voice.

"Don't just stand there," Frau Huber said. "Go and put some coffee on." She turned to Marek. "Your place is waiting for you," she said, "nice and clean. I took good care of it. I would go in there and dust as long as Frau and Herr Gold were there."

"What do you mean, 'were'?"

"They left. Didn't you know that?"

"Where to?"

Frau Huber shrugged. "They didn't confide in me. Once I overheard them talking. They spoke in Polish so I didn't understand exactly what they were saying. Besides, I am not an eavesdropper. What I heard by chance was 'Prague.' They repeated it a few times. After they left, I put two and two together."

"When did they leave?"

"I don't know exactly. About three weeks ago I would say—shortly after the young woman came by looking for you."

"What young woman?"

"I was at your place," Frau Huber said. "There was a leak in the kitchen and Frau Gold asked me to come and mop the floor. I heard a big commotion downstairs and your name mentioned several times. When I came down to return

241

the keys and Frau Gold opened the door, I saw her. A pretty little thing, about that tall," Frau Huber indicated with her hand, "dark hair. I was about to leave when I heard my name mentioned, then yours. I figured Frau Gold was telling her I worked for you. Her name was ... Frau Gold called her, she called her ..."

"What did she call her?" Marek walked over to the woman, took her by the shoulders, his fingers digging into the flesh. "What did she call her?" he repeated, shaking her.

"I don't remember," Frau Huber stammered out, looking at him fearfully. Her shoulder moved under his grip. "You are hurting me, Herr Rodwanski," she moaned.

"Remember!" Marek hissed.

"The door was closed. I could not hear so well. It sounded like, I am not sure ... Elise, Lise ..."

He let go of her so abruptly that she staggered and would have hit the wall if her hand hadn't got hold of a chair.

Marek wiped the sweat off his face. His thoughts were coming in rapid succession. If indeed it was Lisa, the only way she could have gotten his address was either from the janitor in her house or the Search Center. In either case, he had to go to Krakow.

He reached for the phone without bothering to ask Frau Huber's permission. "Information," he said into the receiver, "Srebrny, Ignacy. S-r-e-b-r-n-y ... I don't know the address. There is only one by that name." He got the number and a connection through the operator. He let the phone ring a few times and, when there was no answer, hung up. Going there would mean losing a day. He would call again from Krakow. Alex was the only one left to contact now. It might not be pleasant, but he had no other choice. This was a local number and Marek dialed directly.

"Precision Instruments," a girl answered the phone.

"Maria?" Marek said, remembering the secretary's name.

"This is Nina. Maria is not here anymore."

"Connect me with Alex Lipski," Marek said.

"Mr. Lipski is at a conference in Warsaw. Would you like to talk to Mr. Kowalik?"

Marek gathered Kowalik was his replacement.

"Yes?" a man's voice said.

"I am Alex's friend," Marek said without giving his name. "I need a ride to Krakow in a hurry."

"You are in luck," Kowalik said. "A car is just about to leave."

"Tell them to wait," Marek shouted into the receiver, dropped it, and ran out.

TWENTY-FIVE

"Where do I let you off?" the man behind the wheel asked.

Marek gave him both addresses. "Either one would be fine," he said.

"I will take you to St. Hedwig Street," the man said. "It's on my way."

The girl across the desk looked familiar and Marek wondered where he had seen her before. He asked for Sabina.

"Sabina is not here," the girl said, looking up.

The moment he heard her voice, Marek knew where he had encountered her. Right here, only her hair was different.

"Marek Rodwan," the girl said, "how are you?"

"Fine," Marek said.

"That's good, and your wife?"

It took him a moment to understand her question. "Where is she?" he asked in a choked voice.

"Didn't she get in touch with you?"

"Where is she?"

The girl covered her ears with both hands. "You don't have to shout," she said.

"I am sorry," Marek said. "I didn't know I was. Can you tell me where she is?"

"I hope I can." She took a file. "She is, or at least she was not long ago, on March 29 to be exact, with Adam and Marta Polanski, Lenin Boulevard 17."

"Where is Lenin Boulevard?"

"In the northern suburbs. Streetcar Number 3 will get you there."

He rushed out.

She caught up with him at the door and gave him a slip of paper. "Here," she said, "I wrote it down for you."

Marek had the choice of either taking the streetcar or a horse-drawn carriage. He decided a streetcar would be faster even if he had to wait. He waited for it at the corner, pacing up and down the street.

"You are an impatient young man, aren't you?" a woman in a flowered hat remarked. The tinkling of bells could be heard in the distance. "There it comes," the woman said.

"Do you stop at Lenin Boulevard?" Marek asked the conductor.

"Next to the last stop," the conductor answered.

After a twenty-minute ride, only he and the woman in the flowered hat were in the car.

"You will be getting off now," she said. "Take the street to your left."

Marek thanked her, started toward the door, and stepped off the tram. He looked around. He had never been here before. The houses were new, mostly two and three-story buildings. He turned left into a wide boulevard built up on one side only, with a park on the other side. He checked the number to make sure he was going in the right direction— 10, 11 ... There it was, number 17. He walked into the lobby and looked at the directory—Polanski, Adam he read, apartment 2-C.

He took the stairs to the second floor, found the right door, took a deep breath, and pressed the bell.

Somehow he didn't expect Lisa to open it, but there she

245

was right in front of him, wide-eyed and aghast. Her face turned white, all the blood drained. She took a step back, swayed and would have fallen if not for Marek's outstretched arm. He half-carried her into the room, toward the couch. She sank in, pulling him down with her. Only then did he look at her. Her eyes were closed, her face pale, almost transparent. He touched it with his free hand, the fingers wandering from the hairline to the forehead down the bridge of her nose, across her lips. It was like a hand of a blind man trying to memorize somebody's features. He lifted her face gently by the chin and turned it toward his.

"Lisa," he said, "look at me."

It took a while until she opened her eyes, and when she did, there was fear in them that slowly gave way to bewilderment. "You haven't changed," she said incredulously, for whenever she had thought of seeing him again, she would imagine him emaciated and haggard, just like the men in the camp.

She stretched out her hand slowly and carefully, hesitantly touched his face. He seized her hand and held it there. When he let go of it, he leaned back and began to talk, chaotically, disorderly, the words unable to keep up with his thoughts—how he was searching for her, how he was told she might be dead, how he always knew it was not so, how he finally gave up. About Roman and Paula, about Tamara and Srebrny, about Shimon and Tzvi and Ben Rubin and how he had found out about Kielce and why they could not possibly stay here.

Lisa sat listening to the sound of his voice without paying attention to the words until he mentioned Srebrny. At that point she wondered whether she should tell him what she had heard, then decided that bad news could wait.

"Had you come a few days later," she said, when he finished, "you wouldn't have found me here. Adam and Marta and I were going to leave next week. They are both in War-

246

saw now, picking up diplomatic visas. Oh, Marek, wait till you meet them. They—"

"We too will be leaving," Marek interrupted her. "You and I, soon, I hope. I have to talk to some friends, renew old contacts."

Lisa didn't ask where they would be going, for she was thinking of all the people who were in his life when she was not.

"Marek," she began.

As if reading her thoughts, "You will meet them," he said. "You'll get to know them all."

When she woke up next morning she wouldn't open her eyes, afraid she might have been dreaming. Her hand groped around and found him next to her. She opened her eyes and looked at him, peacefully asleep, his face relaxed.

Under her stare, he half-opened his eyes and smiled. But Lisa did not smile back.

"He would be about a year and a half now," she said absently.

"Who?" Marek looked at her.

"The baby. I never thought about it. Now it suddenly occurred to me. He would be almost a year and a half now."

"What baby?"

"Our son. I am sure it would have been a boy. Remember that time around Christmas when I was so sick?"

Marek didn't get it right away. "Why?" he said finally. "Why?"

"Because we wouldn't have had a chance in the world with a child."

"But why didn't you tell me?"

"Because you wouldn't have let me do it, or you would have been reckless enough to get the money so I could have it done in comfort."

Marek was silent for a long time.

"We will have other children," he said quietly.

"That's what the doctor said then. He was a kind man, a righteous one. So many times I wanted to tell you about him." She paused. "There is so much I want to tell you, so much I want to find out. . . . I've been rehearsing in my mind what I would say to you once we met, and now I don't remember any of it."

Marek stroked her hair silently.

She turned around and propped her chin on the palm of her hand. Looking at him she whispered, "Marek, I am scared."

"What are you scared of?"

"I don't know," she said. "Or rather, I don't know how to put it. It has been a long time. Two years is a long time. I dreamed of you and you dreamed of me. What if we are not at all the way we imagined each other to be? What if it is going to be like the dedication of the temple?"

"What dedication? What temple?"

"I will try to explain," she said. "One day we, Natalia and I—we were in the hospital together—heard over the radio that a temple has been dedicated, and we imagined what it was like, like something out of the Bible. Then it turned out it was different, quite different."

"What does that have to do with us?"

"I know I am not making sense. What I am trying to say is that we might be different from what we thought we would be. That we will have to learn to love each other the way we really are."

"Is that all?"

Marek smiled and pulled her to him.

"Wait," she said, "I haven't finished yet." She paused a moment. Then, "Marek," she said, "do you think we will be able to . . ." She stopped again, searching for the right word.

"Forget?"

"No, not forget. I don't think I ever will and I am not at

248

all sure that I would want to, but ... be the way people should be, happy at times, have carefree moments, be able to really laugh. Do you think we will make it?"

"Together we will," Marek said.

And she believed him.